The Cowboy

By

Douglas Hargreaves

This book is a work of fiction. Places, events, and situations in this story are purely fictional. Any resemblance to actual persons, living or dead, is coincidental.

© 2003 by Douglas Hargreaves. All rights reserved.

No part of this book may be reproduced, stored in a retrieval system, or transmitted by any means, electronic, mechanical, photocopying, recording, or otherwise, without written permission from the author.

ISBN: 1-4140-0563-6 (e-book)
ISBN: 1-4140-0562-8 (Paperback)

This book is printed on acid free paper.

1stBooks - rev. 09/05/03

Dedication

Finally after four years and many exasperating sessions
I dedicate *The Cowboy*
To my Wife Winnie,
To Ken and Peggy,
To my two editors:
Robert Haugen of Lynden, Wa.
Brian Grams of Calgary, Alta.
and to Bobbie Hurst and her
Barnes and Nobel writer group
Thanks to all for their guidance

                      The Author

Table of Content

BOOK REVIEWS vii
THE COWBOY 1
THE HORSES 17
KIDS MY AGE 27
GRANDPA AND GRANDMA 35
HAYING TIME 41
PEGGY'S SWIMMING HOLE 51
THE ONE-ROOM SCHOOL 59
THAT BIG HOLE IN MY HAT 65
MY SECRET 73
THE TRUTH 79
COUNTRY CHRISTMAS 87
BOSSY'S LESSON 93
NURSE "WE" 99
KRAUSE 113
THE COWBOY HALL OF POKE 127
THE STORM 137
BOOTS AND MUD, MUD AND BOOTS 145
BECKY'S BOYFRIEND 161
OLD JIM COWIE 181
SPIES IN THE NIGHT 193

THE ENGLISH KID 205
NO MORE SHORT PANTS 213
WHERE'S MOTHER? 227
ERIC TESTS KEN 239
CALF ROPIN' AT THE STAMPEDE 245
THE FOUND AND THE LOST 255
THE BIG ROUND-UP 261
ERIC VANISHES 269
CHANGING TIMES 283

Book Reviews

Abbotsford and Mission News

July 12, 1997

The Cowboy a gem of a book.

Langley Advanced

October 14, 1997

"A good western. The last of a dying breed."

Langley Times

December 10, 1997

"The book is a true-grit, love-conquers-all story with all elements of a Walt Disney blockbuster."

THE COWBOY

"What the hell am I supposed to do with a runny-nosed little runt like this?" That was the cowboy's first impression of me, his new ranch hand.

"I was told he was twelve and big for his age." he spat. He was furious.

I hung my head and tried to pretend it didn't matter what he was saying, one way or the other. My nose wasn't running and I wasn't a runt. Well, maybe I was a runt.

Mother started to stammer and stutter. I had never seen her at a loss for words before. She did her best to explain that all the arrangements were complete, and her son had had his heart set on this holiday for months. A change in plans now would be most upsetting to everyone involved. "He may be small," she assured the rancher, "but he is strong and certainly bright." She laid it on him good.

I had been preparing myself for this day for the last two months. I was going to spend the summer at a real live cowboy ranch. I had never been on a ranch or even close to horses. The thought of living like the cowboys was enough to excite any ten-year-old's imagination but what did I know about cowboys? We lived in a rich part of the city and our house was one of the biggest there. My parents thought it fashionable to own a large home in a rich district. It was supposed to show you had class and a certain station in life. This was how my Mother explained why we lived where we did, and why I did not have many friends.

Douglas Hargreaves

I think I would rather have had friends.

Our house was located across the street from a large public park in Winnipeg called Assinaboine Park. There were wild animals in cages and places where you could buy peanuts to throw to the animals. There were hundreds of little trails throughout the park but I was forbidden to go into the park unless I was with one of the family. I was told that there might be strange people there or that I might get lost.

Our city did not have a private school, so I was enrolled in the regular public system. Looking back at my life I can see how my brother and I were sheltered from the everyday outside world. Outside of school we didn't see much of it.

Mother's sole aim in life was to attain the highest rung on the city's social ladder. From what I could gather, she was almost there. She was born in the small town of Tillsonburg in Southern Ontario. Her Father had been a share cropper on a tobacco farm. This was his first venture upon arriving in Canada from Germany. Unfortunately, he died young, but not before fathering three girls and four boys. Mother was the youngest. Her Mother died a short time after her Father and she was taken to live with Olive, her older sister.

Olive was married to a successful veterinarian practising in Tillsonburg and could easily afford to look after this child who was to become my Mother.

At six, she went to a convent for her formal education. She completed her education studying business and economics at a college in London, Ontario. She then went on to become executive secretary to the president of a large battery company.

The Cowboy

She was a very clever business woman in her own right.

Father was quite successful in the hardware business when Mother met him and she made certain many large firms sought his expertise. Mother had great plans to help him achieve his full potential in the business and social world. So it was that the largest retail department store chain in Canada, The Hudson's Bay Company, hired him. He became the Bay's senior buyer, a job that required extensive travel.

Mother loved to entertain in our large home and didn't want us under foot, especially if she was preparing for a large party. This never bothered me. I think my brother and I got used to the idea of spending long hours in our rooms. We thought this was what every kid our age would normally do. I would either build models or read. I sometimes fantasized that I was one of the characters from the books I was reading, especially the western cowboy stories. I wondered what it would be like to be a cowboy and live on a ranch.

My brother Billy was five years younger than me and quite big for his age but due to some terrible accident in my genes, we were almost the same size. But this only partially explained our size difference. My health explained the rest. Five years was quite an age gap, so we shared few interests. Billy would spend hours in the yard playing with butterflies, birds, chipmunks and other wildlife. He was timid and gentle. Nancy, our maid, called him a "child of nature".

I, on the other hand, was a pain in everyone's neck. I was told I was too smart for my own good. The kids in school hated me and called me a teacher's pet. None of my Mother's friends liked me, or at least so I thought. I hated everyone and just wished for the day I could get away from all this.

Most of our neighbours were old so there were no kids our age to play with. I had a bike and would ride around our long circular driveway. At least I was moving, even if I wasn't going anywhere. Just like my life.

Our house had three floors. On the top floor Nancy had a large suite of her own and there was also a guest room. My brother and I had separate rooms on the second floor, with a bathroom between. I was in the master bedroom only once and that was when Mother was pregnant with my sister. Uncle Fred, our family doctor and my godfather, came to see my Mother often. She was very unhappy and quite ill most of the time. I don't think she wanted another child. Something happened and the baby died before she was born. Maybe that was the reason for the five years between my brother and me. There was to have been another child in between us.

When we were not having guests, dinner was the most important meal of the day. We had to dress for the occasion and we always wore the same thing. We wore grey shorts, blue blazers (with the Scott Crest), white shirts and dark blue ties. It was Nancy's job to see that we were presentable. Mother must have liked those clothes on us because we always had to wear them at dinner or when visitors came. We would be introduced to our guests and then Nancy would whisk us away.

Father always sat at the head of the table and Mother at the other end, a mile away. Billy and I sat on

The Cowboy

either side, Billy closer to Father, and I closer to Mother, with a huge gap in between. We were instructed in the social graces and table etiquette. We knew how to use the cutlery and table napkins properly and never spoke unless spoken to. If we created a situation or broke one of the rules, we had to finish our meal in the maid's serving room.

I was the academic in the family. I started school when I was five and I skipped grade four. I was smaller and younger than my classmates and never had any problems with school or my homework, just with the other kids. The teachers were concerned that I was not being challenged enough. In that school it was an every day challenge just to keep the bigger guys from beating up on me. To my way of thinking, bigger people were always trying to scare smaller ones.

We had a summer place with a boat house and a motor launch in Kenora, Ontario, on Lake of the Woods. We spent our summers there. In truth, it was more like moving our home from the city to the lake. I saw the same people there as I did in the city, coming and going all the time. They sure looked funny in swimming suits.

In the society world, Mother was well known for having the best and largest parties. Most weekends there would be some splashy affair but neither Billy nor I would be on the guest list. I'd watch people from the upper hallway through the stair railings.

Our Aunt Velna, a good friend of Mother's, would always be there and would give us our baths and bring us some goodies from the party. She was always around and we liked her a lot. I think she felt sorry for us.

Douglas Hargreaves

One night, while I was reading, Nancy came into my room to see if I had taken
my bath. "Skipper, what's that you're looking at?"

"Oh, it's just a story about the cowboys from the Calgary Stampede."

"I'll bet you would like to be a cowboy, wouldn't you, Skipper?" she laughed.

I had never really given it much thought. Me, a real cowboy? The more I thought about it, the more fascinated I became.

I made a promise to myself to become a cowboy some day. I read every book I could get my hands on about cowboys and ranching. It wasn't long before I felt I was ready to take the big plunge.

"Mother," I announced one day, "I wish to spend my summer vacation on a ranch in Alberta." Mother laughed--one of the few times she ever laughed.

"What on earth would you want to do on a ranch? For one thing you're too small and, for another, where would we ever find a ranch to take you? Besides, ranchers and farmers are the hardest working people anywhere," she went on, "why, you won't even get your hands dirty."

I was sure I could handle cowboy work, given a proper chance. I made up my mind to change my school reputation from being the teacher's pet. No more "Where's your Nanny?" or "Who's going to change your diapers?" If only I could go and live on a ranch and get away from this terrible life. One day I'd show everyone. It was humiliating to be so small. People would lift me up like they did Billy, or pat me on the head.

The Cowboy

For once, fate stepped in on my behalf. The Bay offered my Father the position of senior overseas buyer. He would have to live in London, England. Mother was to go with him but no children would be accommodated due to all the travelling. Mother was not about to let a couple of kids get in the way of this move. Father had to accept the position on a temporary basis, at least for the time being.

Aunt Velna was happy to take charge of Billy. He wouldn't even have to change school. Billy was an average, all round normal kid who could play alone for hours. He did as he was told, he was quite good in school and never caused my parents any concern.

I, on the other hand, was a problem and a pain in the neck to everyone. I was not normal. I disliked everyone because they were always treating me like a baby. I had only two real friends in the world, Nancy and Aunt Velna. I was a problem and there was no one who wanted me around. My Father said I had a huge chip on my shoulder. Well, maybe I did because most of the time I wasn't feeling well. My uncle said I had a health problem. He told my parents that the reason I was so small was that I had "Lazy Bowel Syndrome", whatever that was. I learned later that I had a mild case of what is now called "Crohn's Disease". I was always constipated and underwent some horrible and humiliating tests in the hospital to discover my "Problem". My parents were told they had to keep me regular. Mother found the subject disgusting and wouldn't talk about it.

I discovered there was nothing you could add to Castor Oil or Epsom Salts that would make them easier to swallow. I couldn't keep them down, nor any other medicine for that matter. Uncle said it was just in my head and I should be forced to take the stuff. Well, if it was all in my head, why did my Mother make Nancy give me the medicine? I guess it was all right to puke on Nancy but not on Mother.

Mother wrote letters to friends in Calgary (who didn't know me) asking if any of them knew of a ranch that might take a boy for his holidays. Time was getting short and my parents had to arrange something fast.

A letter came, advising that a friend of Mother's had a friend who knew of a rancher. He lived alone in a place called Millarville, right in the heart of the oil fields of Turner Valley, Alberta. His parents ranched in the same area, as did his sister and her family. He rented the ranch and could use a young fellow to help with ranch chores in return for room and board. A working holiday you might call it.

Mother was on the phone, still holding the letter in her hand. In minutes it was all arranged. I was to spend my holidays on a real western ranch! Being away from our parents for the summer didn't upset either Billy or me. Our relationship with our parents was almost nonexistent. There was little hugging or showing of affection--that was left to Nancy and Aunt Velna. What we didn't have, we wouldn't miss. At least that was my thinking.

Several of Mother's friends asked her if she wasn't worried about leaving me with a total stranger, especially a bachelor. What would he know about looking after a ten-year-old? Especially me. Did she realize that living on a ranch was

The Cowboy

a very rough life? "Why, the boy has never done a day's work in his life. How will he survive such an experience with his Mother being so far away?" her friends asked.

Mother promptly dismissed their concerns, saying that I was quite adaptable for my age. She claimed that any friend of a friend of hers must be all right. Nothing was going to stand in the way of her trip to England.

The train ride across the Prairies was terrible. It was hot and dusty and the cars were full of smoke from cigars and pipes. The train was jammed with howling, screaming kids and their parents. I wanted to have the window open but the cinders and smoke just blew in and made conditions worse. There was nothing to see looking out the dirty windows but mile after mile of dry prairie. I wondered who would want to live there.

I thought I might starve waiting in the line to get into the dining room.

A nice black man was the dining car waiter and he picked me up and sat me on my chair. I gave him my meanest look and wanted to poke him in the nose. I wasn't a baby.

Our seats were in a fancy coach called a Pullman car. I think they called it that because the porter came along at night and "pulled" the beds down from the ceiling.

Everyone on the train seemed to have to use the toilet at the same time and we had one in our car that everyone liked. There were line ups to get into it so our aisle was always full of screaming kids and babies with wet and full diapers. I almost wanted to throw up. I'd have never made it to the toilet so Mother made me sit by the window, just in case.

Douglas Hargreaves

I didn't start to get excited until I was able to see some of the foothills towards Calgary. Mother nearly pulled my ears off as I attempted to jump off the train when it came to a halt in the station.

We were met at the station by some of my Mother's friends who provided us with directions and a car for the trip to the ranch. The station was full of people going everywhere and especially Cowboys. I could tell from their hats and boots.

The roads were dusty and the thirty mile trip to the ranch seemed to take forever. I could hardly contain myself as I sat alone in the back seat of the big Oldsmobile . I knew it was an Oldsmobile because I heard my Father telling our friends that he had never driven one before. We had a Studebaker President.

Finally, we turned off the main road into a narrow dusty trail that was lined with tall poplar and fir trees. It looked friendly and warm. It was a pleasant, cloudless day in this Alberta ranch country and a great day to start my new life as a cowboy.

I was excited and a little worried about what the rancher would be like. What would he say when he saw me? I had been rehearsing what I would say when he asked about my age and my size and a lot of other stuff. I had prayed that God would keep Mother's mouth shut about my little health problem. If he found out, that could be the end of it. He could refuse to have me. I was sure Mother would not want to do anything that might destroy her plans.

Now I was going to spend my holidays on a real cowboy ranch. I'd sure show everyone a thing or two when I got back. I would be bigger, stronger and even

The Cowboy

smarter because I would know about horses and steers and all the rest of that ranch stuff.

The Oldsmobile rounded a bend and turned into a lovely valley with a small cabin which was surrounded by a neat hedge. It had to be the most beautiful sight I had ever seen. A dog started to bark and it was everything I had imagined. To the right of the cabin and down a small hill was a barn encircled with fir trees.

The dog came bounding towards the car and a real cowboy slowly strode over to where we had stopped.

Wow! Here was my idea of a cowboy. He was taller and younger than my Father. His blonde hair hung down over his right eye and on the back of his head was a tan Stetson cowboy hat. I got so excited I almost forgot to ask permission to get out of the car.

The cowboy opened the door for Mother and she stepped out. I opened the back door and slid to the ground. The cowboy hardly noticed me as he stood talking to my Mother. I heard him say his name was Ken Wills. When he finally looked my way it was as though I wasn't there. He looked into the back seat to see if anyone else was getting out.

"You ain't the kid who is supposed to be going to work for me?" he asked finally.

"Yes sir." I said. I was starting to shake. This wasn't the way I had pictured it. The cowboy looked me up and down like I was a side of beef. I wanted to crawl away some place and stay there forever. That's when he called me a runny-nosed little runt.

The cowboy considered the situation long and hard. After some further discussion with my parents and a sigh of complete disgust, he agreed to let me stay for a week or so, if only to let me have some sort of a holiday. We had come a long distance just to have me turned away. My family would then have a little while to decide my fate.

Mother was in a stew. She paced back and forth and looked daggers at me, as though it were my fault I was ten and small. I was used to insults and criticism from people I knew but to hear them from this cowboy was terrible. He was a total stranger and didn't even know me. How could he be so sure about what I could or couldn't do?

"Well, come on kid, let's get your stuff unloaded and into the house. God only knows what I'm going to do with you." Ken growled. I hoped God knew.

All this time, Father just sat behind the wheel of the car and watched. He may have been smart in business but he was no family man. He and I never talked much as we didn't have anything to say to each other. Mother did all the talking. Still, even she didn't know how to talk to Billy or me.

Mother patted me on the head and told me to be a good boy and not to upset Ken, no matter what. I was feeling like a piece of the horse pucky that was lying everywhere. It was all I could do to hold back the tears but I guess they were running down my face a little. I hated to let the cowboy see me behave like a little baby. I was about to change my mind about staying when I realized that whatever my mother came up with, it would probably be worse than this.

My parents drove off and I had never felt so dreadful in all my life. My family may not have been the most communicative in the world but at least they offered some security. Here, all I felt was hate. I was

The Cowboy

used to being treated this way by people I knew but not by a total stranger.

Ken looked at me and shook his head. "God, they sure don't feed you very much, do they? How come you never grew?"

"I don't know, sir." His references to God so many times made me think he was a religious man.

"Well kid, you and I have to live together for awhile, so as long as you do as you're told and don't sass back, we'll get along. You step out of line just once and your arse will burn for a week. Understand what I'm saying, kid?"

I really didn't understand what he meant but answered "Yes Sir".

I stumbled under the weight of my suitcase as Ken showed me to my room. It was a nice room with a big double bed. My bedroom at home was four times the size of this one. There was an oil lamp on a little table by the bed and an old chest of drawers for my clothes.

The window looked out over the valley and the barn. I could also see a stream that ran close to the barn and could even hear it gurgling. I lifted my suitcase onto the bed and started to unpack my clothes. Mother had bought me a new pair of jeans, a work shirt with a pocket on each side and also a pair of work boots.

I changed into my new clothes and walked out into the kitchen. I felt strange wearing these work clothes. They smelled like disinfectant and were as stiff as a board. My wool socks itched as they moved around inside my boots. I wished they had been cowboy boots but they were just the work kind. Ken was setting the table for supper though it was still afternoon.

There was a long window that ran almost the whole length of the kitchen which was almost as large as our kitchen at home. There was a wood stove in the corner with a place to heat water built into it. The wood box was beside the wash stand.

In the corner by the door was the cream separator and milk stand and a place to hang our clothes. Ken pointed out everything as I looked around the room.

The kitchen table was almost as long as our dining room table at home. I walked over and stood looking out the window towards the barn, waiting for Ken to say or do something. Finally, as he sat down at the head of the table, he asked, "What's your name, boy?"

"Skipper, sir." I managed to squeak out.

"Well, sit down." He pointed to the chair beside him. He had set a place for me so that I could look out of the window. "How come you're so small, kid? I thought you was twelve. Why are you so little?"

I winced and wondered if I should make a joke about my size. I decided not to. I told him I wasn't twelve, I was only ten, and that I had always been small. I told him I was very strong and could do lots of things.

"Like what can you do? You're too little."

I looked at him and got up enough nerve to ask him if he liked kids. He didn't answer. Finally, he stood up and asked me if I had ever washed or dried dishes or done any work in the kitchen before. I told him no because I wasn't allowed in the kitchen, only the maid and cook. "Well you'll damned well work in this one, kid."

This was certainly not the way I had pictured it. I felt lower than low and had a hard time stopping my

The Cowboy

tears. At least he didn't see them. He didn't like me, that's for sure.

The cowboy stood up and walked to the door. "Get out here kid and I'll show you around the place."

My aunt always told me if you didn't know something, don't pretend you do. Always ask questions. I sure had lots of questions but I wasn't about to ask anything of Ken. At least not yet. Maybe never.

As we walked together, I imagined myself a regular cowpoke. I felt a little important even if I only came just a bit higher than his belt. I resolved that I was going to make a go of this, no matter what. There was no turning back, and besides, I had no where else to go.

THE HORSES

Ken and I walked out into the main yard. We could easily see all the ranch buildings from there. The largest building was the barn and it was huge, with a hay loft on the top floor. There was a door in the front to allow hay to be loaded directly from a hay wagon. I wondered if this would be a quiet place to come and maybe hide sometimes. You could do a lot of thinking up here without anyone stumbling across your hiding place.

There were big double doors at each end of the building on the main floor. One side of the front door was divided into two parts like a Dutch door. They didn't fit together too well, because they had aged over the years and the hinges were loose and sagging. On one side were the stalls for the four cows. Mr Wills told me the cows were brought in and milked twice a day morning and evening. He said the milk was then taken to the house for separating.

There was a gutter or trough that ran the length of the barn. It was to collect animal droppings. The horses' stalls were on the other side. These stalls looked better than the ones for the cows. There was a trough behind them as well. "You'll clean the troughs each day." Ken said. At the head of the horse stalls were eating bins. Hay could be forked down through an opening in the ceiling. There were three windows on each side, but you couldn't see through them, they were so dirty. That made it very dark inside unless you kept the big doors open.

Douglas Hargreaves

Next came the hen house. This was a small building with a wire-enclosed entrance way. There was a gate that let you into the chicken run and another door that let you into the hen house proper. Here the hens nested and laid their eggs.

The floor was covered with hen stuff, and the dust was terrible. Every time you took a step, clouds of dust rose from the floor. I felt suffocated. "You'll feed and water the hens every morning, then gather the eggs." Ken instructed. I quickly learned to hate these birds. They say chickens have no brains, but I swear these birds knew me and sensed my terror. I could imagine them saying. "Here he comes girls, get ready to make him wet himself."

The next building was the chop house. This is where you ground up and stored all the oats and corn for feed. A tractor with a large belt drove the grinder. Working in this building while the grinder was working was terrible, especially in hot weather. The dust was stifling. You could easily suffocate or die from the dust or the heat.

Bordering on the chop house was the main horse coral. It was in a neat little valley, where a small stream from the main creek ran. Horses could graze in this corral and have all the water they needed. Ken had four horses. They had to be the most beautiful horses I had ever seen, but then I had never seen any horse up close before. There were two bay mares, a palomino stallion, and a black Indian pony. That's what Ken said they were. He pointed out the various gates in the corral that allowed the horses to move from one area to another.

The Cowboy

Ken had little to say as we walked around, other than to tell me what the buildings were used for. I had not built up enough nerve to ask him any questions. I didn't think I would have any trouble remembering what he told me as I had a photographic memory. Or at least that's what I had been told.

We walked back up to the house and he showed me where the outhouse was. I had never seen an outhouse before, and he had to show me inside before I realized that this was a toilet. Ken pointed to the Eaton's catalogue lying on the seat beside two holes. There was one large hole and one small one I presumed would fit me. I didn't like this place.

At the rear of the house alongside the barn, was a creek called the "Sheep". It was slow running and crystal clear. "This is where we take our baths." Ken said. We would have our baths whenever we needed one, and always on Saturday night.

The last building was the workshop, or what some called the blacksmith's shop. Inside was a blacksmith's forge, a large old drill press, and an enormous anvil. Along the walls hung bits and pieces of harness, rope, and other parts of machinery. One window allowed some light into the building. In the winter time we would use a coal oil lamp. In the summer, we would open the large doors. Old wagon wheels and rims stood against another wall. In one corner was a large tub of axle grease, jet black and gooey. In another corner was a large grindstone with a bicycle seat on it so you could pedal it and sharpen things at the same time. Finally, I recognized something I had seen before. Hanging above the grindstone was a white porcelain pot with a long rubber hose running down

Douglas Hargreaves

from it to the grind stone. I remember having it used on me when I was in the hospital getting tests. I wondered why it was here in this place. The shop was very tidy considering what went on in it.

So ended my tour of the Bar U Lazy Y Ranch buildings. There were a few out-buildings in various sections of the ranch, but these were just to provide shelter for the cattle or riders in bad weather.

There was an old tractor next to the chop house, and beside it was Ken's half ton truck. It ran okay and was the main transportation into Millarville and Calgary.

Every now and again I would see Ken looking at me and shaking his head. I knew what he was thinking.

We walked back to the ranch house. It was such a beautiful evening that he decided we would sit outside for awhile. He told me what he expected of me and how I was to behave.

"I don't think you're going to be here for long kid, but until you leave, you gotta earn your way. You do what you're told and you'll be all right. You gotta learn to milk the cows, feed the horses, collect the eggs, and feed the chickens. That don't take too long, and we'll see how well you learn. I can't take long showin' you how to do all this stuff, so keep your eyes open."

"Yes sir." I replied.

"And quit calling me sir. Call me Mr. Wills, okay?"

"Yes sir, er, I mean, yes, Mr. Wills."

We headed towards the barn to milk the cows, my first lesson. "All these cows are okay except for this one." Ken pointed to a large holstein cow. She stood looking at me, switching her tail and kicking her legs

The Cowboy

at flies. Ken got a short piece of rope and tied it in a figure eight around her back legs. He told me that this would stop her from kicking the milker and protect the milk from getting knocked over. "Watch her legs and always remember to tie them." he warned. "The others will just stand there and let you milk them."

I watched Ken milk the Holstein. He sat on a stool made from a couple of two-by-six boards nailed into the form of a "T". He held the pail between his knees and pulled on the teats until milk came and filled the pail. It looked easy and I wanted to try it. My hands barely reached around the over-sized teats. But after several tries I got the milk spurting out. I think this surprised Ken. "Keep at it kid." he ordered. "I'll milk one of the others while you practice." My hands finally gave out. I just couldn't squeeze those sausages any longer. I had already set the pail down on the floor, as my knees wouldn't hold it any more. Ken never said anything, but I think he was surprised to see that I had managed to get more than half a pail.

He finished off milking my cow, and the others. We let them out into the small corral where they would stay overnight. We carried the milk pails up to the house. I couldn't carry a full pail but I managed the half pail that I had milked. I struggled, as we had a little climb from the barn to the house. We dumped the milk into a cream separator and cranked until all of it went through. It was really hard work cranking that machine. I couldn't even get it started. Ken had to do that.

It was evening and very quiet in the ranch house. Ken had no radio, only an old gramophone. He put on a couple of old records of Jimmie Rodgers, the

Douglas Hargreaves

"Singing Brakeman". The sound scratched and whined all through the house. Ken still hadn't spoken to me in ordinary conversation, and I was feeling terrible.

Everything overwhelmed me. I could hardly come to grips with the way I was feeling. Why wasn't I happy and excited, like I thought I would be? Instead I was lonely and wanted to cry. No one cared what happened to me, least of all Ken.

"Well kid, you better get ready for bed. I'll wake you in the morning. You don't pee the bed, do you?"

"No, sir." I replied with embarrassment.

I walked into my room and tried to close the door, but it wouldn't close. The hinges needed oil. It was still light outside, but Ken said that we got up early - five o'clock. I had never got up that early in my whole life except to pee. I was feeling awful. I undressed and crawled into bed. I had one cover, but that was enough. It was warm outside.

As I lay in bed looking up at the ceiling, I wondered what I had got myself into. What was going to happen to me? Despite my best efforts to act grown up and brave, I sobbed myself to sleep.

Five o'clock came with the sun just breaking through the window. I was awake before Ken came into my room. "Hey kid, time to get up!" he shouted. "No foolin' around here. This is a working place, not a dude ranch. Come on kid, get dressed and get down and open the west corral gate and let the horses into the creek area. Then get the cows out of the overnight corral and into the barn. I'll be down there by the time you get that done. We'll milk first. You can do that okay kid?"

The Cowboy

"I'll do it, Mr. Wills. I'll see you at the barn." I took off on the run. Now was my chance to prove myself.

There was a light mist on the ground, but I didn't feel the least bit cold. I was glad Ken had finally given me something to do. I had been wondering if he would think I was too small to do anything. I ran to the corral and opened the gate without any trouble. The four horses ambled out. They took off on the trot and it wasn't long before they were over the hill and out of sight. I closed the gate again, and walked back up to the barn. Ken was at the door. "Did you close the gate behind you?"

"Yes sir." I forgot the Mr. Wills title.

"You get the right gate? The one like I told you that lets them into the creek?"

"I think so. It was the one closest to the barn." I felt confident that I had done the job right.

Then I started to wonder if I had opened the wrong gate. Ken kept asking me questions. Hoooolllyy Nellie! What if I had opened the wrong gate? I thought back to the instructions he had given me, and came to the conclusion that maybe it wasn't the right gate. In my hurry to do the job right, I had made a bad mistake.

Ken walked past me towards the corral and immediately confirmed my worst fears. "Gosh all Friday kid, can't you do anything right?" he yelled. "Remember what I told you about listening and doing what you're told? You let them into the outer pasture! It'll take us an hour to get them back. Damn you anyway!"

He was walking towards me. I was scared. I knew he was very mad. He ordered me to undo my pants. The look in his eyes told me I had better do as he said.

Douglas Hargreaves

I undid my belt and my buttons and my pants slid down to my ankles. I was shaking so badly by then, I thought I might throw up.

He picked me up and turned me over his knee. He pulled down my underpants and gave me the first spanking I ever had. He had a way of holding my hands so that I couldn't reach around to protect my swollen cheeks. Those six smacks were the worst pain I had ever felt. He told me I could expect more of the same if I stepped out of line or didn't do as I was told. I was sobbing but not crying. I had let out one major yelp when his hand came down the first time. It was so big and my behind so small he easily covered both cheeks with little effort. The second smack left me almost paralysed. After that it wasn't so bad. I seemed to be numb back there.

I stopped weeping and he put me down, pulling up my underwear. I just stood holding my battered hind end. I retrieved my pants and pulled them back on, sobbing all the time.

"I'm sorry, Mr. Wills. I made a mistake. I won't do it again."

"Best not boy, or you won't sit down again, I can tell you. Now let's go and get those horses. The time we're losing is going to really put our milking back."

I was sure sore as we walked up the hill to the field. My pride was injured, and so was my bum, but at least my bum would heal. I had really goofed up to make Ken mad enough to give me a lickin'. I felt I had ruined my chances to stay.

We found the horses at the top of the hill. They hadn't gone far at all. "Get around them boy and move 'em toward me." Ken ordered." I ran on the outside and

The Cowboy

got around them, and they moved towards Ken and back towards the corral. They weren't too upset at being returned.

I was milking a lot better than last night, and I was getting lots in my pail. I couldn't sit on the stool very well, I was so sore. It took me a long time to get my cow done. I think Ken must have been pleased with my efforts. Perhaps there was hope for the kid after all.

My backside was aching terribly and my hands were cramped so badly, I could hardly carry my milk pails. Full pails were heavy, and I had one awful time carrying my pail up to the house.

When I came in, Ken had the separator turning. He poured the milk from my pail into the machine and told me to carry on turning, while he got washed and made breakfast. Neither of us spoke until I had finished. Then he told me to get washed up for breakfast and to get moving. I jumped and was at the table in a few minutes.

Breakfast was porridge, bread and jam, and a cup of tea. "Well kid, what have you got to say for yourself?" Ken was still angry with me.

"Please Mr. Wills, I'm sorry, and I won't let that happen again. I really was stupid to do that. Please let me stay." I begged.

He looked at me as though he had never seen me before. With a little smile in the corner of his mouth, he said. "We'll see. I gotta say that you took your lickin' like a man. Most kids would be wanting to pack it up and take off for home."

I told him that I would never do that. "I guess I had the whipping coming to me." I whispered. He agreed and told me that you can't make mistakes on a ranch.

Douglas Hargreaves

They cost money, and money was one thing he didn't have. And besides, you could get hurt by making mistakes. Well, my sore bum and I silently agreed with that observation.

It was Friday, and we were going to ride over to see Ken's sister the next day. He would see how well I could set a horse. I smiled, and for a minute I forgot that he disliked his new hired hand so much. "Why you walkin' so funny boy?"

"I guess I must have backed into a hot stove." I hoped I hadn't overstepped my bounds.

He started to laugh and he was all smiles for awhile. I would have taken another spanking to make him smile, look at me and maybe even get to like me a little.

KIDS MY AGE

I managed to get through Friday without further mishap, but my behind was still smarting. Ken selected Nixon, the black Indian pony for me to ride. This didn't help my sore spot. Nixon was named after some distant purebred relative. Ken told me I could ride him and that I had to take care of him while I was there.

"Skipper, never let me catch you running your horse full out." he warned. He put an old rope bridal on Nixon and led him over to the corral fence. He told me to get up on the railing and from there I could mount Nixon. I wondered how I would get on him if I wasn't near a pole fence. I had never been on a horse before and this was the thrill of my lifetime. I was so excited I could hardly contain myself. Ken must have sensed my excitement because he had a little smile on his face.

Ken showed me how to mount Nixon. It was then I started to shake. Silently I prayed, "Oh God, please don't let me fall off." Ken led Nixon around the corral a few times and then handed me the reins. He instructed me on how to rein to left or right using the neck pressure rather than yanking on the horse's mouth. "Just press the reins against the side of his neck opposite the direction you want to go." Nixon wasn't a fat horse but my body was almost splitting. This was going to take some getting used to.

We had no saddle, so I would have to learn to ride bareback. Ken assured me this was the best way to learn anyway. I wasn't about to complain, and rode around and around the corral while Ken saddled

Bonnie, his own bay mare. "Okay kid, let's get going." he said as he opened the gate and out we rode. I think Nixon knew he had a greenhorn on his back. He walked very slowly with hardly any sway that might dislodge me.

We rode onto the lease lands and climbed a few hills en route to Ken's

sister's ranch. I hung onto Nixon's mane for dear life as we climbed the steeper hills. I was afraid I would slip off Nixon's back end. I hoped Ken hadn't noticed. My legs being so short, I couldn't use them to hold on. I didn't let Ken know I was having trouble so I just smiled and felt sore. My rump was sure aching by the time we got to Peggy's place. I had ridden as far as I wanted. Far enough for my first ride, anyway.

I rode up beside Ken as he slipped out of the saddle to the ground. I tried

to be nonchalant as I swung my leg over Nixon's back end and fell flat on my butt. What a way to make my first appearance. Right on my sore spot. Ken, with a look of disgust, was the only one watching my dismount, thank goodness. "Boy, when you're riding bareback, you swing your leg over the horse's neck, not his arse."

We walked into the house where Peggy was baking bread. The good smells coming from her kitchen made me hungry. All of her children were there helping their mom. They ran over to their uncle to welcome him. Then they gave me a thorough once over. Katherine was the oldest. She was twelve. Marie, the youngest, was six. Johnny was nine, and Paul was seven.

Paul was the same height as me. "Hi Skipper." He looked me straight in the eye. "You're seven too, huh?"

The Cowboy

"Hi Paul. I'm actually ten, going on eleven." I tried to cover my embarrassment.

"Gee, you're small, ain't yah?"

I figured Johnny to be fourteen at least, from his size. Hooolllyy! I'm ten years old and a midget compared to these guys.

"I thought you were supposed to be fourteen." Johnny said, looking me up and down. I didn't feel so good around these kids.

"Ken, is this the new hand you hired for the summer?" Peggy asked. Ken looked annoyed at the question and explained that someone had played a trick on him and, yes, I was supposed to have been his hired hand. I felt like crawling away some place and disappearing.

Peggy came over to me and, horror of horrors, picked me up and gave me a big hug. "Welcome anyway, little man. You're sure a cutey," she said. I liked her but wished she would put me down. I was uncomfortable and embarrassed in front of everyone. She put me down and then introduced the kids.

"Why're you so small, Skipper?" Paul said.

"I wished I knew, Paul."

"So do I." said Ken.

"I sure need to grow some, looking at you guys." I said to Paul. "Do you think it would help if I stood in some manure?" It was a pretty feeble attempt at humour.

Everyone but Ken laughed. "You seem pretty smart today. How come you wasn't that smart yesterday?" he muttered.

"You do something wrong?" Johnny asked. I just hung my head, ashamed at the memory of yesterday morning.

"Had to burn his backside for letting the horses go." Ken told them. I think the kids were embarrassed for me, but chuckled and made motions towards my rear end, muttering "ow" and "ouch" sounds.

"Skipper, you mean you should stand in a pile of shit, right?" said Johnny. "From the sounds of things, I think you're already in it right up to your neck." Everyone was finding me a big joke.

"Well, you guys just happened to be along in time for dinner." Peggy said in her good-natured way. I really liked her. She was very friendly and seemed to like me just as I was.

"Let's go and get Dad." Paul said. Paul, Johnny and I took off out of the kitchen. "I think he's in the barn putting a shoe on one of the mares." Paul yelled from up ahead. He was running full tilt down to the barn.

The barn was broken down and very weathered. "It's almost collapsing." Johnny told me as we walked along. "We don't have enough money to fix it, so we just use it as it is. We don't own the ranch, we just rent it. You think you're going to be able to stay with Uncle Ken?" I told him I wasn't even thinking about that. So far, Ken didn't seem to like me and wanted someone bigger. Johnny said he hoped I could stay and we could be friends. There weren't too many kids his age living nearby.

"What grade you in, Skipper?" he asked.

"I'm going into Seven this fall."

"Hey Skipper, you're bulling me, ain't yah? Ha! You're some bullshitter, you sure are."

The Cowboy

"Honest, Johnny, I am. I skipped a couple of grades."

"Golly! Wait 'til the other guys hear that. Wow!"

The barn was as terrible inside as it was outside. Johnny's dad was letting a palomino mare out of the barn into a broken down corral. "That's my horse, Skipper," Paul told me, "ain't she pretty? I paid for her all by myself."

"Hey Dad--this is Uncle Ken's new hired hand." Johnny laughed. Their dad's name was Olie. He held out his hand to shake with me. He was a short man and had a firm handshake. I wondered if I would look like him when I grew up. "Well young fellow, you sure must have surprised Ken, huh? I somehow can't think you're what Ken had in mind. What happened boy, someone goof up some place?"

"Dad," said Johnny, "we'd better get a move on for dinner. We can talk up at the house."

Like the barn, the house was run down, but inside it was clean and tidy. I could tell everyone watched what they said and how they behaved. They were a loving family, and that showed in how the kids talked to their parents.

Dinner was a wonderful meal. I hadn't eaten this well since leaving home. Fresh baked bread, roast pork, potatoes, gravy and vegetables. I never liked carrots but thought I had best not show a dislike for anything. It might just give Ken the excuse he needed to send me home. The kids watched every little thing I did and how I ate. I was on by best behaviour because I wanted to make a good impression. Ken sat right beside me. He wasn't missing much. Peggy kept telling me to take as much as I liked--there was lots. "We may not have much money but we sure eat well." she said.

Olie and Ken talked about the Wilson's new hay stacker. They had built it themselves. "We could do that, Olie." Ken said. "Yeah, I suppose we could if we got the right logs." said Olie.

"I hate borrowing Wilson's all the time." Ken said. They would talk to Grandpa. Grandpa Wills was Ken and Peggy's father. Everyone loved him by the way they talked about him.

"Dad, you know what?" Johnny said excitedly. "Skipper's in Grade Seven at school. Wow! Ain't that some deal, huh?" Even Ken looked surprised.

"That right Skipper?" Olie asked me. "You can't be in Grade Seven at your age, can you? You're ten, right?"

"Yes, sir, I am in Grade Seven. I skipped a couple of grades." Ken was giving me a strange look, like he didn't believe me.

"You must be a smart ass, huh?" Olie joshed. Peggy gave him a scolding look for using bad words at the table. The kids chuckled to themselves. They knew what that look meant.

A large serving of apple pie finished the meal. Hoooollly, was I ever full. I hadn't felt so good since I arrived. Even my bum wasn't hurting so bad. We all helped clear the table and did the dishes. Each of the kids had certain chores to do and did them without a word from their mom.

Ken was talking to Olie and Peggy very quietly. I overheard him say he wasn't sure what he was going to do with me. "What use is he going to be to me?" he said. I didn't want to listen any longer. I couldn't help

The Cowboy

feeling awful every time my future on the ranch was in doubt. What were they going to do with me? I helped dry the dishes and then went outside with the rest of the kids to fool around with an old football. My heart wasn't in it.

"Come on, Skipper," Ken yelled, "let's get a move on. We gotta get home and do the chores, then drive over to Mom and Dad's before dark." He turned to Peggy. "Anything you want me to pick up there?"

"Can I come with Skipper and Uncle Ken?" Johnny asked his mother. Ken said that it was okay with him. One more kid wouldn't upset things more than they were. Johnny could stay over night and come home in the morning.

"Okay, but you mind your manners and stay out of trouble." Peggy lectured. "Your Uncle Ken has a short temper, you know. Get home early so you can get ready for church."

Johnny saddled up while I mounted Nixon from the railing, and we were away. Johnny rode easily in his saddle, while I hung on for dear life.

GRANDPA AND GRANDMA

Ken's old truck snorted and rattled over the mud road. It was dry but the ruts remained from the last heavy rain. Dust flew everywhere as we pulled up to an old gate with tall posts on each side. Johnny and I jumped out and opened it for the truck to get through. The trees lining the roadway were so thick we couldn't see the ranch house until we rounded a corner. There it was, so pretty that it reminded me of pictures I had seen in some of my books.

Ken parked the truck beside another car and Johnny rushed off into the house. I stayed back to go in with Ken.

Mr. Wills was a tall man with slightly rounded shoulders, a sparkle in his eyes, and a full head of grey hair. When he smiled, wrinkles formed beside his eyes. I knew I would like him right away. We shook hands and he welcomed me to their home.

Mrs. Wills was a small woman with a chubby appearance. She too had a smile on her face that glowed with kindness.

"Let me see your muscles, Skipper." Mr Wills said. I grew red but I bent my arm and made a muscle of sorts. He laughed. "Well, Skipper, that looks pretty good to me. Fine and dandy for ranch work." Good--at least someone thought I might be fit to work.

Johnny hopped up on his Grandpa's lap. I could see he loved his Grandpa very much. "Boy oh boy," Grandpa Wills laughed, "you're sure getting too big for your old Grandpa to hold any more. But I think I can still handle Skipper there." Grandma Wills had the tea ready and was making a light snack.

It seemed everyone spent Saturday preparing for Sunday. It was too late in the week to start a new project, and everyone was busy cleaning up the rest of the chores from the week. This Saturday, everyone had lots of time on their hands. They were washing and ironing clothes and shining shoes.

Mrs. Wills served jellied scones and a cup of tea for all of us. I had never had tea before I came to the ranch. I was really getting to like it. The scones were the best things I had ever tasted.

Mrs. Wills took Johnny and me outside to the raspberry patch in her garden. "You boys each get a bucket and pick some berries for supper. Skipper, is Ken feeding you all right? You know he isn't used to having a little boy around the place and he sometimes forgets to eat properly." I told her that I was eating fine and how much I liked it on the ranch. "Well, you just mind that you do what he tells you and don't get into any trouble. Ken always had a bad temper since he was a small boy like you." I looked at Johnny but he wasn't about to say anything about the trouble I already had. I could see Johnny and I would be good friends.

We picked raspberries until my arms were all covered with scratches from the raspberry canes. They were sure sharp. I didn't mind though.

Ken and Mr. Wills were outside talking and looking over some logs that Mr. Wills had cut and hauled down. These were for the new hay stacker they were planning to build. It looked like he had the same idea as Ken and Olie. And of course Mr. Wilson, who had been the first to build one.

The Cowboy

We had a good supper and I can say that my small body was using all the energy it could generate just to move my full stomach around. All day long we seemed to do nothing but eat. I felt good, and Johnny and I talked for hours about the big city, and about ranching and school.

After supper Johnny and I helped dry the dishes while Ken and Mr. Wills sat by the fireplace, which wasn't lit, and smoked their pipes. They were very much alike.

It was getting dark and Mrs. Wills said we should be getting home as we still had the cows to milk. She would see us in church tomorrow morning. I wasn't used to going to church.

Mr. Wills shook our hands and Mrs. Wills gave Johnny a big hug and a kiss.

"Thank you very much for the nice supper, Mrs. Wills." I said. She pulled me over and gave me a hug and a kiss. I was a little embarrassed and hadn't expected this show of affection. I felt happy to have been included . It was the first time anyone had hugged and kissed me for a long time. Everyone was being so nice and friendly that I wanted to belong here and be one of them.

"Bye, Skipper. Nice to have met you, and come back again." Mr. Wills said.

"Thank you very much. I had a good time and I was happy to meet you too."

"Call me Grandpa like the others do." I was really happy now because I had a Grandpa who didn't treat me like an outsider.

We got in the truck and took off for home. Home? I mean the Ken Wills ranch, better known as the Bar U

Douglas Hargreaves

Lazy Y. Ken said, "You sure made a good impression on everyone today boy." That was all he had to say all the way home. Johnny and I talked quietly about school, of all things.

When we got home, Ken told us to move the cows in and get milking. Johnny was really good at it and he told me I was doing really well for a beginner. I told him it hurt my hands but he said that would soon get better as my hands got stronger.

We finished milking and Johnny advised me to pour my milk into two pails. They would be easier to carry and I wouldn't spill any. "Uncle Ken doesn't like to have any spilt." Johnny said. I already knew that. We had the separating done and everything cleaned up by eight thirty. The sun was starting to go below the hill.

"Okay boys, morning comes early!" Ken shouted from the bedroom. He was cranking up the old gramophone and Jimmie Rodgers started to whine away the "Railroad Blues".

We went into my bedroom and Johnny started to undress. I found my pyjamas and was starting to undress when Johnny told me he didn't wear any. "What do you need them for, Skipper? I got some at home for when I go visiting in the city. I just sleep in my skin. Mom says we can't afford such things."

I knew that Peggy and Olie were poor but I never thought much about it until then. I never wore pyjamas either except when I had a guest.

We hopped into bed and talked about the city and the kind of life I had. Johnny asked questions for a long time, wanting to know all about me, until Ken

The Cowboy

told us to quiet up and go to sleep. "Goodnight Johnny." I whispered.

"'Night, Skipper. I really like you. I hope you stay."

HAYING TIME

I got through my first week with very few problems. I was getting to milk quite well. My hands became stronger and Ken even said I caught onto the milking faster than most kids. That made me feel good. I was milking two cows by myself.

I was having some trouble forking hay down to the horses. It was hard to get the hay to stay on the fork unless I took a full fork. But the hay was heavy, so I couldn't lift a full fork. At first I just pushed with all my might. Then I learned to stick the fork in sideways and sweep it over to the opening in the loft floor. This worked very well and I could get it done quickly.

The eggs--well, here was another matter. Those damned chickens are what nearly got me another lickin'. This time it was just a little smack. I hated those critters, and they sure hated me. Every time I went into the coop, one big ornery hen would stand defiantly in the doorway, daring me to try and get an egg. I could almost hear her saying, "Just try and ruffle my girls and see what I do to your arms and legs, buster." She would take a flying run and flap up in my face, scaring the daylights out of me, and I would just about pee my pants. She would peck at my pants and hands.

One time Ken was watching me. When he saw what was happening, he swatted that bird one great smack. It sent it squawking and flying across the coop. Then Ken swatted me on the butt and hollered. "What the hell you so scared of, boy? You bloody baby. It ain't gonna hurt yah. Now get those damned eggs out of there before I bare your butt again." I scrambled to gather the eggs.

The hens produced about twenty-five eggs every day. I had to wash and pack them in an egg crate. Then I'd go into the chop house and get feed for the hens and horses.

I worked out a neat schedule for my morning chores. I got up at five and went down to the barn to let the cows in. If we were going to ride, I would let the horses into the barn and feed them. Then I'd milk the cows and carry the pails up to the house for separating. After that, I would take the separator discs apart and put them on the table for washing with our breakfast dishes. I'd then water and feed the hens and gather the eggs. Finally I'd pump water into the trough.

I developed this routine into a fast operation, and gradually got braver and more confident in the way I did my chores. It was a toss-up as to whom I feared most, the big hen or Ken. To be safe, I didn't fool with either one.

With all the chores done, I'd trudge up to the house and scrub up for breakfast. Ken would have it ready when I came in. He sometimes asked me what took so long. I never answered. I don't think he expected an answer. He was just keeping me on my toes. We would sit and eat in silence except when he'd tell me what we were doing for the rest of the day. I wished he would tell me why he disliked me so much. I was working as hard as I could.

We were starting to hay. This was something I had only heard about and was soon to learn what it was all about. I had heard Ken talking about a new hay stacker but I had no idea what a stacker was or what it did.

The Cowboy

We drove over to Grandpa Wills' place--his fields were the first we would hay. Grandpa had four large fields to do, while Olie, Peggy's husband, had three small ones. Ken had five very large fields to do. A lot of work lay ahead.

Grandpa had already cut some of his hay and it was dry and ready for raking. Ken supplied a team of horses for the rake to move the hay into windrows.

Olie drove the sweep. This was a large piece of equipment with long fingers like fence posts sticking out in front of it. It was about twelve feet wide and mounted on two wheels. The horses were hitched to the sweep on either side of the forks. Olie raised or lowered the forks by walking to the front or the rear of a narrow platform. His weight made the forks go up or down. I thought this was really neat. As the sweep moved along the rows of hay, Olie would stand to the front of the platform. Then he'd walk to the back of the platform and the whole sweep would raise up at the front. This would lift the hay off the ground, and Olie would drive the sweep with its load of hay onto similar forks mounted on the stacker.

The stacker was a huge contraption made of large peeled logs bolted together. There were ropes and pulleys, and a team of horses to raise the stacker's forks up and over the back of the stacker. It was like tossing the hay over your head. After several loads, the haystack was high enough. Then we'd move the stacker and start building another haystack. Sometimes Ken would tell me to stand on the forks and he would hoist me up and fling me into the haystack. This was real fun.

Douglas Hargreaves

My job on the haying operation was to drive the stacker team. When Olie unloaded the sweep onto the stacker forks, I'd give the team a click of my tongue and they'd start pulling the stacker forks up and over. When the forks got to the top of the stroke, the hay fell off onto the stack. I had to stop the horses just as the lift reached the back of the stacker, or they would snap the rope. Then I'd back them up, lowering the forks for Olie's next load.

I had no trouble catching on to this, and my first day went fine. I was lucky, because the two horses I was using were very gentle. Grandpa and Olie told me I had done well and they were proud of me. Ken never said anything to me, even when we sat down for tea break. Grandma always had tea and scones with raspberry jam. Grandpa and Olie sat around telling stories or joking with me during our break, while Ken ignored me. He wouldn't look at me or say anything. Sometimes I felt like crying.

I enjoyed the tea breaks because everything tasted so good and it gave me a chance to sit down. Haying was tiring work. I was starting to feel better about being here and everyone was treating me like I belonged--almost everyone.

We worked late the first day so we could finish Grandpa's fields the next day and move the stacker to Olie's. The men allowed Johnny to come haying the next day, but Johnny was sure upset when they didn't let him do any work. "Skipper's smaller than I am and he gets to run the stacker. It ain't fair!" he protested. No one took any notice, except one look from his father that ended his complaint. Grandpa gave him a

The Cowboy

wink and allowed him to ride with him on the mower. Grandpa had a way of making you feel better.

Johnny walked along with me and the team as I drove the stacker up and down. Grandpa said I was doing as well as anyone who ever helped him with haying. I felt good about that, though I thought he was putting me on. Grandpa would say something nice about me, then give me a big wink. I grew to really love Grandpa Wills.

We were late getting the chores done because we had been haying until dark. We always tried to get as much done in a day as we could. I was so tired I couldn't keep my eyes open. The last thing I remembered was sitting at the supper table. I was in my bed when I heard Ken's voice calling me to get up. I had one wish at that moment, and that was to get some more sleep. I was so sore I could hardly move.

I must have still been asleep during the milking. I was pouring milk into the separator when I lost my balance and some milk spilt on the floor. Ken looked real cross at me. "Gosh all Friday boy, how many times you gotta be told to be careful?" I ran over to the wash stand and wiped the milk up.

It wasn't very much, but Ken was looking for a reason to be mad at me. He usually found one. When he was mad at me I wouldn't look at him but this morning he told me to look him straight in the eye when he talked to me. "Yes sir." I replied. Then it was his turn not to stare at me.

I still had a few more days to go before my holiday would be over and I'd have to go home. We still hadn't heard from my parents. We drove into Millarville to get the mail and to see if there was a letter from them.

Douglas Hargreaves

There wasn't. Ken was sure upset. "What the hell kind of game they think they're playing, huh?" he demanded. I didn't know, that's for sure. I never said a word, but inwardly I was glad there was no letter. The post master asked Ken if I was the new kid he had been hearing about. Ken said I was and that he had expected a letter telling him what to do with me. I may have been happy if there had been no letter, but I was about to cry at the way Ken was talking. So I stepped outside and talked to the postmaster's son. Finally Ken came out and we drove home.

"Well kid, I don't know what the heck is goin' on." he said. "I just don't know what the hell to do with you."

I tried to keep the quiver out of my voice. "Please, can't I stay? Haven't I done everything you wanted me to?"

I guess my eyes gave me away, because he decided to be nice to me for a change. "As a matter of fact Skipper, I'm surprised you lasted this long. Everyone thinks you done just fine for your size and all. I can't find too many things to complain about. You really want to stay, after how hard I been on yah?"

"Oh yes, Mr. Wills, I'll do anything."

"Well, we'll have to see whether or not we hear from your folks and what they have planned for you."

"Please tell them you want me to stay." I pleaded again. He only sat looking straight ahead and we drove home in silence, each with our own thoughts. He had put an old horse blanket on the front seat so I could see out the front windshield.

We finished Grandpa's fields and moved the stacker over to Olie's. Now that was some chore. We

The Cowboy

had to tow the big stacker through fields and then down the main roadway to get it to Olie's. I had nothing to do but to stay out of their way. I might get hurt if I got under the horses while they were moving. Ken could sure cuss when the horses had a tough pull moving the stacker. He'd take the handle end of a pitch fork and give them such a whack, cussing them until they moved. Everything moved when Ken shouted. I didn't feel very good watching the horses get whacked. I knew how they felt.

We got everything set up and Ken said we would start haying first thing in the morning. It would take us two days to finish, counting the time it took to move the stacker.

Ken was starting to talk to me. He was being friendlier. I asked him why he didn't wake me up the other night when I fell asleep during supper. He told me he had tried but I slept sounder than an old maid in heat, whatever that meant. "I picked you up, got you ready for bed, and shoved you under the covers. You never moved an inch. How anyone can sleep that sound I'll never know."

It wasn't the last time he would have to do that. We worked so hard and were so tired when we got home, it was all we could do to finish the chores. I remember coming home one night and falling asleep on my horse as we were entering the corral. Ken caught me before I fell off. He showed me a way to get a few winks while riding. You put your hand on the horse's mane or saddle horn, then lay your head on your arm. He did the milking that night and I went to bed. I was so tired I never ate any supper. I don't think he ate either.

Douglas Hargreaves

On Sunday, Grandma Wills had looked me over carefully. She wondered if I was suffering any ill effects from the hard work. I told her I was just fine and liked what I was doing. "Well little man, you just don't overdo things, or you'll get sick." she cautioned. I think I was sick already because my bones ached like a toothache. I was sore all over but wouldn't tell Ken that. In truth, he was just as sore as me.

The only task I was having trouble with was harnessing the team. I knew where the various pieces went, but I couldn't lift them. I could never get them high enough to put on the horses' shoulders and backs.

I got to know the team well. They liked me and did what I wanted them to do. They knew their job better than I did, and several times they saved me from making mistakes. They probably could have managed without my handling the reins. We finished all the haying by mid-afternoon the next Saturday. Ken pointed to the creek, and I remembered Saturday was bath day. "Okay boy, get your clothes off." he told me as he stood undressing by the edge of the creek. I slowly undressed, wondering what was going to happen and who was going to go in first. The last one in would be a rotten egg. Well, I jumped in but he was faster. The creek was a little deeper where we bathed and ice cold. It took my breath away. It was deep enough to swim a few strokes.

I finished bathing first, or so I thought. "Get back in here you dirty little pig. You ain't done yet." Ken yelled. I wanted to get out of the cold water as soon as I could. He came over to me with a big bar of soap and washed my hair and behind my ears and everywhere else. "Now get under there and get the soap off yah."

The Cowboy

he laughed. That was only the second time I had ever heard Ken laugh.

He was enjoying our bath in the ice cold water. The water was so cold that my little thing just pulled itself inside out. I couldn't see where it had gone. Ken laughed again. I wasn't watching but he came behind me and heaved me far out into the deeper water, laughing like crazy. I liked to hear him laugh. It meant he wasn't mad any more. We dried off, dressed, and went back to the house.

When we got there, we found we had visitors. It was the Wilsons paying a neighbourly call. Ken wasn't overjoyed to see them, although I guess it got boring for him with only a little kid to talk to. As we walked to the house, Ken whispered, "Those buggers never come around unless they want to borrow something or pick up some gossip. They probably want to meet you."

"I gotta do some chores, Ken." I said. (I now had permission to call him Ken.)

"Kid, you come along. If I gotta listen to this, so do you." he chuckled.

So I met the Wilson boys. I liked Phillip the best. Billy and Willie were tough guys--at least I got that impression from the way they talked and behaved. They sure talked tough, as though they knew everything. Mr. Wilson told them to shut up for once. Phillip and I sat quietly together. He whispered that his brothers were really trying to show off in front of me.

"What's the boy do for ya, Ken?" Mr. Wilson asked, looking me up and down.

"He does everything, Tom. There ain't nothin' he ain't doin'. Milks the cows by himself, drives the stacker team. Hell, he's doin' a man's work. If the Wilsons hadn't been there, I would have given him a big hug. I knew at long last that he did care about whether I was there or not."

PEGGY'S SWIMMING HOLE

I had been at the ranch nearly three weeks, and I think Ken was getting a little annoyed at not hearing from my parents. He had received a letter from my aunt the previous week, saying that she had not heard from my parents. She was expecting to hear from them any day. Could I stay for a while longer?

We didn't talk about it anymore. I had been doing my chores and getting better at it all the time. I was to the point where I could milk all four cows myself and my hands no longer hurt.

One day, I rode over to get the mail from Peggy. If we were going to go into town, we would pick up the letters she wanted mailed, and her grocery list. Someone usually went in once a week. I was getting off my horse, when Peggy came over, flipped me upside down, and pinched my butt. She was always teasing me about having lots of padding back there. "I'll get the letters, Skipper. Why don't you go down and have a swim with the kids?" She pinched me again and I hollered. She loved to get a reaction from me. She stood there laughing after she put me down. "Run over past the barn and down the hill. You'll see them." Peggy tied Nixon to the rail outside the house as I ran off.

It wasn't really Peggy's swimming hole, but as it was on her ranch and it was close to her house, everyone called it Peggy's swimming hole. This was the best swimming hole around and kids from neighbouring ranches came there to swim. Beavers had been at work on this old creek for years and had it nearly dammed up. It was like a small lake with bushes and trees all around. The dam was about seven feet deep in the middle and two feet along the edges. The water running through it was perfectly clear and very cold. It warmed up a little on hot summer days. The cold didn't stop anyone from swimming.

When I got to the dam, the kids were having a great time throwing each other in the water and playing tag. I was surprised to see the boys and girls swimming together with no clothes on. Hooolly! This was not going to be for me.

Johnny saw me and came running out of the water. "Come on, Skipper. This is the best day we've had for a long time. Come on, get undressed and get in." He pulled me towards the edge. Well, I thought, if they weren't bothered about each other, then why should I? I had never seen a naked girl before. I didn't want to stare. One girl there was about my age.

They all started yelling for me to come on in. I undressed and jumped in as quickly as I could so no one would notice me. The water was freezing and I nearly choked when I felt it, but the feeling was glorious. I paddled about and got dunked a few times. We had great fun and I really did like the kids. Everyone played well together. Kathy, being the oldest, was the boss. She ran our games. I forgot I was swimming with girls and just enjoyed the good time I was having.

It was getting close to chore time and I figured I'd best get home. The others were getting out too. I ran over to where I had laid my clothes but they weren't there. I searched everywhere. I must have forgotten where I laid them. I was wandering all over looking in

The Cowboy

this bush and that bush trying to find my clothes. I was still naked.

The others were all dressed by now and laughing at my predicament, so I suspected them. I was really beginning to worry. "Please, you guys, give me back my clothes." I pleaded. They all chorused that they didn't know where my clothes were. I had to admit I never saw any of them out of the water while we were playing.

"Well, Skipper," said Johnny, "you must have forgotten where you took them off. You'll have to come home and borrow some of my stuff." Hooolly! How was I going to get to the house without Peggy seeing me?

I sort of sneaked up with Johnny. I was just crawling in through the gate when Peggy grabbed me from behind and hoisted me over her knee. She was laughing so hard that I thought she was crying. The tears were just rolling down her cheeks. "Why, Skipper, are you hiding something?"

I almost turned inside out with embarrassment. "Aw Peggy, please put me down."

"Skipper, where are your clothes, you poor dear?" Then she burst out laughing again. She was the one who had taken them while we were swimming. "You had better watch out from now on. You might never get them back one day. I'm sorry, Skipper, I just had to have a little fun with you." She produced my clothes and I retreated with Johnny to his room.

The kids had a big laugh at my expense, but it was okay. They were laughing with me, not at me. They were just having fun, and they knew their mother had taken my clothes. This wasn't the first time she had

Douglas Hargreaves

done that. "You had better get on home son." Peggy said. "Here are the letters for mailing. Tell Ken thanks."

I got on Nixon, waved goodbye and rode home. It was strange to find myself thinking of the ranch as home. But that was the way I felt.

Ken still didn't talk a lot but we were getting along much better. I didn't think of my parents at all. I was really happy for the first time in my life.

"Where the hell you been, boy?" Ken yelled at me as I rode up. I started shaking. What was wrong? I still had an hour to go before chores. I got off Nixon and let him into the corral. "I said, where the hell you been? Can't you answer me?" He seemed really upset. "I was swimming over at Peggy's--Ken." I tried to sound confident. "I been worrying like hell, wondering if something happened to you. I thought you might have got lost or something. Maybe you fell off your horse. Damn your little hide anyways."

Then I was over his knee and we went through the black and blue business again. I whimpered and sniffed and let out a couple of yells, and then it was over.

"Don't you ever do that again without telling me what you're doin', hear me Skipper? Scared me half to death. Gosh all Friday, boy, just watch out, that's all."

Ken was calming down and my behind was cooling off. He really did care about what happened to me. He really did care after all. "You hungry?"

"No Ken, not very." I sniffed a bit and wiped my eyes. I had tried hard to please him. He didn't have to tell me what to do any more. Well, as much as he hurt my feelings and my behind, I was still going to keep trying hard to convince him to allow me to stay.

The Cowboy

The next day, we rode into Millarville, all the way on horse back. That was the first time I would ride so far. Ken said he wanted to see if I was up to the longer ride coming up in the fall. I couldn't believe what I had just heard. The fall?

It took us three hours. We opened our lunch and ate down by the creek.

When we got to the store, there was a letter from my aunt saying she had heard from my folks. They were being held up in England for another two weeks. Could I stay a little longer? There was also a cheque for fifty dollars included in the letter. I didn't know whether it was the money or me that made Ken chuckle.

"I guess I'm stuck with you for a little while longer." he laughed.

I told him I was sorry, but my parents sometimes lost track of time.

"I'll say they do. Don't they even care about seeing you or your brother? You've been here almost a month now. Maybe the whole summer. What can they be thinking about? I'd miss you if you were my boy." There was a little quiver in his voice.

"They get really busy Ken, and they never have time to think about me or my brother. They like to travel and do things together. I don't think they should have had any kids."

He stared at me for a little while then said. "Well, kid, we gotta go. Get your behind in the saddle." I had no saddle. I was still riding bareback. This was Saturday afternoon and we were going to go to Grandma and Grandpa's tomorrow for dinner. I always liked that.

Douglas Hargreaves

Ken looked up at the building storm clouds. "Skipper, let's get going or we're going to get rained on before we get home." We took off at the trot this time. I guess it was okay, despite what Ken had told me about trotting your horse unless you really had to. Trotting really hurt my behind but I didn't complain. By the time we reached Sheep Creek, it was pouring buckets. We rode under some trees for shelter until lightning started flashing. Under trees during lightning was not the place to be, so we rode on. The downpour drenched us through by the time we got home. We put the horses away in the barn and fed them. Ken said it was important to look after your horse first, then yourself.

We went up to the house and got out of our wet clothes. Soon we had a fire going in the stove, and we made some hot tea to warm us up.

I was drying myself off when Ken picked me up and sat me on his knee. He'd never done this before. What had I done now? I thought he was going to turn me turtle again. Instead he held me close and patted my head. I laid my head on his shoulder and he said. "Skipper, I've really been mean to you, and I'm sorry. I don't know what I'll do when you really have to go home. You are just one hell of a boy." He was sniffling and choking a bit, and I saw a tear in his eye.

I started to sniffle a bit because I was so happy--I just couldn't help it. "I'm glad you're happy with me Ken." Then I really got brave. "I really love you." I told him. He hugged me tighter.

"And I love you too, Skipper. If ever I get married and have a boy, I want him to be exactly like you."

The Cowboy

The great sheet of ice between us had melted forever. Ken said, "I was afraid if I got too close to you, I wouldn't be able to let you go. I tried not to like you or want you around. After those first few days when you started doing your chores, I knew I was stuck on you. The way you tried so hard to do everything just right. You're a fine little boy, Skipper."

Just because our relationship had improved didn't mean that I didn't get his big hand on my hind end a few more times after that. But I knew it was from love, not temper or meanness. I really loved him, and I knew he loved me.

THE ONE-ROOM SCHOOL

The weeks turned into months. I had been at the ranch all summer. The end of August came and it was time for school. I would be staying until Christmas and maybe even longer, and couldn't have been happier. I wasn't the least bit unhappy as I chuckled to myself upon hearing the good news from my parents. Ken wasn't upset by the change in plans either. I knew he was happy the way things were turning out.

The prospect of school was something else. I had never been in a one-room school before, and the thought excited me. I liked school and was looking forward to starting. The thought of school upset some of the other kids.

My aunt had mailed Ken my school reports and documents from my last school. Until then, only my ranch family and my friend, Gordy, knew I was in Grade Seven. To save myself a lot of explaining about my age and my grades, I had lied to everyone telling them I was in Grade Five. That was easy for them to believe. I never thought I would be going to school here. Now I would have to face them all with the truth. It wasn't as though I had done anything terrible.

The summer had finished well for me, and Ken and I were getting along fine. I was his boy. I had learned everything I needed to do on the ranch. I was getting to be a good rider, and as for my chores, they were getting easier by the day. Ken taught me how to use a lariat and to do some rope tricks. I liked it when we would sit and talk in the evenings when he wasn't listening to Jimmie Rodgers or I wasn't reading.

Even though Ken loved and cared about me, he still smacked my arse every now and again. He made sure I would remember what he taught me, even if it meant learning by the seat of the pants. I think he felt he could drive instructions into my head through my backside. I wondered if this system would work in school. The few smacks I was getting didn't bother me all that much any more, except they hurt my feelings. I think Ken felt I was still a little kid instead of being ten. My size must have had a lot to do with it. At least he wasn't threatening to send me home any more. Sometimes my pride got a little bruised along with my butt.

At long last I had finally got what I wanted, and here I was getting ready to go to school. Gordy was my best friend. It didn't bother him that we would be in the same grade, even though he was two years older than me. Gordy lived two miles south of our ranch. He had no one to chum around with except me, and he and I got along well together. I was smaller than Gordy, but then I was smaller than almost everyone around our parts. He told me I talked like a grown up. I hadn't lied to him about my real school grades and he took me at my word when I told him I was in Grade Seven. "You must be smart, Skipper." he said and went on to tell me that he had to work real hard to pass and didn't like school very much.

"It's okay, Gordy," I said, "I'll help you any way I can. It's easy for me."

"Thanks, Skipper. The only time I ever get a lickin' is over that darned school. I wish it had never been

The Cowboy

invented, or at least that I had some more brains." I told him about Ken's method of putting something into my brain. "Yeah, I guess everyone knows about Ken's temper and how you get treated sometimes." Gordy said.

"I wonder how something like that would get around. I sure never told anyone." We laughed.

Ken made sure I was properly set up in my new school, and that the teacher received all my documents. He had ridden to school with Gordy and me.

While he was busy talking to Miss Snowdon, the teacher, I was meeting some of my new school mates. There was Gordon, and there was Phillip Wilson who filled me in on all the routines and introduced me to the local girls.

"Well goodness me, what have we got here?" said one of the girls with a wink. Her name was Becky Mortinsen. I hated that kind of stuff, girls and that kind of thing. I didn't mind them as long as they didn't bother me. The girls just sat and twittered like a bunch of birds. Ugh! The school had the same number of girls as boys.

There was only one other person in Grade Seven besides Gordy, and that was Billy Wilson and he was four years older than me. He was sure annoyed that he and I were to be in the same grade. "How come this punk kid gets to be in my class anyway?" he said to Miss Snowdon.

"Never mind that kind of talk Billy, just take your seat and we'll introduce Skipper to everyone." she scolded. "Skipper, with these marks of yours, I'm sure you're going to do just fine. You certainly have been a little achiever, haven't you?"

Douglas Hargreaves

"Yeah, he sure looks like a little suck-up, if you ask me." Willie Wilson volunteered.

"No one asked you Willie. Now be quiet." said Miss Snowdon. "All the grades are mixed together Skipper, so you won't be the smallest one in the room." I could tell that I was going to like her. She had a nice smile and she seemed to like me. She took to everyone who worked hard in school and did well. That was me, Old Suck-up. Well, I did like school. So what? Miss Snowdon told me she was going to give me a "make up" test, whatever that was, to see how well I would fit in. I sure got some looks from the rest of the kids, especially the Wilsons.

Peggy's kids were happy that I was going to school with them. We had become quite close over the summer, especially Johnny and me.

When I looked at Miss Snowdon's test, I realized she just wanted me to prove my report card was correct. There were questions from Grade Eight and Nine. I think I answered them correctly. The results of the test proved very exciting for me. Miss Snowdon told me I would be taking some Grade Eight and Nine subjects. That sure upset Billy as he stared at me mouthing the words SUCK UP!

Grandpa called Gordy, Phillip, Johnny, and me, the Four Musty Steers. I guess it was because we were always playing or doing our homework together. We liked that name because it was funny and it sure suited us. After school we would come to my place and sit around the kitchen table doing our homework. It worked out just fine in the fall, but as the days grew shorter, we had to get home to do the chores earlier, while we still had some daylight.

The Cowboy

Winter time was more difficult because of the darkness. When it was getting dark by four thirty in the afternoon, I would have to get the cows from the pasture in the dark and milk by oil lamp. Gordon and I worked on his school problems Friday evening or Saturday morning. Phillip would try to come as often as he could, but his father demanded he be home right after school.

One day Gordy came over after supper to do some homework. He always wore his tan Stetson hat which I admired very much. But today it wasn't the tan one but a black one, and it sure didn't fit him very well. "Skipper, how do you like my new hat? I haven't worn it for a long time. Don't you think the black one looks better?" I knew he was kidding because it looked terrible and didn't fit very well. He told me that an aunt had given it to him. He never wore it unless he went to visit her, or she came to the ranch.

"That's sure a nice hat Gordy, but I don't think it suits you as well as your other one." I laughed.

"It isn't mine any more Skipper, because I'm giving it to you." Gordy blushed at the awkwardness of making the presentation. He knew how much I had wanted a western hat. That was all I needed to make me into a cowboy--at least that's what I hoped.

I was so excited. "Gordy, that's the best present anyone's ever given me." I put it on, and it was made for me. I couldn't believe how well it fit.

I ran to the corral where Ken was just closing the gate. "Well, what the heck you got on your head, boy? Gosh a'mighty, you look like a real wild west cowboy." he laughed. I was a little embarrassed. I pushed it back on my head as I had seen him do, and he laughed again. "Ain't you the smart ass."

I was so happy I couldn't thank Gordon enough, and asked him if it really was mine. He told me his ma had agreed that I should have it, so he got on his horse and came right over with it. I would wear it to school tomorrow.

When Gordon had gone home and I was getting into bed, Ken came into my bedroom. "Okay kid, where's the hat?"

"Right here Ken." I pulled it out from under the covers. I had it on my head until I heard him coming into my room. He laughed and told me to make sure I looked after it, as it was a very good hat, and a nice gift.

He was still laughing as he gave me a pat on the shoulder. "Good night cowboy." he whispered.

THAT BIG HOLE IN MY HAT

Riding to school with my new hat set casually on my head made me feel like a king. I was finally going to look like the other guys. Gordy, Johnny and Phillip were waiting when I got to our gate. We usually rode together. Phillip had to leave ahead of his brothers, Billy and Willie, to ride with us.

As we rode into the school yard, Miss Snowdon noticed my new hat and remarked how dashing I looked. I almost bust the buttons off my shirt, I was so proud.

A little while later, Billy and Willie Wilson rode in and glared at me as they unsaddled their horses. "Hey dude," one of them yelled, "think the hat is going to make you look bigger? You're still a little SUCK UP runt and teacher's pet."

"Why do they hate me so much?" I asked Phillip.

"Skipper, they hate everyone, just like Pa does."

The bell rang and we went into school. There were only a few remarks about my hat. We were never allowed to wear our hats into the classroom and kept them in the cloak room. I couldn't wait for lunch time to wear my hat.

It irritated Billy Wilson that I was taking the same subjects he was. He ridiculed anything I had to say and made a general horse's backside of himself. Miss Snowdon tried to deal with his behaviour, but he just laughed at her. This annoyed her and she told him to grow up and pay as much attention to his work as I did. That only set him off more.

Douglas Hargreaves

The girls in the Grade Six class made rude remarks and whistled at me. Becky Mortinsen was the worst because she went around telling everyone that I was her new boy friend. She was really wild when she saw my new hat. She kept making rude sounds to embarrass me during class. Noticing Becky's behaviour, Willie started making the same sounds. Miss Snowdon became very angry. She looked at me as though I were the source of the trouble. She knew I wasn't, but didn't know what to do.

When lunch time came, Billy and Willie were waiting for me in the barn. "Nice hat kid." Billy said.

Willie came over to me and told me I should start growing up if I wanted to wear a man's hat. "I hear tell you're Ken's bastard." Willie snarled.

"Everyone will know before long, huh?" Billy added.

"What do you mean by that?" I yelled.

Willie shoved me from behind and I lost my balance and fell to the ground. I got up and Billy came over to me and pulled my hat down over my ears. Hoooolllyy that hurt! I couldn't see, but Gordy came to my rescue. He shoved Billy away, but Willie nailed him with a fist to the side of the head. We weren't big enough to take on these guys.

Phillip yelled at his brothers to quit or he was going to tell their Pa. Willie kicked Phillip in the behind and told him to shut up or else. Billy and Willie sputtered more threats, and then Willie grabbed the hat while Billy held my arms. Willie took the hat over to the fence and jammed it down on a post. Now there was a big hole through the top of my prized possession.

The Cowboy

I was so mad I could hardly see through my tears. I swung with all my might and caught Willie square on the nose. To my surprise, blood rushed from his damaged beak.

Becky and her friends, who had been watching the goings on, cheered for me. "That's my boy Skippy baby, hit him again." Becky yelled. Hooooolyy! I hated that.

Willie ran into the school. I was sure I was in for it now. As I bent over to pick up what was left of my hat, Billy kicked me in the bum so hard I flew through the air.

Miss Snowdon had seen to Willie and rang the bell for us to resume classes. I was whimpering and sniffling as I came into the room. I could hardly walk. Miss Snowdon said. "What happened to you Skipper, and why did you hit Willie? I am very surprised at you Skipper. I don't think Mr. Wills is going to be very happy to hear of your behaviour at all."

I told her that Willie had made me mad and I just socked him one. I wasn't about to tell her the whole story for fear of making matters worse for me. Billy had a smug look as he watched from his seat. He knew I wouldn't say anything. He'd fix my wagon later.

"It wasn't Skipper's fault, Miss Snowdon." Becky said in her loudest voice. "It was Billy and Willie. They started it." Hoooooollly!

When the school day was finally over, I couldn't sit on Nixon because my behind was so sore. Nixon and I walked with Gordon. He told me I should have told the teacher. But when I explained why I had kept my mouth shut, he agreed that was probably the best thing, and added that I had better stay away from the

Douglas Hargreaves

Wilsons. "But we like Phillip. It wasn't his fault. I'm sure going to get a lickin' when Ken finds out." I moaned. Gordy just looked sad for me.

After a while, he said. "Skipper, what did Willie mean when he said you were Ken's bastard?"

"I don't know, but I think he was just lashing out at me."

I could not remember feeling so low in my life. I knew what lay ahead for me but couldn't think of a way out of my dilemma. Gordy left me at my gate and I mounted Nixon. The time was getting on, and I was already a little late.

I found the cows and herded them to the barn. I put Nixon in the corral and started to milk. I couldn't sit, so I knelt down. The pain was so bad that I wondered if I was bleeding.

Ken came in and asked why I was kneeling down like that instead of sitting on the stool. "Just seeing if I could do it this way." I fibbed.

"Where's your hat?"

"Oh, it got in an accident."

"Yeah? What kind of an accident?"

I got up from the first cow and hobbled over to the next one. Ken was feeding the horses and couldn't help seeing my awkwardness. "What the hell's wrong with you anyway?" he chuckled. "You crap your pants or something?"

I couldn't help sniffling, and then the tears started.

"Gosh all Friday, boy, you get in some kind of trouble?" I had to tell him what happened. I knew he wouldn't appreciate my crying, and tried to hide it as best I could.

The Cowboy

"You get up to the house. I'll finish milking and then we'll see what the heck this is all about."

I walked up to the house and I let myself cry. What was I going to do? I knew I was in deep trouble and Ken wasn't going to put up with this at all.

I was leaning against the porch railing when he came up with the milk. He had to make two trips, doing it by himself. We didn't say a word as we did the separating. When we finished, Ken said. "Lets have a look at your arse."

"It's okay, Ken, it'll get better."

"Get your pants off." he yelled at me. I took them off and he whipped me over his knee like I was going to get the Big Hand, only this time he just looked at my injuries.

As he examined my bruised posterior, he said, "Holy old Friday." Billy's boot had not broken the skin, but I was badly bruised. That Wilson kid had kicked me very hard.

Ken was furious. He got some liniment from the cupboard and smoothed some on my injured behind. That felt good, but I was still afraid I was going to get a spanking.

At last he said, "Skipper, I'm sorry about this. Those bastards will pay, I promise you that." He was red in the face like he got when he was mad at me or the horses.

"Ken, what did Billy mean when he called me your bastard?"

"He was just making mean talk, that's all, Skipper. Don't pay him any mind at all. Gosh all Friday, what I would do to get my hands on those fellahs."

Douglas Hargreaves

As he put me down, there was a knock on the door. In came the Wilson boys' Pa, Tom Wilson. He was just as red in the face as Ken.

"What the hell's that kid of yours doing walloping Willie and giving him a bloody nose?" Ken made me drop my pants again so he could show Mr. Wilson how badly I had been kicked. "Boy, he booted him right dead on huh?" Mr. Wilson sort of laughed. Then he started saying I had it coming until Ken interrupted him and told him exactly what had happened.

Ken said that unless I got a new hat and an apology from his boys, he was going to make trouble. If one of the Wilson boys ever laid a hand on me again, Ken said he would beat the hell out of all of them. "You hear me, Tom Wilson? Just one more time and that's it."

Mr. Wilson drew his horns in and admitted Billy had hurt me pretty bad. Those boys sure caused him lots of grief. He said he was sorry if he had got it wrong. The thought of Ken cleaning his clock was the real fear for him. He told me he was sorry and that the boys would apologize. "I hear tell you and Phillip get along real good. He calls you his best friend." Mr. Wilson said to me. "You'll have a new hat as soon as I can get one." Then he walked out the door.

Ken turned to me. "I'm sorry, Skipper. I didn't mean to doubt your word--you never lie to me. You feeling any better?" I was feeling better.

We had supper and I did my homework and went to bed. Ken finished my chores.

By morning I felt a lot better, although I was still walking funny and dreaded having to see the Wilsons at school. Moreover, I wondered what Miss Snowdon

The Cowboy

was going to tell Ken. Would Ken still believe my version of the story?

When I got to school, Gordy asked me if I had got another tanning at home. I told him what had happened. "Golly Skipper, you was sure lucky. Did you tell him what Willie called you?"

"Yes I did Gord, and he told me that they were just mean mouthing me to make me feel bad."

"Would you like to be Ken's kid?"

"Ha! You know I would. In fact, I practically am, aren't I?" We both laughed.

The Wilson boys arrived with their father. Willie and Billy each came to me and apologized with bloodshot fire in their eyes. I guess their father had laid it on them good last night. Mr. Wilson went in and told Miss Snowdon it was his boys who caused the trouble. "Skipper did what any normal boy would do." he told her. I felt good that he had cleared my name.

Miss Snowdon came over to my desk, put her hand on my shoulder, and told me I was a fine young man for not telling on the boys. "I'm sorry, Skipper. I could hardly believe my best student would stoop so low as to brawl." I grew red and hung my head.

But it was over, at least for now. I knew that one day Willie and Billy Wilson would try to even the score. Still, I think I was just as scared of Becky and her friends.

MY SECRET

There can be no more beautiful time of the year than the fall. The foothills of the Rockies shimmer with the majesty of colour, and present the most magnificent sight one could ever hope to see. Every valley produces its own blanket of colour. The leaves select their own time to change colour. Grandma said it all depended on the kinds of trees and shrubs, what colours they'd be. Riding back and forth to school, and then the round up, provided very exciting times for me.

Grandpa really was my Grandpa--at least he and I thought so, and there was little doubt now that I was a member of the family. It was as though I had always been around. How could I ever bear it when the time came for me to leave? My parents were still in England, but that didn't bother me or Ken any more. I knew it wasn't right, but I was hoping they'd stay there forever. I tried to keep that thought from my mind. I loved my new life, everything about it and everybody in it.

Grandpa championed and encouraged me; I was the shining light in his life. I think he enjoyed me more than his real grandkids. Grandpa and I would sit and talk about all kinds of things. He'd advise me about ranching and all its activities, and what was important to remember. We'd sit by the fireplace where he'd show me books of photos of different ranch people from the valley. They called this area the "Oil Capital of Canada" and we were just on the edge of the famous

Douglas Hargreaves

Turner Valley oil strike. There was oil well drilling going on all over the place.

Grandpa had been here long before any of that started. He had come over from England to homestead, and his British accent was still strong. Grandma also brought some of her Scottish brogue with her. Grandpa said she was very Scottish with their money. If she couldn't make it, build it, or bake it, then she could do without. She said that Grandpa, on the other hand, would buy it if they needed it, because that what was money was for. She said he did that because he was from Devonshire.

Depending on the weather, Ken and I spent most Saturday afternoons and Sundays at Grandma and Grandpa's. Sometimes Saturdays were too busy at home to go visiting. We'd have to make our bread supply last until we could get to Grandma's. She did all our baking for us. Quite often we would sleep over and ride home early next morning to do chores. Sometimes we'd take the truck because it was faster, but mostly we rode our horses.

Ken watched over my studies like a hawk. Quite often he would sit with me as I did my homework, offering help here and there. I liked it when we worked together. He didn't have much schooling but he sure knew a lot. We talked about feed and cattle prices, and how much we could make if we did this or that. I think he valued my opinion more than most others he talked to.

Mother had never told Ken about my stomach problem when I first arrived. My stomach cramps hadn't bothered me too much so far, but now they were getting more frequent, and I was afraid to tell anyone I

The Cowboy

was in trouble. If Ken thought I was ill, he might think he couldn't look after me. I think everyone knew something was wrong because I looked terrible. Still, I didn't tell Ken.

One day when I was at Peggy's, I got the cramps so bad I could hardly stand up. I thought I was going to throw up. "What's eatin' you, Skipper?" Olie asked.

"Nothing really, Olie just an old stomach ache." I lied.

"You all plugged up?"

I told him I was having a problem right now, and couldn't go. "Castor oil works sometimes, Olie. Do you have any?" I asked. Then I said, "Olie, please don't tell Ken about this. He might send me home if he thought I was sick. I know he will."

"We ain't got any castor oil, Skipper, but I got something better that'll fix you up." he said. "Olie please don't tell Ken,"I begged again.

"Come down to the barn, Skipper, and I'll get you unplugged, okay?"

I ran along beside him as he strode down towards the barn. "How you going to do that, Olie?" I wondered with some concern. He didn't answer right away. Olie's kids were getting their horses out of the barn and wanted to know what we were doing. Johnny stayed behind while the others went up to the house.

From and old wooden chest Olie brought out this big metal tube that looked like a giant hypodermic syringe. Just like the one they shot you in the arm with for chicken pox. But this one was a whole lot bigger and had a long tube where the needle would be. Olie went over to the water trough and filled it with water.

Douglas Hargreaves

"Okay Skipper, this is what the kids get when they get bunged up--right, Johnny?"

"Better get your pants off, Skipper." Johnny advised. "It ain't nothin', Skipper--you won't feel a thing and you'll sure feel better."

I didn't have to be a mind-reader to figure out where Olie was going to put that thing. I remembered having it done to me in the hospital one time. I should have thought of this before. At least I never got sick from it and my cramps left me right away. "This'll get rid of your stomach ache right pronto." said Olie. I knew he was right, so I didn't complain.

After my "treatment," as Olie called it, I felt much better and my cramps were gone. "Thank you, Olie," I said as we walked up to the house, "you saved my life." He said I would be a few pounds lighter.

He told Peggy what we had done. "How are you feeling now, Skipper? Why didn't you tell us before?" she asked.

"I'm fine now, Peggy. I was afraid Ken might find out."

Johnny joked that I looked better and wasn't so full in the face. We chased each other out of the house.

Olie told Peggy that he had promised not to tell Ken about my problem. Any time I was in trouble again, Olie instructed, I was to come right over. After that I made several trips to Peggy and Olie's for their help. They kept me healthy and that was all that counted.

We kept my secret from Ken all winter and into the spring. Then one afternoon I came home from school with a terrible stomach ache. It was the first one I'd had in a long time. When I got home I thought about riding

The Cowboy

over to Peggy's, but instead lay on my bed and rubbed my stomach.

Ken came in. "What's eatin' you, son? We got chores to do, let's get at them." I could hardly stand up. "What's wrong, Skip, you got the bloat or something?" I had to tell him about my stomach ache. "It'll go away in a few minutes." I said.

"I don't recall you gettin' belly aches. You ever get them before?" "Sometimes."

"You ain't plugged up, are you?" Ken sounded very concerned.

"I think I am. Sometimes I can't go for awhile. Can I ride over to Peggy's? She gets rid of them easy."

"What she give you?"

"Well, when I get cramps, I go over there and Olie or Peggy flushes me out with water." I was worried Ken might be upset with me for not having told him before.

"Well then, boy, let's get you over there right now." he said. "Can you ride okay? Why didn't you tell me before, Skipper?"

I got off my bed and we walked out to the corral, saddled up, and headed for Peggy's. Johnny saw us coming and by the look on my face, he knew what was wrong. Ken told them I had a stomach ache from being all plugged up. Johnny yelled, "Hey, Skipper, you gonna get the water, huh?"

Peggy showed Ken how to look after me, in case they weren't around sometime. "I got the proper equipment right in my workshop." Ken said. He went on to explain how he had spotted this old hospital stuff in a second hand store in Calgary, and figured that was just what he needed to keep the grindstone wet. He claimed it worked like a damn. He had me fill the can with water one day and said with a chuckle, "You know what that hospital thing is used for, Skipper?" I told him I knew what it was for, because they used it on me when I was in the hospital once.

I was feeling good now. I was happy Ken hadn't been upset with me not telling him about my cramps.

"I can always send you to the Valley Hospital and let them do it if you like." Ken laughed.

"How am I supposed to get there . . . walk?"

"Well, it's either there or the workshop." Everyone was laughing now, even me.

THE TRUTH

When I came to the ranch, Ken laid down a set of rules about how I was to behave and what chores I had to do. He also warned me in no uncertain terms that he didn't like liars. If he ever caught me in a lie, I wouldn't sit down for a week. I believed him, so I never lied. Never.

He seemed concerned when I brought a note home from the teacher. "What's in the note Skipper?" he demanded in his scariest voice. "You in some sort of trouble?" I didn't know what was in it, but I think Ken felt there was trouble in it for him, and then probably me. He had been cross all day because he had put his foot in the bucket of axle grease in the workshop. I was glad I wasn't around. I could hear him all the way into the kitchen. He wasn't mad at me. It was his usual routine when he was furious, and I learned to stay clear of him. First he blew off steam, then went around with a scowl, not saying a word.

I had never brought a note home from school before. It was in a sealed envelope, and I had no idea what was in it. Usually the only time a kid brought a note home, it was to report on some misbehaviour or failing to do homework or some other bad news.

The note said that several of the boys had been caught cheating and borrowing notes from me during a test. Miss Snowden advised that I not be bullied by these boys into giving them any notes, or even helping them with their homework. They were required to do it on their own.

Douglas Hargreaves

"Did you give any notes away, Skipper?" I could tell by the sound of Ken's voice that he was on the verge of yelling.

I tried to sound self-assured. "No sir. They took them out of my books at recess time."

"Skipper, you ain't covering for anyone are you?"

"No sir, I'm not," I replied in a shaky voice.

"The Wilsons or Browns, huh?" He guessed.

My classmates were always asking me to give them my study notes, especially before a test. The only ones I gave notes to were Gordon and Phillip, and only when we were studying at home together. The Wilsons were always threatening to knock my block off. They could too--they were big enough. "I'll tell my parents about what they're doing." Phillip would say, putting on a brave front. He was the third youngest of the Wilson brothers. But we knew he wouldn't dare say a word because his brothers would have pounded him good. He was always coming to school with bruises or black eyes. If it wasn't from his brothers, it was from his father.

Mr. Wilson sometimes treated his boys like they were criminals. Phillip would cry when he talked about it. Gordy and I felt terrible and sad for him. We considered ourselves very lucky. Once I asked Ken if he knew how badly Mr. Wilson treated his boys. "People should just mind their damned business, that's all." he replied. I wouldn't want anyone interfering in my business when I have to punish you." I dropped the subject but I sometimes cried for Phillip. He was my best friend next to Gordon.

Ken didn't treat me like a criminal, but he had a habit of sometimes taking the other person's word

The Cowboy

before mine. It wasn't that he actually mistrusted me, it was just in his nature. In the past he had sometimes punished me first, then asked questions afterward. He didn't do that any more. Still, I got scared sometimes.

So I knew enough never to tell Ken a lie. If I did, I knew I wouldn't sit down for a week. This matter of lying nearly caused me to get in the worst trouble of my ranch life so far, and it was from telling the truth and had nothing to do with school or the Wilson brothers. It had to do with the little shack out back.

I was always having trouble going potty. In the first place, I hated the outhouse because it smelled so bad. It almost choked me. In the second place, I couldn't go anyway. I would sit there for what seemed like hours, trying to get some action going.

One Sunday after church I felt the urge. I had to go really bad, which was very unusual for me. Must have been something I ate. I ran to the outhouse behind the church but there was someone in it. I just about opened the door when I heard a voice from inside. Someone sort of whispering. Hooollly! I didn't know if I could wait. I jumped around a little, trying to squeeze everything back into place. I knew I wasn't going to win. If I didn't get into the toilet right away, I'd poo my pants, and then I would get it. I'd never hear the end of it. I would be too embarrassed to look anyone in the face again. "PLEASE HURRY." I silently prayed. The door stayed closed but the whispering went on. The car horn blew and I knew Ken, Grandma, and Peggy were getting impatient with me taking so long. I had told them where I was going. They said they would wait.

Hooolly! This was it. I felt everything start to move so I ran over to the bushes behind the outhouse. I was

Douglas Hargreaves

afraid my good pants might get messed on so I quickly took them off. I was just in time. Ohh, what a relief. Everyone would have a great laugh if they knew of my near accident.

I was squatting and trying to stay hidden when the outhouse door opened and out came the visiting pastor. He didn't know I was in the bushes. I figured I'd just sneak in to the crapper and finish the job now that he was gone. With my pants and underwear in my hand, I crept over to the outhouse and was just reaching for the door when I heard someone inside. Hoooolly! Not again--and me without my pants on! I couldn't get away. I thought for sure I was caught.

Out came Charlene Isbister. As the door opened outwards, it almost flattened me against the wall. She didn't see me behind the door. I quickly stepped backwards along side of the building. I was safe for a moment. Hoooolllyy! What would anybody say if they found me standing there like that? All I was wearing was a shirt and tie. At least I was hidden from view. I wondered how many more were still in there.

She went into the church by the back door and didn't notice me. I was shaking so bad, I thought for sure I would give myself away. I couldn't hear anyone else in there, so I quietly opened the door. It was empty.

There was a catalogue on the seat, thank goodness. Hooooollly! I couldn't figure how Charlene Isbister got in there. She hadn't gone there after the pastor left. She must have been in there at the same time. It was sure strange to me.

I finished my job but couldn't understand what had taken place. Why were they both in there at the same

The Cowboy

time? Maybe she had got caught, like me. That would have been real brotherly of the pastor to have shared the potty with her. When I finally got back to the car, Ken said, "Gosh all Friday, Skipper, what the hell's been keeping you? You shit your pants or something?" Ken could use that word, but not me. He didn't know how close to the truth he was. This was one time when it would have been better for me had I not said anything, let alone tell the truth.

"I had to go so bad but the pastor was using it. I had to wait but he didn't come out for a long time, so I had to go in the bushes." Grandma sniffed to see if anything was sticking to me.

"That shouldn't have taken so long." Ken kept on.

"I waited in the bushes till the pastor came out, then I was going to go in. I was just going to the door when it opened and Charlene Isbister came out. Hooolllyy, was I ever scared. She didn't see me, though." I was getting redder all the time.

"I thought you said you went right up there after the pastor came out." Ken said.

"Yes sir, I did, but she must have been in there before the pastor came. Maybe she had to go bad too."

Grandma gave Ken a strange look. Peggy was sitting in the front seat but never spoke a word. She just sat there smiling. "Are you telling the truth, Skipper, you little scamp?" Grandma asked.

Peggy came to my defence. "Skipper doesn't lie. You know that, Mother. I'll bet he's just got mixed up or something."

Grandma looked ready to shake the daylights out of me. "You must have made a mistake, isn't that right Skipper? How could you say such a thing? How could you tell such a story?" She sounded almost ready to weep.

"Honest Grandma, that's what happened, I swear. After she got out, she went into the church through the back." I was getting worried now. What was all the big fuss about?

I could tell by the look on Ken's face that there was a "gosh all Friday" lecture coming. "You know what I told you about never lying to me. Why are you doing it now? Why you telling such a rotten thing?"

"Why don't you believe me, Ken? Why do you think I'm lying?"

Now he was really upset, and barked, "I don't know why you would want to tell such a crazy story anyway. You know what? You're going to get it right here and now, you know that?"

I knew it was bum warming time, but there had to be a way to prove that I was telling the truth. Otherwise, what would everyone think of me? They wouldn't believe me any more. I started to cry. "Quit that snivelling." said Ken. "You ain't been licked yet."

We were still parked in the field by the church. Peggy came to my rescue, as she always did. "Why not go back and see if there is anyone in the church?" she said. "Everyone is supposed to be gone, but you never know."

"I'll go look," Ken volunteered, "and there had better be a Charlene in there, or someone's in deep trouble." I wasn't lying--there had to be someone in the church.

Ken walked back to the church and opened the door. I crossed my fingers, hoping Charlene hadn't slipped out the back door. In a moment, Ken and

The Cowboy

Charlene walked out of the church. Hoooollly! I felt like hugging Peggy right there.

Ken offered Charlene a ride home and she got in beside Grandma and me. Grandma never said a word all the way home. Charlene was all talk and making light of everything. Ken asked her why she had missed her ride.

"Well, I had to talk to the pastor for a few minutes and I think my family thought I had gone home with someone else." she explained. She didn't know we were aware of her outhouse expedition with our visiting pastor.

Neither Ken nor Grandma spoke a word. They just sat there, looking straight ahead. Ken looked back at Charlene, then at me. I looked at Ken, but he quickly looked away.

"That visiting pastor is sure a great speaker, and has a good service, don't you think?" Charlene remarked.

"Yeah he's good at servicin'." Ken muttered.

Grandma looked daggers at him. Peggy just sat there, smiling and chuckling. I could always tell when Peggy was laughing--she would jiggle up and down. She didn't laugh out loud most of the time.

No one mentioned my story at supper that night, and I sure didn't want to ask any more questions about it. I felt somehow I had missed something in all of these goings on. Ken never mentioned anything about my story, and he didn't apologize for having doubted my word, either. Peggy did, though, and gave me a big hug and a kiss on the cheek. And, as usual, she pinched my bum.

Things were back to normal for me, but the way they were all talking, things were not going to be normal again for Charlene. The visiting pastor never came back to our parish again. I wondered if he didn't like us. From now on, I would think twice before I told another story, even if it was the truth.

COUNTRY CHRISTMAS

Winter was approaching. Ken was very proud of my school marks and the teacher's report. I was happy too. It looked like I was going to get honours this year, and maybe a scholarship. At least I hoped so.

It was getting close to Christmas and the excitement of the season had a grip on me. Ken had made me a deal that I would get part of the egg money for an allowance. I saved most of it to buy gifts when we went shopping at the Williams Brothers store in Calgary. Ken gave me five dollars to add to my spending money. I was rich!

I bought gifts for some people and made presents for others. I didn't spend all my money. Grandpa said I took after Grandma.

We had been talking about and preparing for Christmas for a month. Now it was Christmas morning. The weather was just right for the season--we had lots of snow. After chores, we took Ken's truck over to Grandpa's. Peggy and the kids were already there, and what a time they were having! Grandpa gave me my usual big hug and Peggy gave me a kiss on the cheek and pinched my butt.

I had never seen a more beautiful Christmas tree in all my life. It was loaded with more gifts than I had ever seen. There were a lot of us, but there would be at least one present for everyone, and maybe a couple more for the kids. Times were really hard, and the grown-ups warned us not to expect too much. They always said that.

Douglas Hargreaves

We ate breakfast then went into the big living room where a fire was blazing in the stone fireplace. I was so excited I could hardly contain myself. I tried to be calm and act like a grown-up but it was almost too much for me. If I got too excited or rambunctious, Ken would get a little upset with my childish behaviour.

"What do you think that big parcel is under there?" Johnny whispered to me, pointing to a huge package.

"Who is it for?" I wondered.

"I don't know but we can look." But we couldn't get near enough without toppling the tree. I didn't want to risk getting my butt warmed on such an exciting day.

"Skipper, have you received anything from your parents yet?" Grandma asked.

"Not yet, Grandma. Probably got lost or held up some place. I got fifty dollars in my last letter. Maybe that's my Christmas present, do you think?" Of course I did not believe my own words. I had also received a card from my brother and my aunt in Winnipeg, who didn't seem to know much more about my parents than I did. The fifty dollars was nice, and we could sure use it. I wondered why they had sent it. Anyway, I had a family and they loved me, and I loved them.

After breakfast we gathered around the tree. Grandpa started to hand out the presents, and the first one was for Grandma from me. I had bought her a new knitting bag. She made a big fuss over that. "Skipper, you are such a dear boy. I needed one, you know."

"Thank you, Grandma."

I gave Ken a new belt with a large cowboy buckle on it. "Just what I needed to hold up my pants and for you know what else." he laughed as he put it on. I

The Cowboy

wondered if that had been such a good idea. He might decide it was easier on his hand if he used his gift on my butt. That would be some present, I thought. The Wilsons always got the belt. Gordy did too sometimes. I never got the belt--only the hand.

Grandpa's eyes shone when he opened up the new pipe I had given him. Ken had helped me pick it out, so it would be the right kind. Grandpa got up and gave me a big hug, and the next thing I knew, I was off the floor floating through the air high above his head.

"Grandpa!" I shouted joyfully, "aren't I getting a little too big for you to be heaving over your head?"

"That will be the day, little man." he laughed.

Johnny got him tobacco for Christmas, so we had both looked after his smoking needs. Grandpa gave Johnny a ride too.

Peggy gave me a new jacket she had made for me with my name embroidered on the pocket. Everyone received little items, mostly home-made.

The big parcel still lay under the tree. "Who's the big one for, Grandpa?" Johnny asked.

"Well now Johnny, let's see who's name is on it. Santa must have had one heck of a time getting that one down the chimney! Well now, look at that--it looks like the name on it is spelled, S-K-I-P-P-E-R."

"Hooolly!" I shrieked.

By the size of the parcel, I had a good idea what it was, but was afraid it might not be. Grandpa picked the parcel up, but the paper started to tear and come off. I saw leather underneath the wrapping. "Grandpa--it's a saddle!"

It was a boy's size, and a beauty. Ken and Grandpa had gone together and found it. Ken said it wasn't brand new, but he and Grandpa had polished it and brought the leather back to new. It had belonged to a boy who had outgrown it, and he had sure looked after it. It was the most beautiful saddle in the whole world. Johnny was as delighted as I was. He already had a saddle of his own.

Tears started to well up in my eyes, and Grandpa said, "It's okay Skipper, you deserve it."

I went over to Ken, who was sitting in a chair beside Grandpa, and threw my arms around him and thanked him. I hugged Grandpa and thanked him too. Ken smiled, and patted me on the shoulder.

I was so happy I could explode and everyone was happy for me, it seemed. What a family I had. "We all love you Skipper." Grandma said as she too gave me a big squeeze. Grandma could sure squeeze.

Hoooollly, what a Christmas! What a life. I was one of the family, and to make it even better, I was finally growing a little. Even my muscles were developing, so I could haul and heave hay like the rest of the kids.

"Skipper, why don't you put your new saddle on Nixon and see how he likes it?" Johnny said. It wasn't cold, so we went out to ride.

Nixon stood calmly as I put his blanket on, and then my new saddle. The stirrups were just right for my legs--nothing had to be changed. Ken and Grandpa must have measured them. I rode around the yard a few times feeling like the King of the Cowboys, sitting in my own saddle on my own horse. I even had a leather thong for my rope. Johnny watched with a big grin. Ken and Grandpa were laughing as I showed off.

The Cowboy

If I had ever had any doubts about whether there was a Santa Clause, they were gone now. Love was everywhere. Happiness I thought I would never know was mine at last.

I tied one end of a rope to my saddle horn and the other to the toboggan. I pulled the kids up Grandpa's road to the big gate and back again. The snow was bright and quite deep except for the ruts made by sleigh runners. I never had so much fun playing around in snow. Even Ken got into the act and joined us.

The happiness we shared had to be what Christmas was all about.

BOSSY'S LESSON

I could milk our four cows by myself in about half an hour. Not as fast as Ken, but getting there. He would sometimes come and help me carry the pails to the house. They were good milkers, Ken told me, except one, and she just gave about three-quarters of a pail. The milk quality was good, and we usually got top price for our cream.

When I finished milking and getting the pails up to the house, we would take off a pitcher of milk for our meals, and the rest we separated. This was awfully boring. I could hardly ever get the separator started by myself. Ken would have to give it a couple of turns, then I would take the thing up to the right speed. In the handle of the crank was this darned bell that would clunk away and drive me crazy. The bell would not stop ringing until the machine was up to speed. The separator had two spouts, one for skimmed milk and the other for cream. Speed was important, as it determined the quality and grade of the cream.

The worst part of the operation was washing the separator parts afterwards. Everything had to be absolutely clean. There were a lot of discs that formed a cone-like drum that rotated at hundreds of revolutions per minute. This spinning drum separated the cream from the milk. I had to dismantle all the discs and wash them, one by one.

If separating had its problems, so did milking. We had one cow in particular that Ken warned me about. Old Bossy was ornery and wouldn't stand still for anyone. I would tie her legs with a piece of rope in a

Douglas Hargreaves

figure of eight. This stopped her from kicking high enough to upset me and the milk pail.

One morning, I was up earlier than usual, finishing off a school assignment. I wouldn't have to ride and round up the cows, as they were in the overnight corral. I just let them into the barn. This saved a lot of time. There was no need to rush getting the milking done, and plenty of time to get ready for school.

I milked the easy cows first, because they gave the most milk and didn't cause problems. Bossy was last. I was hungry and wishing I could eat breakfast. I tied her legs and started milking her as usual. But she was in a more ornery mood than usual for some reason, fussing from side to side in the stall. I pounded her a couple of good ones on her side to keep her from crushing me into the stall planks. My little milking stool was getting wiggly because the nails were coming loose. It had been getting worse each time I used it, but I had put off fixing it.

I was pushing Bossy out of the way, and had milked about half a pail. She kept trying to kick her legs and made me move all over the place to avoid her. I hadn't tied her leg rope as tight as I should have because it slid down around her feet. With one leg free, she kicked and knocked me over. I barely managed to save the milk. The leg rope lay by her feet. I set the milk pail to one side, out of the way.

The next thing I knew, the seat gave way and I went down flat on my behind. That spooked Bossy and she let go with another leg chop that caught me on the side of the head and knocked me into the manure gutter behind her. The old girl knew what she had done

The Cowboy

because she just looked around at me. I think she was smiling. I was covered all over with fresh manure.

I wondered what Ken would say when he found out. I cried a bit because I really hurt, and my pride was wounded too. Still, I managed to get up and tie Bossy's legs again--properly this time--and finished milking her. I sure gave her a pounding for what she had done, just like Ken would have done.

I carried the milk up to the house. Ken hadn't seen me yet. I took my jacket off and tried to clean myself up a little before I came in. My hands, face and hair stunk with manure. I was taking my boots off when Ken strode in. "Holly heck," he said, "what in the sam hill you been in?"

I tried to tell him what had happened without crying, but tears washed down my face.

"Stop that blubbering, you little baby. If you had done as you was told in the first place, you wouldn't be hurtin' now. Get your arse in here".

I was shaking when I had told him the story, but now I was coming apart, dreading what lay ahead. He put the milk in the separator and started the machine. I turned it until it was done. Then he told me to get my clothes off. I stunk so badly that I needed a bath. He had put kettles of water on the stove and had them warm enough for me to bathe in while he washed my hair and my ears.

"How many times I got to tell you about minding what I say? Gosh all Friday, boy, can't you do anything right?"

I was quiet. I knew by now that he had to get it off his chest. I wasn't afraid that he would send me home because Ken and my parents had come to an

Douglas Hargreaves

agreement. My parents would pay for my keep if I could stay until they came back. And besides, Ken and I were getting along just fine. I was here sort of permanently.

Ken lifted me out of the tub and helped me dry off. Then he looked at my head where Bossy had kicked me. "I don't think it's too bad. You got a headache or anything?"

"No Ken, it's just sore, that's all."

I only had a small cut on the side of my cheek, so I guess I came off pretty lucky. At least I thought so, until I found myself draped over his knee and my bum being warmed. I only got three smacks this time, and my trick of holding my hands over my ears really worked. I didn't even cry--just produced a tear or two for effect. Ken knew what I was doing. He sometimes laughed afterwards. He just wanted me to learn not to make mistakes. They were dangerous.

Anyway, it was over and I went to my room to put on clean clothes. I missed breakfast to avoid being late for school.

I had a little difficulty riding to school that morning. Bareback might have been better than my saddle.

When I got home after school, Ken met me and we sat down over cookies and milk. "I'm sorry Skipper, but I just have to make you mind, and be careful. What would I ever do if anything happened to you? I couldn't stand to have anything happen to you. And besides, your parents would sue me to death, and I need you now. I know I act a little tough on you, but only because I worry about you. You know what I'm saying, don't you?"

The Cowboy

I knew what he was trying to tell me, and I knew he was right. I had been stupid about the rickety stool and the loose leg rope. I could get killed if I didn't pay attention. Ken gave me a big hug and asked how my head was. I told him my rear end hurt more, but otherwise I felt pretty good. "I'm sorry Ken, I'll be more careful. It was stupid of me not to check her more carefully. I was in a hurry and I knew better."

"Then we're both sorry--right son?" he chuckled.

Trouble usually strikes when you're least expecting it and often times, it strikes twice. That's what Bossy and Ken taught me. First, Bossy whacked me on the head, and then Ken whacked me on the behind.

NURSE "WE"

Three weeks before the end of the school term and summer holidays, I woke up with a rash all over my body. Hooolly! What the heck was this? Maybe I had got into some poison ivy or nettles. I wondered if I should tell Ken or wait

until after the chores. I didn't feel too bad, just a little hot.

I milked and finished the rest of the chores but was starting to sweat and feel tired. After washing and getting ready for school, I sat down to eat but wasn't hungry.

Ken said, "Skipper, what's wrong with you this morning? You're all red in the face. You coming down with something?" I told him I didn't feel too good and I had a rash all over my body. He lifted my shirt and looked me over. "Okay, son, let's get over to see Peggy right now. She'll know what's going on."

We got in the truck and drove over. Now I was starting to shiver. Peggy's kids were just getting ready to leave for school when we drove up. "Hi, Skipper," said Johnny. "What you doin' here?"

"I don't feel too good."

"You gonna get the water?"

Peggy came out. "What's wrong with our boy?" She looked at my chest and back. "Ken, you gotta get him into Calgary and to the doctor. I think he has scarlet fever, judging from the look of that rash."

Hooolly! I wasn't expecting anything like this. "Ken, it'll go away pretty soon." I pleaded. "Maybe it was something I ate."

Douglas Hargreaves

Ken would have none of that. "Johnny," he said, "tell Miss Snowdon that I've taken Skipper into Calgary. I'll let her know what's going on later."

Peggy wrapped me in a blanket and we drove to Calgary.

When we got there I was really sweating and sure wasn't feeling any better. We drove straight to the hospital. The doctor looked at me and took my temperature. He declared that I did have scarlet fever and he was admitting me to the isolation hospital. Now I was really upset. But the worst news was to come. The doctor later told me I would be there for four weeks.

I started to cry in earnest, mostly feeling sorry for myself. I could hardly imagine having to spend the last three weeks of school and a week of my summer holidays in a hospital.

As we drove to the isolation hospital, I continued my pleas not to go. Ken tried to be reassuring. "Come on now Skipper, you're going to be a big man about this. You'll be home before the rodeos start, and you'll still have all of your holidays left."

"I don't want to go in there Ken. Please?"

"We'll all come to see you, Skipper, almost everyday. You wait and see."

An older lady in a white uniform came to meet us at the door of the isolation hospital. She introduced herself as the matron. I thought she looked kind of grouchy. She told Ken that I could have no visitors until I was to be released. "This is an isolation hospital you know." she said, as though we should expect such rules.

The Cowboy

Ken saw my distress and I know he wanted to hug me, but Matron wouldn't let him touch me. Ken looked as sad about leaving me as I did about him going away. "I'll send some books for you to read Skipper." he said. We were both close to tears.

Matron led me upstairs to the second floor and ushered me into the room she called "C Ward". It looked like what I imagined a jail might look like. I had never seen such a barren place in my life. There was just this large room with white walls. There weren't any pictures on the walls or curtains on the windows. It smelled of disinfectant. I felt like I was being sent here as punishment.

There were ten beds and some baby cribs, but not many kids--just three other boys about my age and two small babies. The beds were about ten feet apart. There was a boy in the bed nearest mine. Across from me was another boy and three baby cribs. There was another kid at the end of the ward. Two babies were crying. I wondered if they had scarlet fever too.

Matron told me to sit quietly, and she'd return in a few minutes. I lay back on the bed and pulled a pillow over my head. I couldn't stop crying, I felt so alone and scared. It was the same feeling I had when I first came to the ranch. How was I going to get through twenty-eight days all by myself in this terrible place?

After what seemed like an hour, Matron finally came back, accompanied by a nurse wheeling a cart laden with all kinds of medical stuff. Matron scribbled notes while the young nurse fussed and fidgeted around me. The nurse made me undress and put on a gown that was too big and open at the back. The other boys watched because there were no curtains around

Douglas Hargreaves

the beds. The nurse kept saying "we" all the time, as though she and I were going through this ordeal together. She assured me everything was going to be all right and that "we" had nothing to be afraid of.

"Are we going to turn over on our tummy now?" she ordered sweetly. I complied and she inserted a thermometer up my behind.

"Hey, I can hold it in my mouth, you know." I said crossly. "I'm not a baby."

"Well, from all the blubbering and noise we couldn't tell." she replied with a smirk. She eyed me all over. "You're certainly a little gaffer--almost like a midget. Well just lay quietly now, and be a big man while we give you a needle in your hip." she cooed. She pulled my gown up over my bare butt.

"Ow! Hooooollly! That's not my hip and that's got to be the biggest needle in the whole world!" I tried not to start crying. The pain was terrible. I wanted to scream. Wowie! Did that hurt! I didn't like this place--especially that nurse.

The nurse wheeled her cart away as Matron stood frowning and writing in her book. "Think you can answer some questions little man?" she asked as I rolled over on my stomach. She looked over the top of her glasses. "How old are you? It says here you're eleven, but that can't be right."

"Yes ma'am, I'm eleven." I snapped.

"When did you last have a BM?" I didn't know what a BM was, so I told her I didn't think I'd ever had one. "You don't know what a BM is, do you?"

"Well, what is it?"

The Cowboy

"It stands for bowel movement." She sounded disgusted. "It's when you go potty, which you should do daily."

I told her I didn't remember when I last had a BM. "Have you had all your vaccinations?"

"Yes, ma'am, as far as I know. You'll have to ask my dad."

"That cow person who brought you in is your father?"

"He's a rancher, and yes, he's my dad." I sneered in my most ferocious manner.

"Well," she sniffed, "that explains a few things then, doesn't it? Your family doctor will be in to see you before long. He says he wants to examine your stomach. I cant imagine what for?" She said .I gave her that "as if I was supposed to know" look ,although I had a pretty good idea even if she didn't.

"I suppose you're happy that you're missing three weeks of school, especially at exam time." she went on. "Well, you might just fail, and wouldn't that be a waste? What grade are you in junior?"

"I'm in Grade Eight."

The nurse came back in wheeling another cart and overheard my reply. "Yeah, yeah, and your bum's sprouting spruce trees." she chuckled loudly enough for everyone to hear. The other boys laughed.

Matron left and the nurse placed a rubber sheet under me. I wondered what was under the towels on her cart.

"You're going to get an enema. Do you know what that is?" She continued to get the bed ready. She assured me that all new patients had to have an enema. Before I could answer, she was uncovering what lay on

Douglas Hargreaves

the cart. I had seen all this stuff before. Ha! We had one of those things hanging in our workshop over the grind stone. It was used to keep the stone wet when we were sharpening blades and things. It had been used on me more than a few times. I didn't tell her that. She proceeded to fill me up like I was a gas tank.

That done, the nurse said she would be back to give me a bath, and not to go away. So where did she think I would go?

The other kids were enjoying my embarrassment and discomfort. The boy in the bed next to me had been through it all, probably, and was taking everything in. He said, "Why did you tell her you were in Grade Eight, you little liar?" I didn't even know him and already he was calling me a liar. This only made the nightmare worse.

"Why did you call me a liar?"

"There's no way you're in Grade Eight, even if you were eleven, which you aren't."

The nurse came in with a glass of milk. She said it was good for us and we should always do the things that were good for us. Why didn't she shut her trap? That would sure be good for me.

She left the room and returned a few minutes later with her trolley and wheeled up beside my bed. "Time for our bath, Junior. Now get your gown off and I'll get you a fresh one. You got a little blood from your needle on it." She said that as if it were my fault the needle was long enough to penetrate all the way up to my heart.

The "bath" had to be one of the most humiliating experiences of my life. Now I knew why there was a rubber sheet on my bed. The nurse gave me the

The Cowboy

smallest towel I had ever seen to cover up with while she washed my various parts. Face, ears, neck, chest and stomach. Then I thought she would go for my legs and feet. No such luck. Nurse "We" went for my "wee" and scrubbed like crazy. The other kids broke apart laughing. I felt like a freak. If I wasn't red from my rash, I sure was from embarrassment. I grabbed for the towel and wondered if the other kids had to take all this abuse from the nurse.

"Over on our tum-tum now." she said. I think she knew she was driving me crazy.

I got a little brave. "What if I choose not to?" I had had enough.

"Oh, you'll turn over, little man." Nurse We assured me firmly. I silently agreed that I would. So much for courage.

The nurse finished my bath then poured some oil on my back and rubbed it in. Finally--something that felt good. I was still sick and running a temperature. That's probably why I was so crabby. Now I just wanted to go to sleep. The nurse left me alone in peace.

I don't know how long I had slept, but woke up with someone shaking me. It was my family doctor. I had met him once before and remembered he was a nice man. "Well Skipper," he said, "I'm sorry to wake you but I'm in a hurry. I wanted to tell you that you have a highly contagious disease, and to make sure there are no complications, we have to watch you carefully. You can be permanently affected by it. You still have a fairly high temperature and we'll have to get that down. That's what does the most harm. Skipper, we're going to send you to the hospital across

Douglas Hargreaves

town in an ambulance. I want to have some X-rays of your stomach. I would like to find out what causes your tummy problems. You'll enjoy the ride, I'm sure."

I wasn't too sure. "When do I have to go?"

"Just as soon as your temperature comes down. Get lots of rest. And no excitement." Excitement from what, I wondered. "I'll contact Ken and tell him what's happening. Perhaps you can see him for a minute at the hospital. Would you like that?"

"I sure would." The doctor left.

"Who's Ken? You call your dad by his first name?" It was Cecil, the kid in the next bed.

"Well, he isn't really my dad. It's just that I live with him and we ranch. He's like my dad."

"You some sort of a cowboy?" asked Donald, the kid at the end of the ward.

"I guess I am. I milk and rope and things like that." I boasted. I began to regret telling them this stuff, but it was too late.

"You in any contests?" Cecil asked.

"I hope to be this July if I'm good enough."

"Hah!--you think you're that good? I wondered what that smell was when they brought you in."

Where was Nurse We's giant needle? I knew exactly whom to use it on.

Time dragged by. Nurse "We" bathed and oiled me every day. She prodded and temperatured until I was turning soft and pale. Each day came the same questions. Did we take our pills, did we drink our milk, did we BM today? How could I BM when there was nothing left to BM? They didn't feed me--just gave me milk.

The Cowboy

The day came when I was to go for the X-ray and I answered "No" to all the usual daily questions.

"We're a smart little turkey, aren't we?" said Nurse We. "We'll see how smart our little turkey is when we come back from our X-ray this afternoon."

We both knew what was in store for me. This was going to be no ordinary X-ray. I'd had one before. They called it a barium X-ray. They fill you full of white stuff.

I got my ride to the hospital and sure enough, Ken and Peggy were there to meet me. I was so happy to see them I almost cried. But I was too big for that, I thought.

"Ken," I said, "please tell them I'm okay now and I have to get home to finish school. This is the worst place I have ever been in my whole life."

"Skipper, I got your final report card and you have three scholarships! You took top honours in the provincial exams. I'm so proud of you, Skipper." I was happy, but would have been a whole lot happier if I didn't have to be here.

Ken gave me a "get well" card from school. Even the Wilsons signed it. I think they wanted me to get well again so they could beat me up some more. Even Becky Mortinsen and the Grade Seven girls signed it. Ughh. They could have

left their names off, for all I cared. Becky wrote, "They had better look after my Skippy baby." Ughh! She was always doing stuff like that to embarrass me.

"I miss you son." Ken said. "It's so quiet and lonely there without you. I got no one to paddle or yell at."

"We miss you too Skip." said Peggy. "Can't wait to get my hands on that little rump of yours again--and hide your clothes." Everyone always wanted to get at my behind, even here at the hospital.

"Is there anything you want or need?" Peggy asked me. "Just get me out of here Peggy, please?"

"I would if I could Skipper, but it will only be three more weeks and then you'll be home again."

"I wrote your parents a letter and forwarded it to your aunt in Winnipeg." Ken said.

A big woman with a nice smile came up to us and said she was nurse Nora Burchill and that she was taking me for my X-ray.

"Can we go with him?" Ken asked.

"I'm afraid not Mr. Wills, but you can see him when he's finished. You can wait in the cafeteria down the hall. He won't be too long."

"You'll look after our cowboy, won't you?" said Peggy

"A cowboy, is he now?" said the nurse. "And do you live on a ranch cowboy?"

"Yes ma'am."

That was Ken's cue to brag. "He's a roper and he's going in the Stampede, the junior events."

"Well now, isn't that nice. I always take in the rodeos, especially the junior events. And what is the cowboy's name?" "Skipper Scott." I said.

"I've heard of you. Well, isn't this something special."

Then they put me on a stretcher and wheeled down a long corridor to a room marked "X-RAY, KEEP OUT." We went in.

"Have you ever had a barium enema before, Skipper?" asked nurse Burchill.

"Yes, ma'am."

The Cowboy

"Really now. I suppose that's why we're taking the pictures. Well then, you know what's going to happen."

She proceeded to give me the soapy water treatment. A "prep" she called it. Hooolly! I had to have the cleanest insides of anyone in the whole world.

I was then wheeled into the X-ray room where she pumped this white, chalky stuff into me. It would show up white on the X-ray and the doctor could see if there was something wrong with my insides. At least nurse Burchill was kind and friendly to me. Not like Nurse We. When it was over, she even said I had been a very good patient. Maybe I was, but the sooner I got out of there, the better, to my way of thinking.

Ken and Peggy met me and thanked the nurse for looking after me.

"I'll be seeing you sometime, Skipper." said nurse Burchill.

"I hope not." I answered back.

"I mean in the rodeo, Skipper." she laughed.

"Where are your manners?" Ken scolded. "You don't talk to people that way." I told them I was sorry.

I said goodbye to Ken and Peggy as the hospital staff secured me in the ambulance for my return trip to jail. "I love you." I cried softly. I could easily have got in the car and gone home. The hospital wouldn't have known.

Back at the isolation hospital Nurse We was her usual sarcastic self. "I see we're back home again after our little trip to the X-ray department. How's our little bum-bum?" I had nothing to say to her. I just kept quiet. "Hmmmpf!" she chortled. "A shot up the rump will shut them up every time."

Douglas Hargreaves

During the next several days three more boys were ushered in and we all watched the rituals. Some didn't take it well at all and cried bloody murder. Nurse We seemed to delight in introducing them to hospital routine. They cried on and off like I had for the first few days. I think they were sicker than me. I wondered how I was going to stand another three weeks of this--especially that horrible nurse.

By the third week, I was completely fed up with this torture and humiliation, day in and day out. I suffered through Nurse We's attempts at retaliation on my body.

Cecil was an even greater pain in my butt than the enemas. I figured him to be a complete loser. He was a low life if ever there was one.

Finally, a small mercy came my way. The day before I was to go home, Nurse We was getting reassigned to night shift. All of us felt the ward would be a safer place without her to contend with. Her new shift started at 10 pm. With luck, we would all be asleep. I was going home tomorrow. Hooolly! Home. There was never any place so dear to me.

I was sleeping soundly and dreaming of Nixon and how much fun we'd had. I missed my horse. I dreamed I was stepping up to receive my trophy for Junior Roper.

Who should interrupt this pleasant fantasy but Nurse We? She said I was to have another enema. It was 11 o'clock--what happened? She was getting even. She knew how I felt about her. Nothing seemed fair as I sat on the pan, pondering what went wrong. I awoke with bright sunshine coming through my window and no Nurse We. Free at last. The new day nurse, who

The Cowboy

was older than Matron, came directly to my bed with the torture trolley. I was starving and wondered when breakfast was coming. I had been off the milk diet for the last week.

"All right, Sunshine." she said. "You're going to be leaving us in a few hours, so let's get this over with. We must be clean on the inside as well as the outside."

"I had one last night."

"Your chart shows nothing of the kind. It's the hospital policy that you have one before you leave."

I decided not to bother resisting and accept this final act of doom. All they knew how to do in this place was humiliate you. I flipped over on my stomach and let her go to work.

At last I got dressed and went downstairs with my little pack to wait for Ken and Johnny to take me home. When Ken came through the door and I rushed into his arms and started to cry he gave me a big hug.

I was still weak, but so happy to be free from that house of soapy water and nasty nurses. I never wanted go back there again.

KRAUSE

I had lived on the Bar U Lazy Y ranch with Ken Wills for over a year with only one stretch away from my new home--those twenty-eight unhappy days in the isolation hospital. I considered myself to be the luckiest boy alive. Learning how to ranch, do the chores and rope steers gave me confidence because I was pulling my weight. Ken certainly thought so.

My parents were still overseas and had come to an agreement with Ken that he would continue to keep me as long as I was healthy and doing well in school. Ken and I found no reason to change the situation. They settled on a sum of money for my keep. Ken told me he wouldn't have let me go anyway. We used the money to buy more cattle.

Grandpa gave me a brand new calf rope for my eleventh birthday. Ken spent a lot of time teaching me how to use it. The rope was a lightweight, and after a while I could make it do almost anything I wanted. I could even do tricks with it. Ken felt I was good enough to enter the Millarville Fair.

Grandpa and I grew closer. He was always aware of what I was thinking or planning and of my hurtings and sorrows, which were getting to be few and far apart. Sometimes I would feel terrible and even cry some, because of a scolding Ken had given me to hurt my feelings. Still, Ken loved me, all right. It was just his way sometimes when things didn't go quite right. He would either give me a tongue lashing or a few smacks on the bum, depending on how he was feeling. One day I asked him if he didn't think I was getting too

Douglas Hargreaves

old for spankings. He didn't answer. I knew he didn't mean it most of the time because he told me often enough. Times were hard, and a young man just starting out on his own had to face many hardships. Ken wanted to prove himself and get his life going. Now, on top of it all, he had to raise me and it was more than he could handle at times. But Ken told me I was a good worker and kept him from getting lonely. Grandpa used to give him heck for treating me badly sometimes, and so did Peggy. Even Grandma would scold him and tell him I was just a "wee bye" you know.

With the fall season winding down and winter just around the corner, we Bar U Lazy Y Ranchers were busy moving our cattle from the reserve lands back home for wintering. It was important to track down all strays and return them to the main herd. Cattle left on the reserve were usually found in the spring--what was left of them after the coyotes had finished with them. All the cattle had to be moved off the reserve before the first snow. I was allowed to miss school, as were most of the older boys, so we could help with the roundup.

Most ranchers left it to the last minute to start their roundup, and the Bar U was no different. Ken and I got together with the Wilsons and Olie to move our herds home.

It took three days on the trail to find our herd. There were fifty head, and for the most part they were pretty well together and in good shape. Tom Wilson's herd was farther south and had crossed the Maclean Creek. Olie's herd, all thirty of them, were even farther south than Wilson's. They were mixed with some other

The Cowboy

herds. We weren't the only ones summering cattle on the reserve. Olie's cattle were easy to spot. They were black Angus, and stood out amongst the Herefords. It was going to take some sorting out, as there were other Angus cattle mixed in with Olie's. Wilson had several hired hands working for him, along with two of his sons, Billy and Phillip. Olie brought Johnny along for the experience, even though he was a little young.

I was a good enough ranch hand to move cattle with the rest of them. I had even been initiated into the Cowboy Hall of Poke. Nixon was a good cow pony and could work cattle with hardly any trouble at all. But he had a habit of heading for the bushy trees to try to wipe me off his back. I was getting used to his pranks, and would lay forward and lift my legs lengthwise along his back. I think he liked that. Ken's horse, Bonnie, was the best cow horse around. As Ken put it, she could turn on a dime and give you a nickel change.

Finding the herds tired all of us. We had been riding almost all day, every day. So after grubbing down, we all crawled into our bed rolls. The moon lit the night like a pale shining floodlight. Ken always placed my roll right next to his so he could keep an eye on me.

I found it hard to get to sleep, even though I could hardly keep my eyes open. I had just closed my eyes when I heard a coyote yelp nearby. I sat up with a start. Standing not three feet from my roll was Wilf Krause, one of Wilson's cow hands. I could tell it was him by the way he stood. No one liked him. He was a mysterious and sneaky type who kept to himself most of the time. I lay back quickly, hoping he didn't see me

Douglas Hargreaves

watching him. But he saw my eyes open and looking at him, and he moved away as quietly as he had appeared. I drifted off to sleep.

At five in the morning we were up and had breakfast. We planned to go off in different directions to look for strays and move them to the main herds.

"Skipper," said Ken, "I want you, Phillip and Johnny to ride to the butte and see how many are on the other side. I think you'll find about a dozen or more swamping around in the coulees on the back side."

"Okay--come on Phillip, lets go find them." I yelled, as Johnny rode up to me and gave Nixon a smack on the rear end. Off we went on the trot, the three of us. No unnecessary galloping I remembered.

We were just leaving when Wilf Krause came riding up and told us that Tom Wilson had assigned him to keep watch over us while we were away from the rest of the herd. I looked around for Ken so I could complain, but he was way back towards the end of the herd. I figured I'd just have to get on with it.

I didn't like Krause. He had a mean streak in him. More than once he had been caught manhandling Willie and Phillip Wilson. Mr. Wilson had hired him, knowing that he had been in jail for being drunk or something like that. I would just stay clear of him as much as I could. I certainly wouldn't get into any row with him. That might upset Ken. I'd been around Ken long enough to know how necessary it was to keep on his good side--not rattle him or give him cause to get angry with me. He couldn't fault me too much any more, as I was certainly holding my own as a ranch hand. I could do most everything now. Ken trusted me.

The Cowboy

Chasing strays and being with my friends was fun and exciting. I'd practice my roping on almost anything that moved. Good roping took lots of practice. I seldom missed a throw. This was the best part of the roundup.

Later that morning, Phillip and I rode over to where Johnny and Wilf Krause were standing. "We'll go up to the top of the butte Wilf." I said. "We'll holler if we see anything."

"Okay kid, we'll move this bunch around the bottom side and meet you on the other end when you come down. Don't rush--it's going to take us a little time."

As we rode, Phillip told me about how Krause had taken a belt to him one day. Krause had found Phillip wandering near his belongs in his bunkhouse. "I wasn't looking for anything, just walking through the building, that's all." said Phillip. "I sure hate him. He told me that if I said anything to my old man about his lickin' me, he would tell my father that I had been stealing stuff out of his belongings. You know my father--he'd give it to me even worse. He always believes everyone else before us kids. I wonder why he does that?"

Phillip and I climbed for about an hour before we got to the top of Square Butte. This was the highest point of land in the foothills around Millarville. The most beautiful sight I had ever seen. "Hooollly, is that ever something! You can see forever, almost to Calgary!"

"Look Skipper--there's some strays over in those trees half way down the side. They must be near the springs."

Douglas Hargreaves

"Okay, let's go get 'em. I hope they're ours."

Going down always took a little longer, and was harder on the horses. We took our time and went down slowly until we finally caught up with the strays. They turned out to be Wilson's. Good. That would save us a lot of time. Just move 'em down and they'd catch up with the rest.

Over the next hour and a half, Phillip and I moved the strays all the way down and were starting to move them around the base of the Butte. We would be meeting Krause and Johnny soon. We could hear them but couldn't see them yet. We'd just keep the herd moving and eventually we'd meet.

Around noon we heard Krause yelling and cursing Johnny. "I wonder what he's hollerin' about." Phillip said. "Hi Johnny." I yelled.

Johnny didn't answer. He just looked away and hung his head. "What's eatin' you Johnny?" I asked.

"Nothin's eatin' me Skipper. Why you askin'?"

"Well, you don't look good. Have you been crying or something?"

Johnny moved off and left the question unanswered. "There ain't nothin' wrong with him." said Krause. "I just get on him a little to make him move."

We continued moving the herd for another hour before we stopped to eat lunch. Sitting around, Johnny kept close to me and I nagged him to find out what was bothering him. Johnny only replied that he was okay, he just didn't feel so good, that was all. Phillip too kept asking Johnny if he had been crying.

"Yeah, I was crying, so what?"

"You got a belly ache?" I asked him.

The Cowboy

Krause snickered and explained that Johnny was just a little baby and shouldn't be on a cattle drive so far away from his momma. Johnny looked daggers at Krause but said nothing. Something had gone on between those two.

Well, we had work to do so we packed up and started off again. Ken would be happy to see that we had got the strays and had moved them so far ahead of the main herd. It would take them some time before they caught up to us. I was feeling pretty good about how well we had been doing. We could stop at a nearby beaver dam for a swim. It was a warm day even for late fall. That often happened when a chinook wind blew warm air in from the west coast.

At three in the afternoon we arrived at the dam. It had a high bank on the far side, unlike the dam at Peggy's. The water was colder too, but looked inviting as usual. Johnny still was not talking very much. He was just being quiet. He was usually fun-loving and always ready to play a joke, just like his mom. If this were Peggy's swimming hole, she'd steal my clothes, sure as anything.

I bet Phillip that the last one in was a swamp rabbit. I knew the water would be real cold but we were used to bathing in chilly water.

We had our shirts off even before we dismounted. Johnny rode over to where I was undressing and told me to watch out for Krause because he was an evil bad man and would hurt me. "What do you mean Johnny?"

"He is bad Skipper." Johnny started to snivel again.

"Why you crying Johnny?"

"Cuz he did something to me and he hurt me Skipper. Just watch out for him."

I wanted to stay around and ask some more questions, but I figured Krause had just given him a boot in the behind. Phillip was bugging us to get into the water. We dove in, but Phillip was faster, so I was the swamp rabbit.

The water was very cold and we screamed as it hit our bodies. Krause was in the water, swimming towards us. "I'm surprised you punks can swim." he said. Phillip swam away from him and over towards me.

Johnny sat by the edge of the dam, looking at us. We yelled at him to get in the water or we would come and get him and drag him in. With that, Johnny started to undress.

Krause swam over to the bank closest to where Johnny was undressing. "Watch your mouth." I heard him say to Johnny. Johnny stepped into the water and swam over to me.

Phillip was farther away, diving and swimming under the water. Suddenly Phillip yelled. I saw that Krause had grabbed him and was dragging him onto shore.

"What the hell you doin'?" Phillip screamed. "Get your rotten hands off me!" "It's your turn kid." Krause grunted as he hauled Phillip out of the water and threw him on the grass. I couldn't understand why he was doing that.

"Krause, what are you doing to him?" I called as I swam over to the shore. "Get off him you big ape."

"Stay away kid, or you're next." Krause yelled.

Phillip was screaming now. I didn't know what was going on or why Krause was hurting Phillip. Krause just laughed and told me to take off. He was doing

The Cowboy

something to Phillip and hitting him on the head. Phillip was screaming and hollering like crazy.

"Help me Skipper! Please!" Krause swung at me and hit me in the face. I went sprawling. I got up again, grabbed a stick and swung at Krause with all my might. The stick caught him on the side of the head. He took after me.

Phillip just sat there a minute then got up and ran into the water. Johnny joined him and they swam towards the other side of the pond.

Krause in the meantime had grabbed hold of my arms and was twisting them up behind my back towards my shoulders. I yelled at him to leave me alone. He pushed me to the ground. I knew then that he had done the worst thing to Phillip, and he was going to do it to me. I yelled at the top of my lungs, hoping someone might hear me. Johnny and Phillip stayed in the water. I quit hollering and started cursing as best I knew how.

"I'm going to tell Ken all about you Krause." I snarled. "Ken will kill you, you rotten bastard."

When it was over and he was getting dressed, he said. "You little brats aren't going to say a word on account of they won't believe you. Ken will tan your little hide for telling lies and making trouble for him. I'm getting out of here. I got my pay and I'm leaving this jerky outfit. Keep your mouths shut or I might just come back and close them for good. Get It?" He mounted his horse and rode away.

Johnny, Phillip and I sat around talking about what we were going to do. I asked them if they were okay, and they said they were all right. They asked about me and sobbed that they were sorry they couldn't help me.

Douglas Hargreaves

They were afraid Krause would come after them again. I agreed it wouldn't have made any difference at that time anyway.

Johnny said we should keep our mouths shut. He wasn't going to wind up dead some place. I wasn't sure how Ken would act if he found out. Phillip and Johnny said they wouldn't tell anyone about my part in it. I thought Ken might feel he couldn't take care of me properly if he learned what had happened.

The rest of the crew caught up to us and insisted we all go in for a swim. We really weren't feeling like it but we had to protect our secret and not make them suspicious. I was afraid Ken would sense something was wrong. He could usually detect when I was having trouble or wanting to talk to him.

It was hard for us boys to carry on as though nothing had happened. Ken did ask about Krause and why he had taken off so suddenly. He wanted to know if I or the boys had done anything to cause him to take off like that.

Wilson only said. "Damned funny guy, that. I'm kinda glad he took off. He was some strange guy." Johnny, Phillip and I looked at each other--we knew what kind of strange Krause was.

I had never heard of such a thing happening before. Phillip told us that a hired hand had done it to him once, so he knew right away what Krause was going to do. And to think we would laugh when we saw steers jumping on top of each other. "Can't make babies that way." we'd shout.

The next morning, Ken had me out of my bed roll and in for a swim before the others were even thinking of getting up. He noticed the bruise on my face, and

The Cowboy

asked what happened to me. I told him I had rode under a branch. "You'll learn one day Skipper." he laughed. Hoollyy! the water was cold. I guess I was still half asleep and if that weren't enough, I had a stomach ache. How was I going to manage getting rid of it out here? I would be home by noon and could have Peggy look after me while Johnny and Olie took their herd home.

We arrived at the Wilson's place first and they drove their herd into their corrals. Phillip gave me a wink when he rode by. Next we dropped off Grandpa's herd. It was almost the size of ours and Olie's put together. We stayed for lunch with Grandpa and Grandma.

"Something eating you Skipper?" Grandpa asked.

"I just got one of my belly aches Grandpa."

"Well, you're going to Peggy's. She'll look after it." That finally made Johnny chuckle. He and Grandpa knew how I was going to be looked after. It was a little joke in the family. Skipper's problem.

We moved the cattle along and came to Olie's. Johnny and I rode ahead of the others and met Peggy at the gate. Johnny hugged his mother, then started to weep.

"Did you miss your mom?" Peggy said. She was really happy to have us home.

"Skipper's got a belly ache Ma." said Johnny.

"You in trouble again, little man? Come on, get off your horse and we'll see what we can do." She asked me how long I had been aching and I told her a few days. Ken was busy opening the gates we used to get through to our ranch. Peggy looked at my rear end and asked me why I was so red back there. I told her I didn't know. I was sure scared that she was going to find out what had happened.

"You sure your bum ain't hurting Skipper?" Peggy asked again.

"It's okay Peggy."

"It looks like a rash of some kind." I agreed it must be a rash.

"You been bleeding a little Skipper. And where did you get those bruises on your back and your arms?" She looked more troubled than I wanted her to be.

"I just fell off my horse."

"You did not Skipper. You're telling me a story, aren't you? I know you, little one. You can't tell a lie if you tried." She kept at me. "I'm going to fix you up, but not before you tell me who did this to you." So she had figured out what had happened. I started to cry. I just couldn't help it. She asked me who it was. I told her it was Krause. She just about went through the roof.

"Where were the other boys when all this was going on Skipper?" she asked. I had never seen her so mad in all my life. "They were swimming Peggy." I hadn't lied. Olie was just coming in the door and looked at my injuries. She told him what had happened.

"Skipper, we better hold off saying anything to Ken." said Olie. "He'll be furious and ready to kill. Is Skipper okay Peg?"

"He will be when I'm done with him. There has got to be something done about that man." I was shaking now as Peggy looked after my belly ache.

I was soon feeling better, in spite of the ordeal. I never told anyone about Johnny and Phillip. They

The Cowboy

could tell in their own time someday. It was only by accident that I had been found out. I got on my horse and caught up to Ken and the herd in time to see them put into our large corral. We would winter them there. "You feeling better now son?" he said. "You did real well on this trip Skipper. I'm proud of you."

Ken never did find out, at least as far as I know. Nor did Johnny or Phillip ever disclose the "happening" as we called it. It was an agreement between us and we kept it.

THE COWBOY HALL OF POKE

By my twelfth birthday, I hadn't grown much but had built some respectable muscles from all the hard work. I felt quite confident from doing most of the chores myself. My biggest triumph was still being on the ranch after two years. Branding time came around. As with the haying, neighbours got together to help each other. So we gathered at Olie's and Peggy's ranch to brand and inoculate their calves. I was quite a good calf roper by that time, so was called on to do my part in sorting out the calves. Still, I really didn't care much for this part of ranching, the branding and that stuff. It had to be done and everyone had to help.

My friends no longer gave me such a hard time about my size. I could keep up with them at most everything except maybe bronc riding. I still was a little too small for that.

Some of the guys working on the branding seemed to think I would make a darned good cow rider. "Yeah Skipper," said Billy Wilson, "the best cow riders are the small guys. They're light and don't bother the cows."

I should have known better than to listen to anything coming from Billy Wilson. I had never heard of a cow rider. "What's a cow rider?" I asked. They didn't spell it out to me but I learned that a cow rider is usually a very small, naive, stupid, hope-to-be cowpoke. He has this burning desire to show off his riding talents to all who can stand to watch without killing themselves laughing. Adding a degree of

Douglas Hargreaves

difficulty makes the event more interesting and hilarious.

The general idea behind cow riding is that the poke doing the riding must sit on the cow facing backwards while holding on firmly to her tail. Digging one's heels into her sides helps the performance.

Billy continued to challenge me. "Skipper! You're just the right size to make a good cow rider." Everyone was watching me and shouting words of encouragement.

Well, I just had to tackle this new task like I did most others, with great zeal and enthusiasm. But I had a strange feeling that I was on a one-way trail to doom. Billy Wilson picked me up and set me on an old dried-up cow facing backwards. He grabbed her tail, handed it to me and told me to hold onto it and pull with all my might. Foolishly, I did.

For a moment, nothing happened. The group of spectators wondered if I possessed some mysterious powers over the beast. Then the cow turned around to see what was on her back. She let out a long MOOOOOO and all hell broke loose. The cow became an out-of-control hydraulic lift, driven by four powerful legs. She leaped sideways once then made a full kangaroo jump straight up. Any bronc rider would have been an instant hero. I held on to her tail though my behind lost contact with her back.

I was flying. It wasn't as though I was anywhere near riding that cow. I still clutched her tail firmly in my hands as if that counted for anything. I was afraid of what might happen if I let go.

Try as I might to stay on board, I only touched her back once and immediately rocketed skyward. There

The Cowboy

would be no marks for spurring--my heels came nowhere near the cow's sides, let alone any other part of her. Somehow, I still had hold of her tail.

Ken told me afterwards that I looked like a piece of dung that sometimes makes a ball on the end of a cow's tail. I couldn't hold on any longer--her tail slipped through my fingers and I flew through the air at least ten feet off the ground. I landed face down at about a hundred miles and hour on my hands and knees in a pile of dry old manure.

It knocked the wind out of me but didn't knock me out. So I survived cow riding. Everyone had a great laugh and I guess I did too, after I got my wind back. They told me that you had to be there and witness the event to appreciate the humour in it.

Well, it was soon time to get on with the job at hand, sorting out calves for branding and inoculating-- and castrating. Now this last part was new to me. I had heard it mentioned before and not only happening to calves. I wasn't about to inquire about what else.

It would start with roping. I had little trouble roping the calves assigned to me and was beginning to feel a part of the whole process. I could get most of them on the first throw. When you got your calf, you'd throw him to the ground and tie his hind legs, still holding his head. The other guys would come and heave him over onto his side. Another cowhand would sit on the ground with his feet against the calf's lower leg, the one closest to the ground. Then he'd grab the other leg and heave it to, almost splitting the poor little calf apart.

Then Ken would come along with his knife. It was sharp as a razor. He would cut into the calf's bag and remove its testicles, one at a time. Then he'd pour disinfectant over the wound. Hooolly, would the calf bellar.

Next, they would brand the calf with a red hot iron showing our "Bar Y Lazy U" brand. The cowboy holding the back legs got a face full of smoke every time. Finally, someone would come along and stick the calf with a hypodermic needle full of anti-black-leg toxin. Now the calf was free to get up, if he could, and stagger away to tell his friends about what happened to him.

After I had pulled down a few calves I was told I was going to be the leg man. I didn't think I was strong enough to hold a calf but they assured me that if I got my feet against his lower leg and pulled hard on his upper leg, I could hold him.

As the leg man, you're right close to the action. You watch the poor calf lose his manhood. I counted my lucky stars that I wasn't a calf. He would squirm and roll around something awful as Ken cut his testicles out. I could almost feel it myself. Needless to say, I sure didn't like being the leg man. The smoke from the branding iron almost made me puke.

I stood up after I finished my first calf as leg man. Without warning, three guys grabbed me and ripped off my boots and pants! Horrified, I yelled towards Ken, "What the heck are you guys doing anyway? Come on! Gordy, what are they doing?"

The next thing I knew, I was laying on the ground the same way the calf had been, only spreadeagled. Morris, Gordy's brother, and one of the other cowhands came over to me with the knife. The

The Cowboy

cowhand knelt down beside me, telling me it wouldn't hurt hardly at all if I just held my breath.

"Oh yeah!" I cried. "I heard how those calves bellared. How am I supposed to hold my breath, anyway? Ken, please, Ken!" They terrified me into thinking they were really going to do it. I was going to lose my jewels, just like the calves. These guys seemed very serious about the whole thing.

Ken strode over and asked them what was going on. Morris dragged the back edge of the knife across my privates. I honestly thought he was about to cut them off. "Oh please Ken, stop them!" I cried.

Ken knelt beside me and I felt him smearing something sticky and greasy all over my supposed wound. It was only axle grease. It was all over my stomach and everything else. Everyone was laughing and yelling and jumping around.

So that's how they duly initiated me into the Cowboy Hall of Poke. They now considered me a full-fledged cowboy. Right now I was a full-fledged mess. Gordy grabbed my hand and hauled me away. Ken followed and took me into the blacksmith shop and cleaned off the grease, then washed me off with kerosene from the barrel. It stung like crazy, and I was a deep brown colour around my private parts for some time after.

"Kid, I'm proud of you." said Ken. "You came through that like a man. Every cowboy goes through it one time. They have to prove they can hold their own with the rest of us. And you surely did Skipper. I really am proud of you." He gave me a big hug.

I guess I was really frightened of being castrated, even though I couldn't see them really doing it. And

Douglas Hargreaves

there was my best friend, laughing with the rest of them. "Fine friend you turned out to be." I said to Gordy.

"Well Skipper, if I had said anything, you know what would have happened to me? I had it done to me once."

I really did feel proud though. I hadn't cried, just yelled a lot. Gordy later told me he had spotted a few tears in my eyes. The real humiliation came later when the guys were sitting around talking about the day's activities. They complained they had a hard time trying to find Skipper's hose and jewels. "Skipper," said one of them, "you nearly had us believin' you was a girl." I may have been deep brown down below, but I was bright red around my face. I knew enough not to try to argue.

Day by day, my roping skills improved. Grandpa told Ken that I should enter the Junior Roping section of our local rodeo and fair. There were three categories, and Ken decided I should enter all three-- Thirteen and Under, Novice Roper, and Intermediate Roper (fourteen to sixteen years of age). He did this to get out of paying the entry fees for all three events. If you entered all three, you could qualify for the next event without paying a fee, provided you won your first event.

When the time came, I was very nervous and didn't want to let my friends down, especially Ken. I drew small calves, a lucky break. And I found there was little serious competition in my challengers. To top it off, Nixon performed perfectly for me in all the events, and I never missed a throw. So . . . I won all three events!

The Cowboy

Boy, was Ken ever proud. He walked around showing me off and boasting about his kid and how well he had taught me. I was overjoyed, but a little shaky.

When we got home, everyone was waiting for us to have a party and celebrate. I got to stay up until 11 o'clock. Hooollly, was I ever excited, and so bushed that Ken had to pack me off to bed, although I didn't remember that. I must have fallen asleep in the chair where I had been talking to Gordy.

When I awoke the next morning, all three trophies stood grandly on my dresser at the foot of my bed. I could hardly believe it. Some money went along with each trophy and Ken put it in the bank for me. Grandpa suggested we spend a little of it on a new, softer rope for me.

Ken and I did get a chance to go into Williams brothers the next weekend to look over their ropes. I was standing by the harness rack looking at bridles and bits when a kid came running past me and knocked me into the stand. It toppled over and the whole thing spilled out all over the floor. Ken was there in a shot and had me by the arm. He was ready to haul my arse over his knee. Then out of nowhere came a very stout matronly-looking lady, waving her finger in Ken's face. She told him that it wasn't the dear little one's fault, it was that other brat of a kid.

Whooooey--rescued! Ken put the dear little one down, and we both started to pick up the goods. We had them back in place when the clerk come over. He thanked us for picking everything up and even discounted the new rope we had picked out (a real beauty) even though it had been my body that had slammed the fixture to the floor. The other kid got his behind kicked out of the store.

Driving home in the truck, we were both very quiet. I was feeling brave, thinking about having held my own on the Bar U for two years now and I was a roping champion to boot. I felt I could speak up and say what was on my mind.

Taking a deep breath and sitting as tall as I could on my seat blanket I said, "Ken, how come you're always ready to believe someone else before me? If something goes wrong or something bad happens, you're always ready to blame me and spank me, rather than find out what happened. You never ask me what happened. I know you like me and consider me like your boy but if it was really true wouldn't you want to be on my side rather than everyone else's and take my word for it?"

Well, he just stared at me every now and again while he drove. He didn't say a word. I decided to continue.

"Remember the time I let Old Bossy's leg ropes slide down and she kicked me in the head and I landed right in the manure gutter? I was so unhappy, and hurting that I thought you would give me a hug and make me feel better. Instead, you had me take a bath, patched the wound on the side of my head then you spanked me. I could never understand that. I thought you really didn't care about me or care how badly I was hurt. I couldn't bear it. I thought I might run away some place but I didn't know where to go."

Still he didn't say anything. So I went on.

"Remember the time Phillip and I were riding on the south side and we rode through the creek to catch

The Cowboy

those strays of the Wilsons'? We took the short cut home. Remember what you said to me when I got home and Nixon's blanket was wet? You only told me that I had sweated him and there was no excuse for that. Then you spanked me. You didn't even give me a chance to tell you what had happened. When I finally got to tell you about it the next day, you told me you already knew from Tom Wilson. He told about how good Phillip and me worked together getting the strays into his upper pasture. You didn't even tell me you were sorry. I felt you wouldn't care if I never came back. I was just a big pain under your saddle blanket."

I was sobbing a little. Neither of us said anything for a long time. I wondered if I had gone too far.

Finally, Ken said, "Gosh all Friday boy, can't you ever see nothing?" He was getting all choked up and emotional. His voice cracked a little.

"Course I care for you. You're my kid and I do love you. I don't know what I will ever do when you have to leave. I'm sorry I have such a bad temper. I was brought up by the big hand method and I don't think it did me any harm. I didn't think I was wrong to use it on you. I just thought you would understand I was only doing it for your own good. I wouldn't have bothered if I didn't care. Remember how I worried and fretted over you when those bastards of cousins belted you when I was away? Of course Skipper, I love you. I'm sorry, if that's what you want me to tell you. I am the most proud parent in the valley, you gotta know that. I just want you to learn well and grow up to be the big man you can be. You may be just a little guy but you have made yourself a mighty big man in the hearts of all my family and all your school mates."

Douglas Hargreaves

I could see his eyes were glistening with tears. I too had tears in my eyes and a lump in my throat. He pulled me over close beside him. I lay against his arm and sort of snuggled up to him and dozed a little. I dreamed of all the people who were most precious to me. Ken, Grandma, Grandpa, Peggy and her kids, Phillip and Gordy. I was glad I had the nerve to open my heart to Ken. I was his boy. He hugged me even closer as we drove home.

The next morning was bright and beautiful. With our chores all done we sat down to breakfast.

"Well, little man, you've had some busy times lately, haven't you?" This was Ken's way of giving me permission to speak my mind.

"I guess so. You know Ken, I really don't mind getting my arse booted. Booted sounds more manly than spanking, anyway. But when I do things wrong, please let me try and talk you out of it first?" We both laughed.

"Champion Roper" had a neat sound to it but I wasn't about to let it go to my head.

THE STORM

"Oh Skipper, Skipper, what have I done to you?" I heard Ken asking, as tears streamed down his cheeks. I've been sick with worryin' about you. You shouldn't have gone out on a night like this. Damned cows could have waited until morning. You're worth more them those danged things." Ken said as he carried me up to the house. I had never seen Ken cry before and all because of me.

It all started when the snow storm blew in around three o'clock, just as we were getting out of school. By the time Phillip, Gordy and I arrived at our gate the storm had turned into a full blizzard. The wind was driving the snow so hard, it kinda cut your skin. I had a scarf wrapped around my face leaving just a little slit to see through. Phillip and Gordy headed for home on the double

while I rode on down to our barn. I had to get the cows in out of the weather.

My heart stood still when I noticed the corral gate was open and the cows were no where to be seen. The weather had been threatening when I left for school and Ken told me to give them some feed and leave them in the corral. The gate had never been opened as far as I knew. The cows had been there for milking and when I let them out of the barn there was no place else for them to go but into the corral . We used that corral when we didn't want to have to go looking for cows or horses.

Ken had driven into Calgary and left me to milk and do my regular chores. He said he'd be home for

Douglas Hargreaves

supper. Most times being as we were bachelors, we ate at Peggy's, Ken's sister. She was a much better cook than either Ken or me. It was like a second home to both of us.

The cows had somehow got out of the corral and without taking my school bag up to the house, I laid it on the oat bin in the barn and headed to the gate to see what had happened. Maybe the cows had broken it themselves. I wondered if it was my fault. If that was the case my bum would be aching when Ken found out.

I started to panic wondering what I should do.

The blizzard was getting worse and it was getting colder. The wind seemed to blow right through my coat. I thought I was dressed warmly enough, I'm sure I had ten layers of clothes on. Still I shivered under the icy blast.

The gate was not damaged. Someone had opened it or had left it unlatched. I don't know whether I was shivering from the cold or from what was going to happen to me. Ken was not very tolerant of mistakes, especially mine. "I expect better from you boy." He'd say.

I decided to take the North Fork trail up over the hill towards Isbister's. This trail led to the Mortinsen's field gate. It was about two miles and mostly inside the tree line. I broke out of the trees and the wind nearly blasted me right off Nixon. To make matters worse it was getting very dark and with the snow blowing like it was I could hardly see.

I followed the fence line. I knew I wouldn't get lost as long as I had that in sight. Sometimes I couldn't even see the wires and I was riding right beside them.

The Cowboy

Hooolly! It was cold. There was no way I would hear the cow bells with all this wind blowing.

I figured I was almost to the Mortinsen's gate and still no cows. There were no tracks cause the blowing snow would have filled them in. I was really starting to worry now. I wondered what Ken would say when he found me gone. He got quite upset when I'd take off without letting him know where I had gone.

I turned Nixon around and we started back down the fence line again. Nixon sure didn't like this weather but being a Cayuse pony, he should have been used to it. I'd often brag about Nixon's ancestors. He was part Indian pony and part quarter horse with a mind of his own.

I was almost to the Sylvester gate that led to Peggy's when I discovered it was open. Well, there was the answer to where my cows had gone. There were sure lots of places they could go from here. I narrowed it down some, thinking they probably headed for the creek.

No cow bell yet, just the howling wind and the driving snow. Nixon's head was all covered with the stuff. He was sweating from walking in the deep snow and it just stuck to him. I kept brushing it off his eyes. I guess I looked about as bad.

I rode through the gate but the thing that bothered me was I'd no longer have the fence line to guide me. Now I was really starting to shake. I hoped the cows had headed down to Sheep Creek for the water. I was pretty sure I could find my way there.

I finally came to the creek but no cows. I rode across and looked for any signs of tracks in the new

Douglas Hargreaves

snow. Nothing. Well I had had enough of this and knew that I needed help.

I turned around and was heading through the creek when a coyote darted out from under some brush startling Nixon. He jumped sideways throwing me into the freezing water. I got out fast but not before my boots and pants were thoroughly drenched. Now I had to get home and fast. "Nixon, you dumb bell, why did you do that for. You've seen hundreds of coyotes before." I scolded.

My clothes were freezing already and I was in trouble. I had to find the fence line that led back to the gate. I knew which way the creek ran and I knew the fence cut over it. If I rode along it I'd come to the fence. My teeth were chattering by this time. I knew I was slowly freezing. I couldn't feel my fingers nor my toes. It was a good thing my coat didn't get wet.

If I ever got home again I would take my lickin' like a man and be thankful for it.

The snow was about eight inches and drifting badly. Some drifts I rode right into before I saw them . Nixon didn't like that at all and would veer away. I guess he sensed the drifts before I did. A couple of times I couldn't even hear the creek, I was so far away and the wind didn't help either.

I figured I had to be getting close to the fence and that made me feel better but I was still freezing. Nixon whinnied. Now what would make him do that? I had no way now of seeing anything. If I got home, it would be more from luck than from anything I did.

All of a sudden I heard the cow bell and standing knee deep in snow beside the creek were the cows. Hoooollly!. " How'd you get down here you crazy

The Cowboy

girls?" I screamed. I half thought about leaving them and getting Ken but figured they might freeze as well. Maybe I could get them moving easily enough.

I got behind them and they started wandering along the fence towards the gate. I wasn't sure how far I had to go but knew I had better make it quick. My hands were numb and I couldn't feel them to know whether I had my bridal lines in my hands or not. I had lost all feeling in my feet and they weren't hurting any more.

A huge snow squall blew in and I couldn't see the cows even though they were

right in front of me. I felt real fear for the first time. I thought I was going to die out here in the cold and wondered if Ken would feel bad. I knew he would. He loved me now like I was his own. Why didn't I leave him a note telling him about the cows? I was stupid. He'd figure it out easy enough.

Nixon found the cows for me and we continued until we reached the gate. They went through it and started for home. They knew where to go even if I didn't.

I had tried to keep my arms and legs moving and even thought of getting off Nixon and walking to keep my blood circulating. I guess I should have done that but I was just too tired. I felt like I wanted to go to sleep. I wondered if I could stop for a minute and just rest with my arm resting on the saddle horn and laying my head on my arm. Ken had shown me how to do that. You wouldn't fall off your horse that way and you could even grab a few winks.

I was beginning to panic when I couldn't see the tracks. The cows knew they were going home but where was home? "Nixon you old hay bag, you take

Douglas Hargreaves

me home please?" I was starting to cry. Why would I do a thing like that? That wasn't going to help. Ken didn't like crybabies. "Gosh All Friday boy, grow up and be a man." Ken would lecture me when I had hurt myself. I wanted to be but I was only twelve and I was freezing to death and no one knew I was here.

Nixon kept on walking and bucking the drifts. I knew he was tired too. Maybe I'll just let him rest a few minutes. It wouldn't hurt either one of us to rest a bit. "Nixon. You want to rest boy?" I snivelled through me tears. The tears were frozen onto my scarf and my eyes were almost frozen shut.

"Ken. Oh Ken, please find me. Please look for me." I cried, willing Ken to hear my thoughts. Nixon stopped by a large drift. I could hardly see the pile of snow. " Come on Nixon, I'll let you rest." I yelled at him. I think he knew the predicament I was in. I tried to get down but fell off Nixon into the snow. My legs wouldn't hold me up.

I sat down in the drift holding onto Nixon. "Nixon, you find a way around and I'll walk along behind you." I talked to him. He just stood looking at me, as I lay back in the snow. I remembered folks say that the first thing that happens before you freeze to death is the want to go to sleep. I tried to stay awake but couldn't any more. I fell asleep.

The first thing I remember was Ken carrying me up to the house. "I'm so damned sorry Skipper it was all my fault. I almost killed you." He was crying. I was crying. Nixon had stopped at the drift by the side of our barn. We were inside the barn corral! He had brought me home. Ken said he spotted the cows first, then Nixon.

The Cowboy

Ken worked on getting my circulation back while I hollered and screamed. I think I cried most of the time. Ken never said anything, just kept massaging my body with snow. Why did he use snow?

After what seemed like half the night, he finally got the circulation back into my legs and arms. I was very hungry and Ken made me some beef broth. I never tasted anything so good in all my life.

I was sitting at the table all wrapped up in a blanket. My clothes were drying in front of the stove. He pulled up a chair and sat down beside me. We just looked at each other knowing what the other was thinking. He reached over and sat me on his lap. I fell asleep on his shoulder.

I didn't suffer too much frost bite, just a little peeling of my hands and feet. Had I stayed there much longer I would not have been alive in the morning. Ken was shaken and cried often. He told me how he had left the gate open after letting the team in. He remembered he had forgotten to latch it. The cows nudged it open. "Skip, I'm sorry. You'll never know how frightened I was that I might lose you. I knew where you had gone. I'm very proud of my cowboy. More than you'll ever know." he said. Outside, the wind continued to scream, piling huge drifts everywhere. No school tomorrow.

BOOTS AND MUD, MUD AND BOOTS

One day we drove to Williams Brothers in Calgary in Grandpa's 1928 Chevy touring car. It was one of the few times Grandpa and Grandma came with us. As usual, I was oohing and aahing at all the neat western clothing for kids when Grandpa came over and told me to sit down. The man wanted to measure my foot. "What for Grandpa?"

"Just because I told you to, that's why." he said gruffly. I knew better than say another word and sat down.

The store clerk said, "Take your right boot off boy." I took off my shoe and was glad that I had clean socks on with no holes in them. Peggy used to say having a hole in your sock was like going to the hospital in dirty underwear. The clerk measured my foot, went away, and came back a few minutes later with a box in his hand. He sat down on a little stool in front of me and opened the lid of the box.

Hooooolllly! I almost died. There in the box were the most beautiful pair of western boots I had ever seen.

"I don't know if we got a pair small enough for your boy." the man told Grandpa.

"Try them on anyway Skipper." Grandpa said. I must have been living under a star because when I got those boots on, I swear they were made right on my foot.

"Well, I guess I was wrong." the clerk said. "They fit him fine and there seems to be plenty of room for him to grow."

Douglas Hargreaves

"Ha! Skipper ain't going to grow too much." Grandpa said. "Sorry son, I was just kidding."

"Walk around in them boy." the man told me.

I already had walked around in lots of boots--other peoples, just trying them on and pretending they were mine. The clerk gave me the other boot to slip on and I think it fit even better than the first one.

"Ha!" said the clerk. "Well sir, the boots fit the lad. Shall I wrap them up or will he wear them?"

"Oh, I think he will want to wear them, huh, Skipper?"

"Hoooooollly!" I hollered. I could hardly believe it! Brand new boots for keeps. I tried to contain myself and act grown up but the excitement was just too much. I hugged Grandpa and thanked him over and over again. He chuckled and told me they were my birthday present from himself and Grandma.

I remembered the new bridle Grandpa had made for me. "Grandpa, I already got my birthday present from you and Grandma." I said.

"This is the big present for both your birthday and your good marks in school my boy. You need proper boots for your rodeoing and that's for sure. We can't have you entering the rodeos in an old pair of boots, now can we?"

I strutted around the store like I had become the new owner. I was really all fitted out for good now. New jeans and boots. I had also got a new plaid western shirt and a brand new jean jacket that fit perfectly. Ken had bought me a Stetson some time ago and getting it cleaned and blocked made it look like new again. Ken told me how badly he felt for me when I was in the rodeo, not having proper western boots for

The Cowboy

riding. But he just couldn't afford them, that was all. Grandma said I looked like a ragamuffin, whatever that was. Now I had proper boots for this year's events, that's for sure. I was so happy I almost cried when I thought about what Grandpa had probably given up to buy them for me.

Earlier in the day, we had taken the eggs and cream in to the dairy next to the Williams store. Then Ken had gone with Grandpa to Williams. But Ken wasn't in the store when I got my new boots. He didn't let on that he noticed them. I walked around him, almost tripping over him in the parking lot.

"Boy," he said, "did you get the money from the eggs yet?"

"See anything different about me Ken?" "Yeah, come to think of it. I think you should have shaved this morning." he laughed.

"Aw Ken, boy you sure got blinders on this morning. Look down on the ground."

"Well, I'll be go to hell. Will you look at those jeans, now. Damned good looking pants there Skipper. But then you had them on when we left, didn't you? You telling me you come in here without your pants on?"

I was through playing his little game. "Ken! Look at the new boots Grandpa and Grandma got me."

He almost killed himself laughing, then heaved me up into the air, letting me almost hit the ground before catching me. He liked to see the fright in my eyes when I thought he might miss me.

I went into the Williams store office which also served as the dairy office. I liked going in there because I knew everyone and we'd joke around. They

Douglas Hargreaves

liked to tease me. "Are you sure you collected those eggs yourself, Skipper?" they'd ask. I wondered if they had heard how much I hated chickens.

They were always asking questions about the fairs coming up and if I was going to win the junior roping events. "Skipper, you going to keep those trophies you won last year or are you going to give someone else a go at them?" one of the ladies asked me.

"Hey Skip, don't forget, there's a few guys out there who want to take that bit of silver away from you this year." joked Sylvia the office clerk.

"I guess you're right Sylvie, but then maybe it's their turn, and I'll have to settle for less this year."

"Oh Skipper, I'm just joking. Of course you're going to take first again this year. Everyone knows that for sure." I was turning red.

"Sylvie, you know I'm not that good."

"Come around here." she said, showing me around the counter. She gave me a big hug. I always liked that, especially when there was no one in the office to see. "Come on in and sit for a minute, Skipper."

"I better not keep them too long or you know who'll come looking for me." I said. I sat down in the big office chair behind the boss's desk. I swung the chair around a couple of times so that I could look out the window. I swung the chair back again and hoooolly! There was Mr. Williams himself, looking down at me.

I shot out of the chair like a bullet but he caught me and heaved me back in it again. In a big deep booming voice he said. "You going to take the championship this year, boy? I'm just kidding you, Skipper. Of course you're going to take first again this year."

The Cowboy

"I'm sorry Mr. Williams, I didn't mean to be sitting in your chair." I wiggled out of the chair and stood looking up at him. He just about busted out laughing. "Skipper, I hear tell you're having the trophy engraved already with your name on it for this year's rodeo."

"Aw, come on, Mr. Williams, you know I couldn't do that." I laughed.

"Well son, my money's on you. If you do only half as good as you did last year you'll win hands down. You want me to put in a good word with the judges?" he joked.

"Do you know the judges?"

"Well I know one really well. In fact, it's me." he laughed. "How do you like that, Skipper? You better be nice to me."

Well, Mr. Williams sure was a nice man. I always enjoyed talking to him because he never talked down to me like a kid but like an adult. Mr. Williams also owned a half interest in Tip Johnson's trucking company that hauled oil well equipment in the valley.

I forgot about Tip Johnson until Ken reminded me a while later. It was a Saturday morning.

"Gosh all Friday boy, you gonna sleep your whole life away?" I had been up late working on a school assignment and was sleeping the sleep of sleeps. Sometimes on a Saturday, I was allowed to sleep for an extra hour. Today was not going to be one of them.

"You forgot we promised we'd go into the valley and help Tip Johnson with a few things today." Ken reminded me. "Get your little butt out of that bed and let's get the chores done so we can get going."

Sometimes when I didn't want to get up, I'd pretend I was sleeping. Ken would come into my room with a

Douglas Hargreaves

jug full of cold water. He would pull back my covers and simply dump it all over me. We'd have a good laugh and it got me out of bed. Today, I decided to avoid the water treatment.

Sunshine poured in through my window and that made me feel especially good. After all the rain we'd been having, it felt wonderful to see the sun again. Day after day we'd had rain, rain, rain, rain, rain, until we were waterlogged. It was a real chore to get to school and back, what with the roads being so muddy and the ditches so full of water. I'd get home from school soaked through and needing a complete change.

Mud was everywhere. It stuck to your boots like gumbo, building up into huge balls of guck that made hard walking. Sliding was what it was. I'd walk Nixon down through the creek to wash off his hooves and then wash off the stirrups and other parts of my saddle. So I was really happy when the rain stopped.

I got dressed and headed down to the barn. We had left the cows in the barn corral over night so we wouldn't have to go looking for them in the morning. I milked them almost as fast as Ken and that pleased him.

My hands had sure toughened up since the first time I tried milking, over three years ago. It didn't seem that long. It was as though I had always been a part of the Wills family. I knew some folks thought it strange that my parents were never around. Grandma and Grandpa didn't think it strange. They considered me to be their boy, right from the very beginning when I arrived. I had never been homesick for Winnipeg. Never. I had a real home now and that was all that mattered. In spite of the difficult time I had to start

The Cowboy

with, I had found what I was looking for. Love and caring and purpose and many good friends. My new boots showed me how tall I stood with my ranch family. At first I had been wearing my old broken down work boots, the ones my mother had bought me when I first came to the ranch. Then, for most work and chores, I used a pair of western boots that Gordy had grown out of. I could get a good shine on them if I worked at it.

I had just passed into Grade Ten and would be going to Turner Valley for the next school term when Grandpa decided I deserved a new pair of boots, especially for this year's rodeos. There was no doubt I would be competing. It was a big day in my life, the day I got those new boots. They were black and had a metalled design engraved into the sides. Not too fancy but just beautiful and they just fit me perfectly.

On that Saturday morning, the sun may have been shining, but the yard was a terrible muddy mess. Even walking to the barn carrying our empty milk pails was a chore. The mud clung to our boots. Just to keep from falling was a task. We finished the milking and put the cows out so they could get into the upper pasture for the day. For me, getting those milk pails back up to the house was almost impossible. It was too slippery. I decided to empty the big pails into smaller pails so they would be lighter and less likely to spill. I made four trips back and forth through the muck.

On my last trip up, I only had one pail to carry and it was only a little over a third full. Sure enough, my foot slipped and down I went, covering myself with mud and milk. Now I was going to get it. On top of having spilt the milk, I was going to make us late for our meeting with Tip Johnson in Turner Valley. I'd have to change and clean up.

Ken saw me and of course wasn't pleased. "Gosh all Friday boy, can't you be more careful? Can't you even do a little thing like carry up a pail of milk? We're late as it is. For a penny and a half I'd just leave you here by yourself." At least he was laughing.

"I'm sorry, I just couldn't help it Ken." "Get your towel and get down to the creek and wash all that crap off you quick, before I change my mind."

He handed me a towel and I ran off down to the creek. I was a terrible mess. I undressed and splashed into the creek. Wow that water was cold! I got out and towelled myself off. I was running back up to the house, trying to stay on some of the grassy parts. My foot slipped again and down I went, bare-arsed into the mud.

Ken was laughing so hard I thought he might fall down into the mud himself. The anguish on my face made me look even funnier. Back again into the creek. This time I took it a little slower and made it back to the house. Ken and I sometimes laughed when we talked about what would happen if someone came into the yard when we were on our way back up from the creek. Wouldn't that make a great picture?

As I was putting my socks and my shirt on, Ken said, "You're gonna have to wear your new boots, Skip. You got no others to wear. They're too wet and filthy and your old work boots don't fit any more."

"Ken, I can't wear my new ones in all this mud." I complained.

"Well, it's either your new ones or you go barefoot or you stay home. Your old boots are just too wet and

The Cowboy

muddy. You can't wear them. Now let's get a move on."

He fetched my new boots and I tugged them on. I would have to walk as carefully as I could and look for dry patches. I sure wasn't going to spoil my new boots.

The town of Turner Valley was just the worst mess for mud I had ever seen. Teams of horses pulled big trucks down Main Street. Tractors slipped all over the roads even with their big tire cleats. They just plugged up with mud. The board sidewalks were covered with mud from people walking on them with muddy shoes.

I looked out of place with my brand new boots all shiny and clean as we walked down the sidewalk to Tip Johnson's office. The office was empty but there was a note for Ken from Tip saying he would be back as soon as he got one of his trucks pulled out of the mud. He'd be coming up Main Street as all the side roads were impassable.

Even if you were just passing through town you had to go down Main Street. The mud was at least a foot deep, even deeper in places. Trucks wallowed up to their axles. Teams of six or even eight horses strained and slid in the goop as they pulled trucks. One such truck we recognized as Tip's.

"Come on Skip, let's go walk down the sidewalk to meet him." Ken suggested. We walked down the boardwalk which was almost as muddy as the road. Still, I had managed to keep my boots pretty clean so far.

We were almost abreast of the team when the hame strap on the front outside harness that hooks onto the double tree broke away. The lead horse on that side shot forward. The big Belgian mare reared up and

Douglas Hargreaves

started pulling away from the other lead horse. This frightened the rest of the team and they pulled to one side.

Ken jumped off the boardwalk and slid through the mud trying to get hold of the breakaway mare's bridle. But his boots slipped and he fell into the gooey mess almost under the horse's stomping feet. I ran up the boardwalk until I was abreast the jumping horse and ran off into the mud. I managed to catch the mare when her head was down. I hung on like crazy and she settled down.

They all kept on moving and the team slowly pulled the truck through the mud.

"Don't let them stop Skip, or we'll never get going again." Tip Johnson yelled.

All of a sudden the Belgian mare whose bridle I clung to heaved her head high into the air, bringing me up with her. But she pulled me clean out of my brand new boots! I looked back to see where Ken was and where my boots might be. The last I saw, the truck slowly rolled over them, crushing them into the slime and the guck.

"Ken! My boots!" I yelled. "Please Ken, can't you get them?"

He never looked back because he didn't hear me. I knew I had to stay with that mare until we got to drier ground and could stop. Well, we never did find a dry spot. That stamping and stumbling horse half dragged and half lifted me through the mud.

After a while, another driver came up and relieved me, taking the mare's rein. I ran back through the mud to where I had last seen my boots. Nothing but as sea of clay and mud.

The Cowboy

We finally got to Tip's truck yard. The big truck came to rest on the gravel base of the parking lot. I was in my stocking feet. Someone found one of my boots, but only one.

"Ken, how am I going to tell Grandpa?" I said.

"Boy, that was sure great work you did." Tip said to me. "You guys sure happened along at the right time. I don't know how to thank you. That wasn't really what I had planned for you to do today. I wanted you to drive this unit to Spence's place so we can start rigging up on Monday. You think you can still do that?"

Both Ken and I looked like drowned rats. Ken looked much worse than I did. "Sure Tip," he said. "We need the money so we'll just scrape off some of this crap and we'll go."

Tip looked at my stocking feet. "Here son. Here's an old pair of rubber boots. You can borrow them for the rest of the day."

I took off my socks and tucked them in the pockets of my jacket and put the boots on. They were ten times too big and my feet just wallowed around inside.

The truck needed refuelling. I climbed up on the big fuel tank at the back of the main deck and held the hose as Ken pumped in the fuel.

"Whoa, Ken! Stop!" I yelled. But the fuel kept coming. It sprayed all over me and into my big rubber boots.

"Ken! Why didn't you stop when I yelled at you?"

"Well, you should have been more on the ball and caught it quicker. Right?"

I wasn't going to win this one. Still, if this had happened a year ago, I would have had my bum tanned and that's for sure. "Jump Skipper, I'll catch you." Ken said. I leapt off the top of the truck and into his arms. The big rubber boots kept on going.

"Gosh all Friday, you sure stink kid." he laughed. Diesel fuel is terrible stuff to get on you, especially on your skin. Well I was soaked in it and there wasn't anything I could do about it.

Somehow we were able to complete the trip to Spence's without once getting stuck. Ken knew what he was doing, driving the big rigs. He was better than anyone else in the valley. They were often coming to him to help them out.

Ken also drove the municipal grader now and again. Most times, if my chores were done or I didn't have anything else to do, he would take me along. I liked to go with him on his road grading trips. He was the best around and I sure liked to watch him work. The oil drillers were always asking him for advice. I knew quite a few of them and they knew who I was. I got to climb all over the rigs. The roughnecks would take me up to the derrick platform and let me slide down the safety rope out into the field alongside the rig. Of course, they would also play tricks on me, like throwing me into the mud tank. Then they would take me into their wash room and spray me with a big pressure hose. It must have had a million tons of pressure in it. It would blow me across the room and nail me against the wall. Sometimes it hurt but I never cried. Ken was always around to see they didn't go too far. Ken firmly believed I needed to be tough if I was going to survive.

When we got to Spence's they were setting up a rig. The roughnecks started to unload right away.

The Cowboy

"Ain't you guys supposed to wait until Monday?" Ken asked. "Nope," said the tool push, "we were waiting on this stuff and now we got it, we can get going." The tool push was the rig boss.

After they unloaded, the roughnecks picked me up and carried me into the wash room and put the big wash hose on me. They laughed when they saw me. They got the mud washed away but the smell of diesel fuel still clung. Mr. Spence came over to the wash house, handed me a monster towel and told me to get out of my clothes. "You get dried Skipper and come up to the house."

The towel was so big it dragged on the ground as I walked up to the house. Mrs. Spence showed me in. Ken, Mr. Spence and Will Perkins, the tool push, were sitting at the table drinking coffee. "What kept you boy?" Ken smiled. He looked all clean again, better than me, that's for sure. Mrs. Spence brought me some clothes and told me to change into them in her son's room. The clothes belonged to Lynn, their twelve-year-old. I knew him a bit from school.

The clothes fit perfectly and I guess I came out looking pretty good. "Hey Skipper, you look better in those clothes than Lynn does." said Mrs. Spence. "You wear them home and then bring them back when you're done with them."

She gave me a glass of milk and a large piece of cake. "Thank you ma'am, I sure was getting hungry."

"I've heard all about you Skipper, from the kids and from other people in town. What a fine young roper you are and how polite and well-mannered you are."

Mrs. Spence was embarrassing me.

Douglas Hargreaves

"Skipper," said Mr. Spence, "you going to take the trophy again this year?"

"He'll walk away with it. There ain't no one in the valley can rope like your kid." Will Perkins said. "Ken, this boy of yours is something else when you think of how he grabbed those horses this morning and how he did it in all that crap. Yessiree, he's some kid." I was blushing again. Ken was beaming.

Tip had followed us in his truck and we left Spence's place with him. I stood on the rear deck as we bounced along back into town where our own truck was parked.

We finally made it back to the ranch after skidding our way through miles of mud. The warm sunny day had dried the roads a good deal but they were still pretty treacherous. I was tired and had blisters on my feet from wearing those big rubber boots. My only worry was how I was going to tell Grandpa about losing my beautiful western boots in the mud.

After milking, Ken and I went over the day's events.

"Skipper, I'm real proud of you. You really saved the day for Tip." He walked over to where I was standing by the porch railing. He picked me up and set me on the rail. Now we were eye to eye. He gave me a big hug. I always liked it when he did that.

The next morning, Sunday, we went to church as usual. I was dreading it because Grandpa was there and I would have to tell him about my boots. I gingerly walked up to him to explain my misfortune but he was ready for me. Ken had filled him in about my mishap.

"Skipper," said Grandpa, "I know about the boots and don't you worry, I'm not mad at you son. These

The Cowboy

things happen to hard-working men. Couldn't be helped. Just part of the job. Some day you'll get another pair but we just can't afford it right now."

After church, as we were about to get into the car, Tip Johnson and Lynn Spence drove up. They had come all that way through the mud to see Ken and me.

Lynn said, "Skipper, my mom says you're to keep the clothes because I'm grown out of them anyway. Mr. Johnson has something else for you too." Lynn gave me a friendly punch.

"Here Skipper," said Tip with a smile. "A new pair of boots for the hard working man. They're the best they had in town so I think you'll like them. It was my fault I got into trouble with those horses. If it hadn't been for you and your dad I would have been in real serious trouble. You guys really helped me a lot." Then he handed Ken and me an envelope with our names on it. It was our pay. Ken knew he was going to be paid but I wasn't expecting anything. I opened the envelope and there were two bills, a twenty and a ten. It was the most pay I had ever earned. "Thanks very much, Mr. Johnson." I said. And thank you Lynn, for the clothes."

Grandpa was looking on and I could see the sparkle shining in his eyes whenever he got a tear in them. I'm sure he could see the same sparkle in mine.

BECKY'S BOYFRIEND

Most Saturdays, when we visited Grandma and Grandpa, we'd get our clothes mended and our laundry done. Grandma would also give us our baking for the week. Ken and I never had to do any bread baking ourselves and we probably
couldn't do it anyway.

Peggy would help us out foodwise by baking us scones or muffins. Not bran muffins--that was the one thing I had learned to bake myself. During my first year on the ranch, someone had given us a hundred pound sack of bran . The stuff lasted us throughout the Winter and Spring. Sometimes it was all we had to eat--bran porridge, bran biscuits and bran muffins. We were hard pressed for money but we always ate well even if we didn't have any extras. With all that bran, no one could understand how I could still have trouble with my bowels.

Into my third year on the ranch, everyone found it hard to believe I was still living there and actually growing some. I had filled out a little bit too, and was able to do a lot of the heavier chores. I was growing up and Grandpa bragged to everyone about his young man.

Ken was real proud of me. (My reputation as a rodeo performer helped.) He now had confidence that I was responsible enough to manage the ranch alone if he had to spend a couple of days in Calgary.

No one in our community worked on Sunday, except the Wilsons, and then only sometimes. Grandma saw to it that we were always bright and shiny for church. She wanted her brood to set a good example. We'd go on a picnic after church if the weather was good.

For me it was a lot of fun to visit friends on Sunday after church. Church service was pretty routine for me until this one memorable Sunday. The visiting preacher asked me if I would read the lesson for the day. I looked at Grandma and she was beaming all over, nodding her approval.

"Sure," I said, "what do I have to read?" He asked me to read Chapter 14 of the Book of John, verses fourteen to twenty-two. Grandma was so proud that I was to read. She believed it was due to her strong influence that I was such a good church-going boy. This was something new for me so I was a little nervous as I went up to the front.

I was getting through the reading quite well until I got to verse twenty-one. "He it is who loves me; and he who loves me will be loved by my Father, and I will love him and will disclose myself to him." Becky Martinsen started to giggle, then laugh outright. I couldn't help looking at her as her father gave her a burning glare of disapproval.

"I love you too, Skipper." she blurted out, and started to laugh again. The congregation chuckled--all except Grandma and the preacher. Grandma stared daggers at Becky, then more daggers at me. I could tell I was in for it, even though I never once ever paid her any mind, let alone gave her any ideas about you-know-what.

Completely thrown and embarrassed, I stumbled through the rest of the reading as best I could. I couldn't wait to get back to my seat. Such a thing had

The Cowboy

never happened in church before. I sat down between Ken and Grandma. Peggy had a smile on her face and all the kids were winking and casting smiling, knowing looks at me. Becky and me?

When I came out, Becky's father was laying the law down to her in no uncertain terms. They were talking to the preacher. I think he was making her apologize for her behaviour. I thought she should be apologizing to me for embarrassing me like she did.

We got into the car before she and her father had finished. I sat in the corner of the back seat, afraid to say anything. "Cat got your tongue, Skippy love?" Peggy said.

"Aw Peggy, what's that supposed to mean?" All I could think about was how I was going to be in for it at school.

Grandma announced at dinner that we were going over to the Mortinsens for the afternoon. "Grandma, I can't go over there after what she did." I protested.

"Stuff and nonsense." Grandma scolded.

"Is there something wrong that we can't visit with our friends?" Ken chuckled. "Please Grandma, don't make me go over there." I begged.

"Skipper, you're going like the rest of us, so never mind about it. You must have said something to encourage her to make such a scene."

"Grandma, how can you say such a thing?"

"Hmmph. I know one thing. That girl had spunk to do what she did. She must be in love." I had never heard her carry on so, and at my expense.

I ate in silence for most of the meal but Johnny insisted on goading me. Finally, I told him to leave it

Douglas Hargreaves

alone. "It's okay love, you'll see her this afternoon. You two can be alone." he promised.

"Grandma please make him keep still."

"That's enough now. All of you leave the boy alone." Grandma said. Her words were always law. Grandpa gave me a wink and a smile and I felt better.

We helped with the dishes and Ken said he and I would drive home and get our horses. We'd ride over a little later. It was a beautiful afternoon. Johnny begged Peggy to allow him to come with us. She agreed. I knew this was going to be one of those terrible ordeals.

We rode through the Mortinsen's large gate and up to the house. Becky's family was well-to-do, like the Wilsons. They owned a huge ranch. We sometimes worked with Becky's two brothers, moving our cattle off the lease lands. They were always on hand to help with branding. They were with the group that tried to brand me after my cow-riding adventure. Everyone kidded me at school for weeks about that one, especially the girls.

Grandma, Grandpa and Peggy were at the Mortinsen's when Ken, Johnny, and I arrived but I didn't see Becky. I was looking around so I could avoid her. Johnny and I walked over to the verandah where all the men were gathered, telling stories and passing on bits of gossip.

"Hi-yah Skip," said Olie. "I hear you gone and roped a steer you can't ride, huh?" Everyone laughed but me. They talked about my having won another trophy for cow riding. Gossiping was something everyone did on visiting days. That's how news got around, good news or bad. That way and from the travelling Watkins salesman.

The Cowboy

Johnny and I decided to walk down to the corral and see the Mortinsen's new Arabian horses. They still needed breaking. We ran along side the barn and over the remains of an old haystack to get a better view. All of a sudden I was hurled off my feet into the air by a flying tackle. It was Becky. She was wearing jeans and looked like a boy. I fell flat on my back in the hay. Becky was on top of me.

"Hooollly!" I whooped. "Becky! What the heck you trying to do?"

She planted her big ugly lips right on my cheek. I thought I would throw up. Johnny was screaming and laughing and jumping up and down. "Get her off of me Johnny, you dumb-bell!" I yelled.

"Skippy's got a girl friend! Skippy's got a girl friend!" he chanted at the top of his lungs.

Becky sat astride me, holding my arms above my head. I couldn't move. "Becky, let me up." I hissed. I sounded desperate as she started kissing me again. I squirmed and tried to get away from her lips. She was sitting on my stomach and choking me. I couldn't get my breath.

"Becky, you little bitch, you get off of me right now or I'm going to tell." I threatened.

"Oh Skippy, I heard what you said. And who you going to tell anyway, lover boy?" she giggled. "Everyone knows you were coming over here today. I told them what I was going to do to you."

"How could you do such a stupid thing? Come on Becky, please let me up."

"Not unless you promise to be my boyfriend." She tickled me and I gasped for breath with forced laughter. Johnny saw I was choking and took a flying

Douglas Hargreaves

jump onto Becky's back. She tumbled off me and I got up and ran as fast as I could back to the verandah. I stood beside Ken and stayed there for the rest of the afternoon.

When it was time to go home, Ken said, "What's eating you, son?"

"Please Ken, keep that girl away from me. She's crazy."

"You talking about Becky, Skip?"

"Ken, she's crazy. She tried to make me be her boyfriend and kiss her." "Skip, you should be flattered to have a girl make such a fuss over you. It isn't every day you get a big chance like that."

"Ken, please, this is serious. I hate her. She's such a pig. I don't ever want to see her again. What will she tell the kids in school? She told me she had this planned. All the kids knew what she was going to do to me."

"What did she do to you, Skip?"

"Well, I told you. You know."

Johnny came over and told Ken what had happened. "She wants to make love to Skipper." Johnny concluded.

Ken laughed and told me he would protect me from the giant lady vampire.

What Johnny had told Ken scared me more. Surely she wasn't crazy enough to try anything like that, was she? I saw Becky walking with her mother and sister as we were getting on our horses to leave. She waved at me and blew me a kiss. I turned away and didn't look at them.

When we got home, I talked worriedly about what Becky was trying to do. "She just wants attention

The Cowboy

Skipper." Ken said. "She wants attention from the smartest and best-looking kid in the school. So she'll do anything."

I wasn't convinced that was all she had in mind. "I can't fight her Ken. I'm too small."

"Look son, she isn't going to hurt you. Just ignore her and she'll soon let up."

"I sure hope so. I can't stand her."

I could hardly sleep that night, and when morning came I was almost too tired to get up. I struggled through my chores, ate breakfast and rode off to school. Gordy was waiting for me by our gate and I told him what had happened. He laughed and said everyone knew Becky to be a boy-hungry brat. I really should be afraid of her.

"You can't hit her Skip. You can't hit a girl." he chuckled. That was out of the question. If I ever raised a hand to her, she'd break me in two. You didn't tangle with Becky. She had given one of the Wilson boys a black eye. On the other hand, I had to do something drastic. I was in a real dilemma.

As expected, everyone at school had heard of our escapade at Becky's place and were having a great laugh at my expense. They were laughing at Becky's romp with me in the hay.

"I never did such a thing. She just knocked me down." I claimed.

"Oh sure Skippy, we know," they giggled, rolling their eyes at me. Becky kept looking over at me during class. How could a small Grade Niner handle this female bully playing her dangerous game? I decided to talk to Peggy. Tell her what I was afraid of. She always knew what to do.

Douglas Hargreaves

I was having a rotten day at school. Miss Snowdon kept telling Becky to pay attention to what was going on in her own class and to stop looking at me. I asked to be excused and was allowed to go outside.

Olie happened to be going by with a load of hay. He saw me and stopped.

"What's up Skipper? What you doing out here?" I told him what was going on in the class. He told me to watch out for Becky, that she and her sister were wild ones. They were just plain mean.

"Will you tell Peggy that I want to see her after supper?"

"Skipper, you got another belly ache?"

"It's not that, Olie. It's this thing with Becky."

"Sure Skip, we'll work something out."

He continued on his way and I returned to class. Miss Snowdon said. "Are you feeling poorly, Skipper?"

"No Ma'am. I just needed some fresh air, that's all."

Billy Wilson said. "What Skipper needs, only Becky can give him."

"You watch your tongue, Billy Wilson," said Miss Snowdon, "I don't want to hear any talk like that."

Everyone started to laugh. I grew redder each moment. The class was breaking up and getting out of control and Miss Snowdon was getting upset. Becky sat there enjoying every minute of it. "See you after school Skippy." she said.

"Quiet, everyone! And get back to work!" shouted Miss Snowdon.

That Becky. What a brazen rotten bitch, I thought. How was I ever going to get out of this?

The Cowboy

Miss Snowdon contributed the last straw. I don't know why but she told the two of us in Grade Nine to open our books to biology and turn to the section on reproduction. That did it. Becky and three of her classmates started making moaning sounds and mumbling, "Ohhh, Skipper . . . Ooohh, Skipper." I picked up my books and left the class.

I rode home but Ken wasn't there. I rode over to Peggy's and told her what had happened.

"Skipper, they're only joking with you. They see how upset you get and know they're embarrassing you. That's all they want. They just want to upset you and have a little fun at your expense."

"But Peggy, what if she beats me up or something? How will I ever live it down?"

Peggy tried to make me feel better. "Come on Skipper, you may be small but you're not that weak."

"I can't hit her Peggy. You know that."

"You won't have to Skipper. Just tell her you've had enough. You watch. She'll back off. I'll tell you what I'll do. I'll talk to her mother. I'll see her day after tomorrow."

"I don't know if I can wait that long." I sighed.

"You feeling alright these days Skipper? Your tummy behaving itself?"

"After all of this, it won't be."

Friday night after school, Gordon, Phillip and I decided to go for a swim at Peggy's swimming hole. I had taken enough razzing for one week and the swimming hole seemed like a good idea to get away from it all.

We were throwing an India rubber ball into the middle of the pond and diving for it. I was diving for

Douglas Hargreaves

the bottom when someone grabbed my privates! I screamed and gurgled under water, trying to get up and away from whoever it was. It couldn't be Gord or Phillip. Billy would often sneak up on us and grab us, but not these guys. I saw long hair floating past and then, horror of horrors, Becky surfaced! She was laughing and still holding on to my thing.

"Ow!" I screamed. "Becky, you let go now, you hear?"

Phillip came over and saw what Becky was doing. He tried to pull her off, without success.

"I'll let go of your stinkin' little thing if you promise to be my boyfriend!" she yelled. She was hurting me and I couldn't do a thing to get her to let go. Both Gordon and Phillip tried getting her off but the more they scrambled, the more she squeezed. She was pulling me out of the water onto the shore, still holding on. I started to cry and she let go. She just stood there as bold as could be and told me either I became her boyfriend or she was going to tear them off next time. Then she ran off.

"Hooollly! What am I going to do?" I asked my friends as we got dressed.

"Did she hurt you Skipper?" Gordon asked. "Yes, and I darned well couldn't do anything about it."

I went up to the house and Peggy saw I had been crying. "Why Skipper, what's wrong?" she asked.

"Becky got me in the pond Peggy. She was holding on to me and I couldn't get out. She told me that unless I was her boyfriend, she was going to pull my thing off." I started sniffling again.

The Cowboy

"I saw Mrs. Mortinsen and she told me she would talk to Becky. She said they were only funning you and kids will be kids."

"Peggy, when she grabbed my dink, that was not funning."

"She did what?" Peggy sounded alarmed.

"And she grabbed my Jewels (as Ken called them) and squeezed hard. That really hurt bad Peggy."

"No it wasn't funning. I'll talk to Olie and Grandma."

Church the next Sunday was just frightening. Becky had told some of her friends what she had done and they were all making little cat calls at me. I couldn't stand any more of this.

Ken went over to Mr. Mortinsen and told him what Becky had done to me. There would be no more of that sort of thing. "What kind of a daughter are you raising there George?" Ken said. "What kind of a girl would go around attacking boys like that?"

"Well, I'll tell her to lay off." he said. "Gosh, I don't see what she sees in your puny kid anyway."

Regardless of how badly I felt, everyone seemed to think Becky's behaviour was quite normal and cute. A little forward, mind you, but otherwise quite funny. She told the girls I had a nice body. They whistled and joshed each other about what Becky saw. "Becky, can we come and see too?" they yelled, loud enough for me to hear. What did they mean, "come and see"?

When we went visiting to Peggy's that afternoon, the general talk was about the behaviour of young kids today. How their parents were not disciplining their offspring. They weren't talking about me or any of my friends. All of us got disciplined on the behind. We

Douglas Hargreaves

toed the line or we didn't sit for a few days. Simple as that. And that's what Becky Mortinsen needed, I thought. Someone to warm the daylights out of her backside. Probably no such thing would ever happen.

I got through the next school week with only a little snickering and kidding about my tangles with Becky in the hay and the swimming hole. "I think we got it all fixed up." I told Ken with relief. "I think she has given up on me as her boyfriend."

"Guess she thought it over and decided your equipment wasn't good enough." said Ken.

"Aw, please don't say things like that."

"Okay son, I'm sorry. Just joshing you a bit."

I jumped up on his back, pretending to wrestle him and beat him up. He just simply flipped me up and over his knee in the old whacking position.

"That's no fair." I complained. I knew he was joking--but you could never be sure. Ken told me I was getting too old for spankings. I agreed. Then he said he wanted me to know he still could.

Shortly after the second week of Becky's attempt on my body, mean little things started happening. First my lunch went missing from my saddlebag. Then my homework got scribbled up. A note appeared on my desk telling me I had better watch out for "you know who".

I had to explain what happened about my homework to Miss Snowdon. She knew I always had my homework and assignments done on time. She questioned Becky directly.

"Why would I want to have anything to do with that little worm anyway?" Becky replied, loud enough for everyone to hear. I avoided looking at her. Gordy

The Cowboy

gave me a wink and we went on as though nothing had happened.

After school, Phillip told me he had overheard some of the girls talking with Becky about me. "I don't care." I said, trying to sound confident.

"They were talking about Friday after school." Phillip said.

I tried to dismiss his warning. "Oh phooey, not again."

"I wouldn't put anything past her, Skipper. She is terrible and can be real mean."

Friday came, and the only thing I had planned for after school was to get the cows in from the north pasture, milk them and then I was free. Ken was going to meet me at Peggy's for supper. I would ride over after I milked.

I had completed separating and had put the cream down in the well where it would keep cool until we took it into town. I was walking down to the barn to get Nixon when Sarah Billingsly and Wendy Carstairs came riding into the yard. I hardly ever saw them outside of school. They were both in Grade Eight--like Becky.

"Hi," I said nervously, "what are you guys doing here?"

"Oh, we were just riding around and decided we would come and pay you a visit." said Sarah. "We're on our way to Peggy's."

"That's just where I'm going. You came this way as a short cut, right?" I said hopefully.

"Well you might say that." Wendy said with a little laugh. "We wanted to see what you were up to."

"What do you mean, what I'm up to?"

As I was opening the gate to get Nixon, Becky came barrelling around the corner of the barn and tackled me. I fell down and the big slob pinned me.

"You gonna be my boyfriend?" she demanded. "I ain't askin' you again, you little twerp."

"No, I'm not going to be your bloody boyfriend or anyone else's. Get off me right now."

"Hey Sarah, did you hear what the nasty little man said to me? He needs some lessons in manners doesn't he?" I struggled to get up but she was too big and strong. "Get hold of his arms." Becky instructed her gang.

"What the heck you think you're doing?" I yelled. My worst nightmare was coming true. "I'm sure gonna tell on you guys." I threatened.

"Yeah, sure you are, Skippy baby." Becky laughed.

Sarah held my arms above my head while Wendy held my legs. Becky undid my belt and proceeded to pull my pants off! I was screaming at the top of my voice hoping someone might hear me. Becky pulled off my undershorts and invited the girls to see what all the fuss was about.

"You bitch girl!" I yelled.

"Now, now, Skippy." Sarah said as she patted me on the stomach.

"You're right." Wendy said to Becky. "It's even smaller than my baby brother's."

"You're all going to get it when Ken finds out about this." I warned.

"Turn him over on his stomach." Becky ordered. They flipped me over and Becky grabbed a riding crop from her saddle. "Well now, Skippy boy," she said, "are we going to talk business or am I going to lace

The Cowboy

your little bum with this whip?" I was terrified and tried to bargain.

"Why do you want to do this stupid thing? I'm too small for you. Why not just let it go at that? I won't tell anyone what you did."

Becky brought her whip down hard across my behind.

"Becky! Please! No!" I yelled out. "You don't really want me to be your boyfriend, do you?"

She whacked me another one. It hurt so bad I started to cry. "Why do you want me so badly for your boyfriend?" I sobbed. "Because, little smarty, I just do, that's all." She lashed me again.

Wendy decided she wanted a turn too. She said I thought I was so good. This would teach me not to be so smart from now on. They were just getting warmed up. Wendy whipped me three times and laughed at my screaming. "See, Becky, he ain't such a big shot now, is he?"

Sarah took the whip from Wendy and gave me three more.

I was bleeding. My backside was so numb I could hardly feel the lashes any more.

Becky told me I was going to be her boyfriend so she could do whatever she wanted with me. It was that or more lashes. I couldn't stop crying. I hated them seeing me cry.

"What a cry baby you are Skipper!" Sarah said and lifted up my shirt so that Becky could whack me a few more times on the back. This, they figured, would hurt even more.

Douglas Hargreaves

"Okay Skipper," Becky said with a smirk, "I'll ask you one more time. Then I'm really going to tan your ass." She leaned over and kissed me.

"Okay! Okay! Please Becky, please, no more! I can't stand any more." I begged. I was about to throw up or maybe pee. "You gonna do what I tell you Skipper?"

"Yes, honest I will, Becky. Please don't hit me any more. Sarah, please make her stop."

"Just remember one thing Skipper." Becky warned. "You go back on your word and I'll get you. You know I will." She turned to Sarah and Wendy. "Let him up."

I could hardly stand up and ached all over. "How could you do such a sick thing?" I said to Becky.

"You're my boyfriend, right, Skipper?"

"Yes Becky, I'm your boyfriend. What am I supposed to do anyway?" I just wanted to get to Peggy's as fast as I could.

Sarah said, "Oh, what about--you know what we said we were going to do?"

"Oh yes." Becky sneered. "Just in case he forgets he belongs to me."

The three of them picked me up and threw me into the creek.

"Bye sweetheart." Becky called out as they rode away.

I was just getting out of the creek when I heard Ken riding towards me. Everyone at Peggy's had been wondering what was delaying me.

"Ken!" I yelled.

He came running up to me. "Skipper, what the hell have you been up to? Oh God, son, what's happened to you?"

The Cowboy

I was standing by the creek in only my shirt. He saw my cuts and bruises.

I started crying and couldn't stop. I clung to him like my life depended on it. My clothes were still lying by the barn where the girls had left them. He picked them up and carried me to the house and into my bedroom and laid me on the bed. I had stopped my crying but continued to sniffle.

"Ken, it was Becky and Wendy Carstairs and Sarah Billingsly. They whipped me with Becky's riding crop. She wouldn't stop lashing me until I promised to be her boyfriend. Ken, what am I going to do? I had to promise her I would do anything she wanted me to."

He got a wash cloth and wiped the blood off, then put some salve on it. "You just lie there for awhile until it feels better." he said. "I'll get you something to eat."

"Ken, please, I want to go to Peggy's."

"You think you can ride with your bum so beat up?"

"I'll stand up in the stirrups." I told him.

"Okay son, if you feel up to it." he said.

"Ken, what am I going to do about what they did?"

He was furious. "I'm reporting them to the Valley police, Skipper. They can't go around doing things like this. I sure ain't heard of such a thing happening before."

Ken saddled Nixon and helped me onto his back. Even Nixon sensed things were not right. He kept looking back at me all the time we were riding.

When we walked into the kitchen, Peggy knew right away there had been trouble.

Douglas Hargreaves

"Show Peggy, Skipper. Show her your behind," Ken said. "Skipper!" Peggy cried out, "who did this to you?"

Everyone had a look at the damage.

"It was Becky and her classmates from school," said Ken. "You're going to the police, aren't you?" Peggy and Olie said in one voice.

"I'm going to see Mortinsen first. Let him stew for awhile." Ken said.

Ken made me go to school on Monday. We had to see this thing through. I continued doing all my chores. I could hardly sit on the milk stool, I hurt so bad. Ken's worst spanking never hurt as bad as this horse whipping.

No one in class said anything about what happened. The girls didn't look at me.

About eleven o'clock, Ken arrived with Mr. Mortinsen and a policeman from the Valley. Ken talked to my teacher then they called Becky outside. After a few minutes, they called Wendy and Sarah outside.

The girls did not deny what they had done. They figured it was okay. They felt good about it. Becky smiled the whole the time.

Since all three were only fourteen, nothing much could be done to them except put them on probation to their parents and the courts for several months. The policeman went to all three girls' homes and told their parents exactly what they had done.

It must have had some effect, because they never spoke to me again. School was never quite the same after that. At least I was not going to have to be Becky's boyfriend, that's for sure.

The Cowboy

All the guys in the school wanted me to tell them the gory details.

"Bet she didn't find your dink again, did she?" said Billy.

Gordy, Phillip and I talked about it sometimes when we were alone or at the swimming hole. They couldn't believe such a thing could happen. Sometimes we even laughed about it. But they laughed more than I did.

OLD JIM COWIE

I don't know how many times I rode past the old cabin without taking any notice. It was set back in the bushes. The yard, if you could call it that, was really just part of the hay field alongside. It looked like a shack the miners used to build in the early days. It seemed it had always been there and I never paid it any mind.

I never saw anyone around the place but we knew that an old man by the name of Jim Cowie lived there.

One day, Gordy, Phillip and I were taking our time riding home from school. It was very warm and quite muggy. We made plans to head for Peggy's swimming hole. We still had lots of time before chores.

"Ever been to Old Jim's place?" Phillip asked me as we rode by.

"No. I didn't know anyone lived there." I replied.

"Well, Old Jim Cowie lives there, and he's a bad one. My pa says I'm never to go around there."

"I saw him outside once and he sure looked old." said Gordy.

"He owns the quarter from the road to our place." said Phillip. "Pa has been after that quarter for years but the old man won't let it go. I was riding home after chasing some strays. They broke through a hole in Jim's fence. They were in some scrub behind his house. I never thought about whose place it was and I rode up there and moved them out. I just got smokin' em' when I come across Jim's cabin. I'd never seen it from the back before. I didn't think I was that close to it."

Douglas Hargreaves

" Well, the old guy comes hobbling around the side of the house and scares the heck out of Kachook. He rears up and chucks me on my rump. The old guy comes over and grabs me by the shirt. Nearly ripped it off. Boy, was I scared. He never said a word. Just stared at me, never blinking an eye or smiling or nothing. I guess he knew I was darned scared of him. He just stood there holding on to me. I told him I was sorry and didn't mean to ride on his place. I was only chasing our strays."

"I tried to move but he was holding on to my arm and my neck. He was squeezing hard too. He kept looking me up and down, then turned me around and then around again. I was almost ready to scream. I told him I wouldn't come near his place again."

Phillip went on to repeat that Mr. Cowie never once said a word, just held him tight and turned him round and round.

"Then all of a sudden he let me go. Boy, did I ever leave that place in a hurry. I won't ever go back there again."

What Phillip was telling us was really scary. I decided to ask Ken about Old Jim Cowie. I wanted to know what he was like and why he lived all alone.

We had our swim at the beaver dam. Johnny and Mark were already swimming. We fooled around for awhile and had a great time as usual. No girls this time. Our best fun was diving for an India rubber ball. It was heavy enough to sink, and being white, it was easy to see under water. We sometimes stirred up a lot of the bottom when we were swimming but you could see that ball no matter how dirty the water got.

The Cowboy

I heard someone coming down to the dam, whistling. It was Peggy. I started to make for the shore to get my clothes before Peggy found them. She had a habit of hiding them and making me sneak up to the house in my nothing. Then I had to search for them. I swear this gave her more pleasure than a card game, watching me hide and run around to find my clothes.

"Boys," said Peggy, "you guys come up to the house after you finish your swim and you can have some scones and tea. Skipper, where did you put your clothes?" She wouldn't have asked me if she hadn't already swiped them.

"Peggy? Have you taken my clothes again?"

"Why Skippy, Peggy wouldn't do anything like that, now, would I?"

"Aw, Peggy, please give them back to me." I pleaded.

"I'll see if I can find where they are when you come up to the house."

Everyone always got a real laugh out of Peggy stealing my clothes. Today was no exception. I was used to it and didn't mind so much, as long as it was just us guys.

I found my clothes, all right. They were hanging on the clothes line drying. After Peggy had taken my clothes to the house, she had washed them and hung them to dry. They were still wet, of course, so I had nothing to wear.

"Johnny," said Peggy, "get Skipper a pair of your jeans while his are drying."

She was always doing things like that. Sometimes I never came up to the house because there were visitors

Douglas Hargreaves

or strange girls around. Peggy's own girls were used to me bouncing around looking for my clothes.

As we were eating Peggy's scones, I said, "Peggy, why does Old Jim Cowie live by himself?"

"Well," she said, "as I heard, his family don't live anywhere around these parts. They live in the Maritimes some place. I heard they never want to see the old man any more. They had some kind of a row or something."

"Is he very old?"

"He was here when I was born. Someone told me they think he might have hurt or even killed someone in the family. But I just heard that--don't know for sure. You boys just stay clear of Old Jim, you hear?" she warned. "Phillip, I hear you had a run-in with him once."

"Yeah, it was a few years ago. Boy, did he ever scare the heck out of me." We finished our scones and Gordy and Phillip rode on home.

"Skipper, get one of Johnny's shirts. Ride home and do your chores, then come back for supper. We're going to Grandpa's after supper. Ken's there."

Johnny and I rode over to Grandpa's. I decided to find out what he knew. "Grandpa, why does Old Jim Cowie live all by himself?"

"Skipper, he's just too darned miserable to be near anyone."

"Doesn't he like anyone?"

"Well son, no one ever goes near him to ask him if he does or he doesn't. He's just one miserable, cantankerous old man." He advised me to stay clear of the old coot. Old Jim Cowie was harmless enough, but just stay away.

The Cowboy

That was good enough for me. I wouldn't go near his place, even though it was just down and across from our gate on the main road, set back about a hundred yards or so. There were a few bushes here and there in the front but mostly hay. The shrubs around his house never grew high enough to cover the windows. About a week later I was picking saskatoons by our roadway. It was after supper and still light out. Grandma had asked me to get her some of those berries before the birds finished them off.

I had picked two pails full when I saw two of Wilson's steers crossing the road to Old Jim's place. I looked around and figured I could get them out of there before Old Jim saw me. No one would know they had been out. I remembered Grandpa's and Phillip's warnings about Old Jim. I walked over to the two grazing steers and shooed them out of Jim's field and back towards Wilson's. Old Jim's hay was so good that they didn't want to leave and kept trying to come back. I was starting to worry. Suppose Old Jim saw me and came out? Hoooolly! What would I do then?

I got closer to the cabin and it seemed deserted to me. I chased those steers all over the place, making a lot of racket. Finally I got them heading out of Jim's hay, when I turned around, there was Old Jim standing right behind me. I just stood there shaking. I wanted to run but the legs didn't get the brain's message.

"H- H- Hello, Mr. Cowie." I stuttered.

He said nothing--just stood there blocking my retreat and staring at me. He looked like he'd fall down any minute. He was shaking too. Sweat ran down his forehead and he smelled awful.

Douglas Hargreaves

I found some courage to say something. "Are you all right, Mr. Cowie?"

He just stood there, quite still, but shaking. At last he said in a crackly quivering voice, "You're Skipper, ain't you?"

"Yes, sir. I live across the road from you."

"I know who you are. You're Ken Wills' boy."

"Yes, sir. I live with Ken."

"Where's your folks, boy?"

"They're in England."

"You miss your folks?"

I was feeling a little more at ease. I would have liked to have been somewhere else though, with him just staring at me like that. At least the urge to wet my pants was leaving me.

"Not very much, Mr. Cowie. They're very busy with business. They don't have much time for kids."

"One day you'll miss them son. I know. I have a family who I didn't think I would miss but I do. Now it's too late. They don't want to have anything to do with me."

This was turning into a strange conversation and I was feeling very uncomfortable.

"Ken good to you, is he?"

"Yes sir. He's like my dad."

"He give you lots of lickin's, does he?"

I wondered how he would ever know about that. "I guess I have it coming, Mr. Cowie. He really loves me. I wouldn't leave for anything."

"Well, he's very lucky to have you, Skipper. I hear everyone likes you because you are a good boy. I knew I would like you, Skipper, just hearing about you." he said in a shaky voice. I reddened a bit. "I don't feel

The Cowboy

very well, Skipper," he went on. "I'm getting too old. I can't fend for myself any more. Get on home now and I'm glad I finally got to meet you boy." He tottered towards the house.

"Can I help you, Mr. Cowie?" I said as I walked him to his door. Hooolly, did he smell bad. He leaned on me so much I thought I would cave in under the weight. I really felt badly for him, and I didn't even know him.

"Would you get me a pail of water Skipper, please? I don't think I can carry it." He handed me a pail.

"Sure, Mr. Cowie."

"The pump is around back by the workshop."

It took me a long time to get the pump primed. The water that came up was kind of rusty. I wondered how long it had been since he had used that pump. I worked the pump until the water came clean, then filled the pail. He asked me to set it on the porch. "I'll take it in for you, Mr. Cowie." I said.

"Well, all right, just inside the door. There's a stand where I keep the pail."

I wished I hadn't volunteered to take the pail inside. It had to be the scummiest place I had ever seen. I felt so terrible for this old man. The cabin was only a single room with a bed at one end and an iron wood stove to cook on and provide heat at the other. In the middle was an old tattered chesterfield and chair. There was a side board against the wall and in front of it was a an old wooden kitchen table with two chairs. There were two windows, one at the front beside the door and one at the back.

"Mr. Cowie," I said, "can I help you clean things up a bit? Where do you keep your food?" I looked

Douglas Hargreaves

around the room. He had settled into the chesterfield, which was covered with old newspapers.

"I got some, some place. You just get on home now. I'll be fine and thank you son."

I took my pails of saskatoons home. Ken asked me where I had been and what had taken me so long. He gave me a good scolding for having gone over to Old Jim's place. He told me I wasn't to go anywhere near there.

"I'm sorry Ken, but I had to get Wilson's steers out of there." I said. "I have to tell you what I saw and what I was doing."

I related the whole story to him and for once he listened to what I had to say. He said that we should have the authorities look in on the old guy.

"Ken, he hasn't any food. I know he doesn't." I didn't want to drop the subject.

"Okay then, let's put something together and you can take it over."

We packed some biscuits, scones, a jar of jam and some tea. There was still some milk left, so I poured it into a bottle. Ken and I walked up our road and over to Jim's.

"You go on up, Skipper. I'll just stand back here. He don't like anyone around here."

I went to the door and knocked. "Mr. Cowie, it's Skipper." I called.

"What you want, Skipper?" he answered in a feeble voice. "You better get on home. It's getting late."

"Mr. Cowie, I brought you something to eat and some tea. Please can I come in and make it for you?"

"Go home now, boy. It's late, really late. You get on home now." he whispered.

The Cowboy

"Mr. Cowie, I'm coming in."

I opened the door. He was still sitting where I had left him. I brought in the things we had packed and poured some water into the kettle. I couldn't get the stove going. It was too full of ashes.

Ken walked in and didn't say a thing. He went to the stove, emptied the ashes and got the fire started. He put the kettle on and then went out.

I opened the things we had brought, buttered some scones and put some jelly on them. Jim Cowie remained silent the whole time. When the kettle finally got boiling, I made the tea.

"You like anything in your tea, Mr. Cowie?" I asked him.

He still hadn't moved or said anything. The cup was all dirty and mouldy, so I cleaned it. I set the food on the table beside him. He made no move to take any of the food until I stood beside him and put my hand on his shoulder.

"Mr. Cowie, please drink some tea. I made it for you."

Slowly he turned his head towards me. There were tears in his eyes.

"Please, Mr. Cowie." I said again. "I made this for you."

He looked at me through his tears. I almost started to cry. "Now I know why everyone talks about you so much." he said, his voice quivering with emotion. "You are a very special boy, Skipper. Thank you. I will eat and drink, thanks to you." Now I was embarrassed.

"I'll be back tomorrow to see how you are." I said. Ken was standing just outside the door and heard everything. "You know," Ken said, taking my hand in

Douglas Hargreaves

his as we walked home, "you are something special, Skipper."

The next day we got the word around that Old Jim Cowie was in dire straits and needed his neighbours' help. Peggy, Grandma, Gord's Mom, Mrs. Wilson, and Miss Snowdon all came right away. Others showed up later. Mrs. Billingsly and Mrs. Mortinsen were there too. Not Becky.

Over Jim's protests, they cleaned the place and washed his clothes and bed sheets. They all agreed the Old Jim's living conditions were the most dreadful they'd ever seen. Soon it was the talk of the community. Everyone chipped in with food and other things to improve the health and well-being of an old guy they had come to either fear or hate. All the time, Jim just sat there on his couch, watching the fuss without a word.

After that, whenever I visited Old Jim, he always had a tear in his eye and wanted to talk. How everyone had come round for him was too much for him to fathom. He was still shaking. He could hardly stand up. One time when I came by, he had peed his pants. Hooollly, what a stink.

My school mates asked me about Jim and why I was going over there. I told them I wanted to help him. He was very old and couldn't do anything for himself. I heard that the authorities were going to come and put him in a home for old people. I hoped they would come soon.

We left Jim with quite a bit of food--enough, we thought, until the people from the home came to look after him. I went in to see him on my way home from school each day. Phillip and Gordy would wait outside.

The Cowboy

I went in one day and Old Jim was sleeping. I put my hand on his shoulder to make sure he was alright. He woke up and put his arm around me, and told me I was his boy. I hugged him back. He pulled me to him and kissed my cheek. I was kind of scared and wanted to pull away, but didn't. "Get on home now, boy. I'll remember you. Goodbye, Skipper boy." he whispered. He had tears in his eyes again.

I didn't tell the guys what had happened.

The next day when I went in to see him, he was still sitting there on his couch, his eyes closed. I went over to him like I usually did and touched his shoulder. His eyes didn't open.

"Mr. Cowie, it's Skipper." I said. I shook him just a little and he slumped over on his side. He wasn't breathing. I sat down beside him and cried. I didn't know what to do or even say at first. So I recited the Lord's Prayer. Then I just said. "Goodbye, Jim Cowie." He had already said goodbye to me.

I went outside and Gordy asked me why I was crying. "Mr. Cowie is dead." I told him.

The authorities came and took charge of Jim and his belongings. A policeman came to our place one evening and told Ken that they had found a note on a piece of brown paper.

"How he had been able to write, no one knows, but he managed." the officer said to Ken. "His family tells us it's his handwriting all right. Jim Cowie has left his quarter section of land to your boy."

Old Jim's family agreed that the old man had every right to do with his property as he chose. They had heard about what we were doing for their father before he died. They were glad he had given the land to me.

Everyone for miles around was talking about it. Phillip told me that his father was going to make me an offer to buy the property. "He's been wanting to get his hands on it for years." he said. I already knew that.

At school, Miss Snowdon made special mention of what we had done and how important everyone was in the sight of God.

"God rewarded Skipper for his being a Good Samaritan." she said.

"It wasn't God, Miss Snowdon," I said, "it was Mr. Cowie."

Ken and I decided to keep the quarter section and give the hay to Olie and Peggy. They could sure use the feed. Ken said the hay was the best anywhere and we had plenty and didn't need the extra.

In my bedtime prayers I thanked Old Jim Cowie for his gift. I knew I would miss my visits with him.

SPIES IN THE NIGHT

Oil drilling was changing the way of life in our valley in many ways. It was a growing industry and I had to admit that it was exciting. As the valley prospered, new people moved in. There were rigs going up all over, even in our own back yard, so to speak. For ranchers who had the mineral rights to their homesteads, it meant almost instant wealth. The oil companies paid for the rights to use their land, the rights to use their water, and the rights to the oil itself, if they found any.

Our friend Tip Johnson owned and operated Johnson's Trucking Company, which moved almost all the rigs in the valley. He had the largest fleet of trucks and the only really heavy equipment capable of moving in the big rigs. Gone were the days when the rigs were constructed of wood. The new ones were all steel and looked like power transmission towers. They were portable, and had to be assembled and disassembled each time they were moved.

Every so often, Ken announced, "Skipper, I have to work for Tip for the next few days. I'll be home on Friday. You have to run the place until I get back. You can handle things okay?"

"Sure I can handle it." It made me feel really happy and grown up when he would leave the ranch in my hands.

Ken and I were getting along just like father and son. I had lived on the ranch with him for three years but still never pushed my luck. He had a terrible temper and could easily lace my behind if I fouled up.

Douglas Hargreaves

I didn't worry any more about Ken sending me back to Winnipeg. I was now part of his family. He was proud of my school marks and roping trophies, like any father would be. Things had sure come a long way from the days when I first arrived.

There was a drilling rig just to the east of our land. Sometimes we could hear the big engines at night. Ken had told me I could go to Peggy's for supper every night if I wanted to. I always liked to do that. Peggy was like a mom to me.

I had some homework to do one evening and was getting ready to go home. "Skipper, you watch, it gets dark a little earlier these days." said Peggy. "I don't want you to ride in the dark."

"I'm okay, Peggy." After all, I was the big boss of the Bar U Ranch.

Johnny was about to put his horse away when he saw me getting ready to leave. "I'll ride you to Sylvester's gate Skip." he said.

"Okay, let's go."

Johnny rode with me until we came to the main fence and I leaned over and undid the gate. All the wire fence gates had been fixed up so that I could reach the top wire. Otherwise I would never have been able to close them. This was the only swinging pole gate between our place and Peggy's. At most of the other gates, I had to get off my horse and undo the top wire, lay the gate down, walk Nixon through it, then stand the gate up again and put the top loop over the post.

I said goodnight to Johnny and he turned and trotted away. I rode for about twenty minutes, then heard what sounded like someone whistling. It

The Cowboy

sounded like a signal. I didn't hear a reply, so I rode on.

It happened again. My curiosity was getting the best of me. I was a little scared too. I was torn between finding out who was whistling and riding on home before it got dark. I decided a minute longer wouldn't hurt.

I rode over to where I thought the sound had come from. Nothing. It was getting darker now and I was just on the edge of our neighbour's fence line. I could see the lights of the oil derrick and hear the rig drilling away. It seemed awfully close.

I continued along the fence for about a quarter of a mile, then heard the whistle again. It was closer than before. Darkness made it hard to see anything well, so I decided I had better go home.

Then--what was that? Someone was talking. Not loudly--it was almost a whisper. I couldn't tell what they were saying. Why were they talking in the dark, up the hill from the rig? Suppose they were bad guys on their way to rob me, with my being alone and all? Lots of crazy ideas ran through my head. The boss man of the Bar U got scared and headed for home. The hair on the back of my neck stood on end. I thought they might be following me.

I was still scared as I walked up to the house after putting Nixon in his corral. The shadows created monsters and villains about to tear me limb from limb. I ran to the house and locked the door. I had been walking that path to the house every night for three years and here I was, acting like a little baby.

I slept with my clothes on and felt terrible in the morning. I wondered if I should say anything to anyone but convinced myself it was nothing. Everyone would think I was a scaredy-cat and just imagining things. Well, I wasn't imagining things--I knew what I heard.

Riding home from Peggy's the next evening, I took the path closer to Sylvester's upper gate, which would take me almost right to where I had heard the noises the night before. It wasn't quite so dark, so I could see much better. As I crested the hill, I saw a man sitting on the grass with a pair of field glasses, looking towards the rig. I pulled Nixon up sharply, dismounted and tied him to a small shrub. I didn't have to do that. He always waited for me, even if he tossed me off sometimes. He would just stand and look daggers at me.

The man hadn't noticed me. I walked quietly along, staying behind the short scrub poplars. There was just one man. I decided to wait for a few minutes as it wasn't too dark yet and I wanted to see if anyone else would show up. I had a strange feeling that someone was watching me just as I was watching the man. Nothing happened, so I decided to go home.

This time I undressed for bed. I was pretty confident that whoever the man was, he wasn't interested in a little kid like me. Hard as it was, I thought I had better keep my secret. All the kids were talking about the new well and mysterious things that were happening.

"Did you hear about the shooting the other day over by Wilson's rig?" Gordy asked me.

"Yeah Skipper," said Phillip, "my pa says they were shooting at someone who was spying on their drilling rig."

The Cowboy

"Spying!" I said with some alarm. "What do you mean spying? Why would anyone want to spy on a drilling rig?"

"Well, I heard my pa say that these spies work for other drilling companies," said Phillip. "They want to find out all about the other rigs drilling around here."

Phillip sounded like an authority. Hmmm. I had never heard of this sort of thing before, but what did I know? Well, one thing I did know--someone was spying on the Sylvester rig and that was for sure. I considered telling my friends what I had seen but thought I'd better wait until Ken came home the next night. He'd know what to do.

On my way over to Peggy's for supper, I took the route close to the hilltop overlooking the rig. Sure enough, there was a man sitting in the same place as last night. He didn't see me and I turned around and rode on. I thought about riding down to the rig and telling the workers what I had seen but thought they'd probably think I was telling a story coming from a kid and all. I rode on to Peggy's.

Over supper, I asked Olie if he knew anything about oil rig spies. "What you want to know about them for?" Olie asked me suspiciously.

"Just wondering. The guys were talking about someone shooting at one the other night." I said.

"Yeah, well, they're around all right. I'm surprised there ain't none around Sylvester's."

"What do they need to know about other rigs, Olie?"

"Why you so interested, young feller?" I waited, and he went on. "They want to learn all they can about the other guy's drilling, so as they can tell whether or

Douglas Hargreaves

not they should buy up or lease other adjoining property. By watching what's going on, they can tell how deep they're drilling. How hard the engines are working tells them what kind of rock they're in. They can tell if there's going to be oil or not and how good the well is, even." Olie seemed to know a whole lot about the drilling business.

"I guess it's pretty important to know as much as you can about things like that, huh? It would give you an edge over the other guys, wouldn't it?"

"You're right Skipper, that's exactly the truth of it." Olie said.

Peggy handed me a dish towel and told me to get drying and do less talking. I got my usual pinch on the behind. "I'm either pinching it or filling it, huh, Skipper?" she laughed.

Johnny and I finished the dishes and Olie advised me to get a move on. There were some rain clouds forming and it was already getting dark.

I got on Nixon and thanked Peggy for supper. "See you tomorrow." I said. "Ken should be home for supper too."

Johnny came running out of the house. "Skipper, just before you go, will you help me with this one arithmetic question?" he asked.

By the time I had finished with Johnny it was quite dark. "Maybe I'd best ride you a ways." Olie said.

"It's okay Olie, thanks. I can get home okay."

"No," he insisted, "I ain't going to let you ride by yourself. I'll ride until the Sylvester's gate."

When we got to the gate, Olie held up his hand and told me to be quiet. He could hear what I had heard the night before. We rode over to the trail leading to the

The Cowboy

hillside. He motioned me to get off my horse and stay behind while he checked out the sound.

"You stay put right here Skipper, you hear?"

"Sure, Olie."

I was afraid. I thought maybe I should tell him what he could expect to see. But he would find out for himself in a minute or so. I kept my mouth shut.

I held his horse but then decided to tie up both horses. I peered into the darkness but couldn't tell where Olie was. He must have gone over the edge of the hill, out of my view, I thought.

"Hey!" I heard someone shout from down below. That's all I heard. I waited and waited. Still no Olie. Everything was quiet, so I decided to creep down and see what was going on.

I could almost see the lights of the drilling rig when I stumbled over Olie. He was lying face down in the grass.

"Olie! Olie!" I whispered. No sound. I felt where his head was. It was wet and sticky. "Hooooolly! Olie are you okay? Please say you're okay!" I shook him, but he didn't move. Hooolllyyy! I knew I had better get some help. I ran back to Nixon and decided to get to the rig. It was closer than Peggy's.

I rode as fast as I could, taking the steepest part of the hill. That would take me almost right into the drilling yard.

"Hey! What the hell you doing there kid?" a man from the rig yelled at me. I could hardly hear for the drilling engines. "Please! My uncle has been hurt by a spy on your oil well!" "What the hell you saying there boy?"

Several men got in a small truck and drove over to where I was standing.

One man said, "Give me your horse boy and tell me where your uncle is. You go with the truck and show them where to go."

I got into the truck with two other men and showed them the route to get to Sylvester's gate. When we got to where Olie was, the man who had taken Nixon was already there. He had Olie sitting up. They got him into the truck and the two men drove back down with Olie.

"We'll take him to Turner Valley and you tell your folks we'll look after him." said the man who had taken Nixon.

I got on Nixon and rode back towards Peggy's. It was really dark now and I could barely make out the gate. As I swung it open, someone stepped up to Nixon's head and grabbed the reins. "Who's there?" I said, sounding a lot braver than I felt. "What are you doing here? What do you want?"

A man I couldn't see grabbed me off Nixon and set me down on the grass. I was so terrified I was about to pee myself.

"Okay little man, if you're smart, you're going to listen to what I have to say." I couldn't make out his face in the darkness but his breath stunk of beer. "You like your horse, huh? Well, if you don't want something terrible to happen to your nag, you just forget you saw anyone around here. We saw you the other night looking around."

He pressed a piece of paper into my hand. "Take it. It's twenty dollars, kid. That's to keep your mouth shut and your nag alive. You never saw anything, hear

The Cowboy

me?" he whispered in my face. The beer stench was sickening. "One word," he went on, "and you're going to be short one horse. You might even wind up getting hurt yourself. Okay?"

Before I knew it he had vanished. I couldn't see where he went. For awhile I thought he might come back and hurt me or something.

I rode to Peggy's and told her Olie was on his way to the hospital. "Oh my God, Skipper! What happened to him?"

"I think somebody hit him over the head. I found him after he went looking for someone spying on the rig." I told her about going to the rig for help.

"You did right by telling the rig crew about it, Skipper. I'll take the car and go into town. You better stay here with Johnny and the kids."

I wondered if I should have told her about the spy giving me twenty dollars but figured it would be better to wait till Ken came home. I just couldn't handle everything that was going on.

Olie had been knocked out and had a slight concussion. They released him from the hospital after an hour or so. He and Peggy got home in the early hours of the morning. I was waiting up for them.

"Skipper, you are one smooth thinking little kid." Olie said. "Going to the rig first and then telling them it was a spy was just the right thing to do. How did you know that? The oil company guys said we were right. They're giving us a reward for having put the run on those guys. Plus, they're paying me for my sore head."

"We can sure use the money." Peggy said. She had a worried look on her face. When she gave me my usual pinch, a hug and a kiss on the cheek, I knew she would be okay. She sent me off to bed.

I was up real early, rode home and did my chores. I was just getting on Nixon to go to school when a car drove up. On the door was painted, "Cascade Drilling Co."

"Hi son." said the driver. "You the youngster who stopped our spy?"

"Yes, sir. Can I tell you something else that happened?" I said in a low voice, almost a whisper.

"Sure boy. What you got to say?"

I told him everything, from when I had first spotted the guys up to getting the twenty dollars. I pleaded that they wouldn't let anything happen to Nixon. I showed them the money and they assured me I had done the right thing and I was a real hero.

"Your daddy should be real proud of you son. Your uncle sure is. You helped us a great deal." I got a little red and told him I had to get to school. "Okay, son, we'll see your pa when he gets home."

I worried about leaving Nixon in the school yard by himself but the man had told me that nothing was going to happen to Nixon. They had their man locked up. Hooolly, what a story I had to tell Ken! I wondered if he would be happy or mad that I had got myself into trouble.

Well, he was happy and I got a monster hug from him just to show he missed me and was really concerned about me.

"You never cease to amaze me Skipper." he said, shaking his head. "I go away and you catch oil well spies. What if something had happened to you? I could never face losing you, you know."

The Cowboy

He had that lump-in-the-throat sound in his voice. He told me he had heard all about it from the police in the Valley. Then he gave me another hug.

THE ENGLISH KID

Riding past Old Jim's place after school one Thursday afternoon in June, Phillip and I noticed tire tracks across the front yard to the cabin. The hay grew just as tall and thick here as it did in the main hay field. It had never been cut.

"I wonder who was here, and when?" said Phillip. "I don't see any truck around. Someone snooping around, do you think? Can't figure why anyone would want to come up here. Old Jim's cabin is empty. Olie ain't using it for anything, is he?"

"No, he's just haying the property." I said. "We're going to start on it as soon as it dries a bit more." Everyone was busy getting their hay off. The sooner you could get it off, the sooner you could get another one off in the fall if you were lucky. We could use all the hay we could get. Buying hay made things unprofitable, Ken said.

There were two more weeks of school but Miss Snowdon told me I could quit for haying anytime Ken wanted. I knew I had passed. I had worked hard and it was worth it. I was going into Grade Ten and would have to go to school in Turner Valley in the fall. That would be some change from attending a one-room school for the past three years. It had been a relief to see Bill Wilson leave to go to school in the Valley. But now he and I would be going to the same school again and that didn't sit too well. He was always trying to slap me and Phillip around when we were swimming at Peggy's beaver dam. He was such a bully.

"Skipper, we're going to start on Jim's field on Saturday." Ken said when I got home. "We got to get going on our hay pretty quick. You make tomorrow your last day. Then we'll get started on Saturday."

"Ken, did you see those truck tracks up to Old Jim's cabin?" I asked.

"Yeah, I saw them. I figure Olie may have been in there to look at his crop for haying."

I agreed that had to be where the tracks came from. We let it go at that as we wouldn't know for sure until we asked Olie.

On the way to school Friday morning, Gordy, Phillip and I noticed the tracks had been run over again and had flattened the grass down even more than yesterday. Coming home from school, we saw even more tracks. Also, there had been some activity around the house.

"Skipper, you better find out what's going on." said Gordy. "Someone's doing something over there."

"Should we ride over and see who's been there?" said Phillip. "I can't right now." I said. "I got to get my chores done early 'cause we're going to Peggy's for supper."

"You're sure lucky Skipper, getting out of school early. I wish I was smart like you." said Gordy.

"Me too Skip," said Phillip. "Think of us suffering, day in and day out."

I promised I would help them with their exams if they were having any trouble. We agreed to meet for a swim Saturday after work, if I could make it. "I'll have to see how late we are with the haying." I said. "Anyways, you guys go without me. If I can come, I'll be over."

The Cowboy

Ken had gone to Grandpa's to arrange for getting the stacker up to our place. I was just finishing the milking when a kid about my age came walking into the barn.

"I say, am I troubling you?" he asked in a very English accent. Hoooolly! You could have knocked me over with a feather. His accent was very British and correct. Mr. Sylvester had an accent almost like this boy's.

"Hi," I said, "what are you doing here?"

"I've come to see if I can buy a jug of milk from you. You see, me and my mother and my little brother have just moved in across the road from you and we really need some milk."

I could hardly believe my ears. This kid was saying that he and his family had just moved into our house, on our land--and we didn't even know about it? That explained the tracks. They had been moving in, right under our noses!

"How come you're living there?" I asked the kid. He had short curly blonde hair and a pleasant face.

"Well, if you must know, my mother is Olie Nystrum's sister-in-law or some connection like that. You know Olie and his family just down from you?"

"Peggy's my aunt."

"Well now, isn't this a pleasant situation. Already we have relatives in this foreign country." he sort of smirked.

"I'm sorry." I said, realizing I had been a little rude. "I guess I wasn't expecting anyone to be coming to visit, especially from up at Old Jim's place."

"How old are you?" he asked.

"Twelve."

Douglas Hargreaves

"Goodness! So am I, but you certainly are small for your age, aren't you? Look how much taller I am than you." He moved over beside me. Here we go again, I thought. Well, I wasn't about to let young master smarty pants get to me, especially on our first meeting. He'll have some trouble with the other kids in school if he acts like this, I thought.

I asked him how long he was going to be living there. He told me his family had had a bit of tough luck since coming to Canada. This was their last resort. He said they would never have given this place a second look if they had anything to say about it. His father had just taken off somewhere in Toronto and they hadn't seen him since. They had written a letter to Olie asking if he could help them get on their feet.

"We are really suffering in this terrible place." he said in his uppity way. "I wished we had never left home. I suppose your school is that one-room place we passed when we were coming here?" I confirmed this fear.

"Do you like living here and doing what you're doing?" he asked.

"Yeah, I do. I milk these four cows, then I separate the milk into cream."

"What's your name?"

"Skipper."

"Oh yes, I remember the name. My Uncle Olie told my mother that there was another boy living very close to us that I might make friends with. So you're Skipper."

We continued talking as I milked. I told him I'd give him some milk when I finished separating. I

The Cowboy

started up to the house carrying my pails while he walked alongside.

"Hey, why don't you carry those other pails for me?" I suggested.

"Oh, really?" He was not enthusiastic. "Well, I'll help if I must."

He helped me with the pails, then watched while I separated. "Want to try cranking for awhile?" I asked him.

"Well, all right, I can do that, I'm sure." I thought he was acting pretty hoity-toity.

I asked him what his name was. "Michael." He looked like a Michael, I thought. As for his size, he was about normal for his age and about the same height as Phillip. His voice was lower than mine. I took him to be one strange character. I was going to find out what this was all about.

I scooped some milk out of the top of the separator and poured it into a big jug.

"There you are, Michael. I'm going to have to go to my aunt's in a minute, so you'll have to go."

"Do you have your own horse?"

"Yes, I have a black Indian pony named Nixon. He's a quarter horse."

"How lucky you are. Will I see you in school next week?"

"No, I'm finished. We have to start haying tomorrow and all next week." "But I was told school had two weeks to go yet."

"Yes, but I've already passed into the next grade and the teacher said I didn't have to write any exams."

"Well I'm in the Eighth Form."

Douglas Hargreaves

"You mean you're in Grade Eight. We go by grades here."

"Well, what form--I mean what grade are you in, Skipper?"

"I'm going into Tenth Grade."

"Surely you're telling me a big lie, aren't you?"

"No I'm not. I'm going into Turner Valley next year, into high school." I wanted to get on with things. "I have to go now, Michael. I'll probably see you tomorrow sometime. We're haying on your place."

He thanked me for the milk and walked off. A minute later, he called back, "I have money to pay for the milk Skipper." "Sometime later, maybe." I said. When I got to Peggy's, I sure had a lot of questions for everyone about what was going on up at Old Jim's. It turned out that Olie was Michael's mother's brother-in-law. Everyone was very interested in my story about meeting Michael.

Olie had been working for the past week in Turner Valley and didn't know when they were arriving. Peggy knew, but we just hadn't seen her all week. Their English relatives were going to stay at Old Jim's cabin for a while until they found something in the city where the mother would be working. Their name was Stacey-Barnes. Hmmmm, I thought . . . Michael Stacey-Barnes. Hoooollyy! How was the kid ever going to handle a name like that in our school? At least he wasn't shy.

The next day I saw Michael watching us as we stacked hay next to the tool shed. My job was driving the stacker team, which I was quite good at. The hay on Old Jim's was the best we had taken off from

The Cowboy

anywhere in a long time. It was heavy and tall and we made monster stacks.

We all sat down at tea time for scones and jam. Grandma always had them for us for our break. I waved Michael over to join us. I wanted the whole crew to meet him. He came over a little reluctantly and was a bit embarrassed when I introduced him to Ken and the others. Olie had seen him before, although he had never talked to him.

"Sit Michael and have a scone and some tea." I offered. "Thank you awfully, Skipper." He sat down and took the scone. He was wearing short pants, and I'm sure the hay was sticking into his bare legs. He never complained, though. As we talked, he just sat there and listened.

"Want a ride on the stacker, Skipper?" said Ken. I always liked to ride the stacker. All us kids did. We finished our tea and I called to Michael to get on the stacker so we could get a lift up.

"Golly, isn't this exciting. Are you sure it's safe Skipper?"

"Come on," I urged, "you'll really like it."

Ken and the team of horses took us up and over. The haystack was quite high so we had lots of hay to land in. Ken knew exactly how far to throw us and when to stop the team. Michael laughed and laughed, even though the hay stabbed harshly at his bare legs. We had two rides and then I had to get back to work.

"Thank you very much Skipper." said Michael. "That was most enjoyable."

He walked back to Old Jim's cabin and I went back to work. He stood watching us for most of the afternoon. I thought I was getting to like him.

NO MORE SHORT PANTS

Haying Old Jim's place went fast, despite the heavy crop. We heard there was supposed to be rain, so we worked long hours, well into the night. The rain didn't come but heavy dew delayed our getting stared in the morning. The hay had to be dry before the sweep could gather it.

I saw Michael watching us a few times. Sometimes he ventured over to where we were working. Whenever he did, I invited him to join us during our break. Grandma even started to include a few extra scones in case our visitor appeared. He was very quiet and listened intently to everything we were saying. He would sometimes laugh at our accents, as he called them.

One morning in the middle of the week I decided to ride over to the Stacey-Barnes "homestead" to see how things were. The ground was too wet to start haying, so I had some free time after chores. I thought Michael would be in school but he was sitting on the front porch. I rode up to him and saw he had been crying.

"Hi." I said.

"Good morning, Skipper." he sobbed.

"You in trouble or something, Michael?"

"Skipper, I hate this place and I hate the school and I wish I was dead. That's what I wish."

I got off Nixon and sat down beside him. "Michael, haven't you any long pants? You're always wearing those short ones. It's very hard on your legs and besides, the other kids all wear jeans." I was trying to be helpful.

"That's part of the problem you see." he complained. "They laugh at me and my brother because of the way we speak and they make fun of our clothes. Skipper, we don't have any other clothes. My father took most of our things with him to the States. The rest is back home, you know."

"Why don't you go back and talk to the teacher and I'll introduce you to my friends, Phillip and Gordon. They'll help you out at school. I know they will."

He wasn't completely convinced. "Well, I think it is Phillip's brother who knocked me down when I told him to stop behaving like an infant. Boy, did he hit me hard, right on the side of my head. I didn't cry though."

"Did you hit him back?"

"Well, I was going to, but some other kid knelt down behind my knees and then I was pushed backwards. I fell really hard. Everyone laughed. I felt so terrible. Then Miss Snowdon called us all into school and I handed in our transfer papers and reports for me and my brother. Miss Snowdon read it out in front of everyone. She told me she thought the children would get to know more about us this way."

Michael went on to tell me that the whole school found the two of them highly entertaining, as he put it, and laughed at them. "It was most distressing." he said sadly.

I asked him if that was why he was home instead of at school. " Skipper, I just can't stand this place another minute. Everything is so primitive here. I'll never fit in." he complained. His brother wouldn't leave the

The Cowboy

class, so he left by himself. His mother was in Calgary for the day, tending to financial matters.

He talked pretty grown-up, for only being twelve, I thought. He was really upset. I assured him that all the kids were not like Willie and Billy Wilson, and that he just had to be patient.

"Why don't you come along with me for the day?" I said. "Then you won't get bored and you won't be thinking about yourself."

"Wouldn't I be putting you out?" he said.

I smiled, jumped on Nixon, and took my foot out of the stirrup so Michael could get his foot in and haul himself up behind me. We rode down to my house. I took him into my bedroom and dug around in my dresser drawer for a pair of jeans that Gordy's mom had given me.

"Here, put these on," I said. "They're good ones but they're too big for me."

"Thank you very much Skipper." he said.

"May I really have them?"

"Sure, put them on right now."

"Will you step outside while I change into them Skipper, please?" He looked very embarrassed when I just stood there.

"What for?" I asked. I tried being funny. "You got something to hide?"

"Really Skipper, you do embarrass me," he said earnestly.

"Hooooooly!" I said, surprised. I thought a little man-to-man talk might help. "Get your pants off. I'm not going anywhere."

He turned his back to me and slid his pants off.

"Where's your underwear?"

Douglas Hargreaves

"See, I knew you would embarrass me."

"Don't you wear any underwear?" I asked. For a moment, I thought it might be what English kids did.

"Well, if you really must know, Skipper, I don't have any. So now are you satisfied?" I saw tears forming.

"Sorry. I didn't mean to give you a heart attack." I went into my dresser drawer again and fetched him a pair of under shorts. They were a little tight, but he said they would do. When he pulled on the jeans, they fit him like they were made for him. I dug around again and found an old brown belt I had never used. Ken had made it for me from a harness.

Well, Michael looked at himself in the living room mirror and a smile came over his face. "Goodness, that does look better. And I feel better, too."

"I'll say you look better. Lets go. I have to start work soon. Come,

I'll show you how to ride Nixon."

We were the first ones at the hay field. The hay was still quite damp but drying fast as the June sun rose higher. I dismounted and told Michael to stay on and just let Nixon's reins loose. That way, Nixon would get used to him. I led Nixon around the stacker a few times, then let Michael ride by himself. He sat on Nixon just right and seemed quite at home on him.

Grandpa arrived next, then Ken and Olie with the three teams. Ken had been at Grandpa's, working on some harnesses. He was surprised to see me there already.

"Well Skipper, I see you've brought your friend along. He certainly looks a lot more like a poke than he

The Cowboy

did the other day." Ken said. Michael rode over, smiling.

"Well boy," said Ken, "if you're going to be around here, you're going to have to work. How come you're not in school today?"

"Ken I'll tell you about that later." I spoke up.

"So you're wearing some of Skipper's clothes, huh?" Ken went on. "Well, that's a smart idea. You can work in that stuff. Skipper never does." Ken laughed.

Ken lifted Michael up onto the hay rack and showed him how to drive the team up the rows while he loaded the rack. We were going to take some hay to our own loft.

The day went quickly. Michael was right in his element. He couldn't have been happier. It had been a hot day and by the end of it we were some dirty. We unhitched the horses and Ken decided we would finish up tomorrow. Michael and I got on Nixon and I told Ken he would find us at Peggy's swimming hole. We were going to have a bath and swim.

Even as late as it was and as hungry as we were, we still had to swim. Ken came by in a while. Michael was bound and determined he was going to leave his under shorts on but Ken sure fixed that. He picked up Michael, squirming and fussing, yanked his shorts off and tossed them into the water. I was nearby, just in case he couldn't swim. It turned out he was a very good swimmer.

Soon we were having the best time swimming and chasing each other and of course diving for the India rubber ball. Michael's troubles at school were long forgotten.

"Suppertime for you fellows." Peggy called.

Douglas Hargreaves

Hoooollly! I had almost forgot about Peggy. I made a beeline for the shore. Over my shoulder, I told Michael about Peggy's custom.

When we got to where I had left my clothes, sure enough, they were gone. So were Michael's. We looked at each other and started to laugh. Michael asked me where we had to go to get them and I told him that they would be up at the house. Ken was laughing at us because Peggy never took his clothes.

We ran up to the house in our nothing and Peggy's daughter, Eilene, came roaring out and chased us away. Michael was just looking for some place to hide. She caught up to both of us and smacked our behinds with a towel.

"Want some more?" she yelled. "Please, Eilene, just let us get dressed." I pleaded.

"This is quite shocking, to be undressed in front of a girl." Michael said.

"Michael, she's seen everything we have." I turned to Eilene. "And most of the guys in the valley."

"Skipper, I have not. I only seen our own family." she said. She left us to get dressed. Michael was laughing quite hard. As he put it, the whole thing was such a lark, really. Most of his concerns had pretty well gone.

We went into the house and I introduced all the kids to Michael. Phillip and Gordy had been swimming with us. They were very happy that Michael was at least going to be able to get along with everyone, after all. Peggy apologized to Michael for taking his clothes but told him he had better get used to it, as she liked little boys' bare bottoms. "Right Skipper?" she teased.

The Cowboy

Everyone was finding Michael to be a likeable kid. He told us the story of his father leaving them and going to the States, taking everything they owned. The family had hardly any money and no clothing other than what they had on their backs. The only people they knew in Canada were Olie and Peggy, way out west in Alberta.

"I thought I might try and take my life." Michael said. "It was terrible."

Ken said, "Well, you did a great day's work, and we'll pay you something for it. In fact, you can work tomorrow too, if we didn't work you too hard today."

"Oh yes, indeed, I really would like that." Michael could hardly contain himself.

"Well boy," said Ken, "as of right now, your name is Mike, not Michael. Okay? We can't say "Michael" that good, and Mike sounds more like you belong out here."

"Oh really?" he said, as though Ken had given him a present. "Thank you, Ken." Then he looked at Ken sheepishly for a moment and said. "I am sorry. I didn't mean to take such liberties by calling you by your first name."

"Mike, you call me Ken, that's fine. And everyone else you can call by their first names. We're all equal. Well, all except Skipper, that is. I still warm his behind now and again." he laughed, making a grab for me. "I'll warm your's too if you step out of line, you hear?" He looked stern but his eyes were laughing.

Mike looked a little scared but saw we were all smiling. "I will certainly follow the rules Ken, I assure you of that. Our old school master use to cane us when we were misbehaving and that really smarted. Then my father would hear about it and I would get another strapping at home. So I know what it feels like."

It was getting dark and Mike had to get home. We wondered where his brother might have been all this time. We had forgotten him entirely. I decided not to ask about him now. The three of us rode to the ranch.

"I'll walk from here Skipper." said Mike.

"It's okay," I said. "Maybe I should explain where you were all day, in case your mother gives you a hard time."

Mrs. Stacey-Barnes looked old, more like a grandmother than a mother of children who weren't even in their teens. She wore lots of make up on her face. She spoke little, but nodded and thanked me for helping Michael and said she appreciated Mike being able to work. He really didn't have to be in school, as he too had completed his grades. Mrs. Stacey-Barnes remarked how well Mike looked in his western clothes. It made me think back to the days when I first came from the city to the ranch and how Gordy had helped me get settled in. The main difference was that I didn't have parents who really cared about me. At least Mike had his mother with him.

She had made supper for her younger son, Eric. He was about ten and quite pleasant. His mother thought he should stay in school to get adjusted and get to know some of the children a little.

Ken was really taken with Mike and thought the boy had great potential. I agreed and told Ken that I would take him under my wing. "Good for you son." he said. "You know what it feels like to be alone, don't you?" He gave me a hug.

The Cowboy

We finished Old Jim's place and then we moved the stacker over to Olie's. Gordy and Phillip were at my place a lot, especially right after school. We included Mike in all our activities and little adventures. Peggy loaned Mike a pony and Gordy loaned him an old saddle he had. Mike was told the horse was for him to use but it had to be kept at my place.

Mike was really settling in and getting along with everyone. One day we were getting ready to go to the beaver dam and Mike said he would like to bring his brother.

Eric was a little too quiet. We had no doubt his new life was not going well for him. Neither was school. The kids didn't pick on him like they had Mike but still he was made to feel like an outsider. As the smallest kid around, I knew what that was like.

Eric at first didn't want to come with us to the dam but Mike insisted that he had to come. We lifted him onto Nixon and rode on down. Mike and I hid our clothes from Peggy. Eric wouldn't get undressed. He looked shocked to see us naked. Mike pleaded with him to come for a swim. He wouldn't budge. I winked at Mike and we took hold of Eric's arms and heaved him in, clothes and all. Mike told me that Eric could swim as well as he could. Eric coughed and fumed and sputtered for a few minutes, so we pulled him out of the water. He was blubbering and laughing hysterically.

"Okay Eric, get your clothes off so they can dry." Mike ordered.

Eric undressed and we placed his clothes on a bush to dry. His shoes would take longer. We went in and swam some more. Gordy and Phillip teased him the most. Poor Eric sure was getting his welcome to the western world. But he surprised all of us when he picked up a piece of horse pucky and threw it at Mike. It nailed his older brother right on his chest and everyone laughed. Eric broke into a big grin and he laughed with us. Mike did not retaliate. He only told his brother that horse shit was what made people and things grow. Gordy said it sure didn't work for you-know-who. I would get him for that.

It came time to get out and head for home. Mike and I and the others got dressed.

Eric said, "My clothes are gone! Did you chaps hide my clothes?"

"Peggy!" I called. "I think I know where they are Eric."

"Well for goodness sake, please return them. I'll wear them even if they're still wet. I mean, look at me! I have nothing to wear!"

"Sorry Eric." I said. "You'll just have to get them yourself."

"Skipper, why must I do that? I'm quite naked, you know."

"Come on Eric, lets go and get them." I said as we walked up to the house. Gordy and Phillip were laughing themselves silly. They headed off for home while Mike and I and Eric sneaked up to the house.

Eric did his best to cover himself up. Mike assured him repeatedly that it was no big deal. "Don't worry about it Eric." he kept saying, as Eric darted behind the bushes in the front yard and then crept over to the tool shed.

He was kneeling down, peering around the side of the building, when Peggy nabbed him from behind.

The Cowboy

She lifted him up and hauled him toward the house under her arm. Eric didn't know it but you could never get one up on Peggy, not ever. All the while, Eric squirmed and yelled bloody murder. Mike, Johnny and I just about killed ourselves laughing.

She took Eric into the house and sat him down on a chair and handed him a towel which he hastily put over himself. He was beet-red with embarrassment but there was a trace of a smile coming on his face as well.

"Well you little rascal," Peggy teased, "what are you doing running around the country side in your birthday suit?"

"Please ma'am," said Eric, "did you take my clothes?"

"Well, as a matter of fact I did. They needed a wash anyhow." She handed Eric a pair of Mark's old jeans and a shirt.

"He needs underpants Peggy." Mike told her. "He doesn't have any."

Peggy found a pair of shorts for Eric and told him to get dressed.

"Here? Right here?" he asked incredulously.

"Yes, right here and right now, young man." Peggy said firmly.

Eric fumbled around under the towel until Mike whipped it away. "Just get used to it Eric." said Mike. "No one is going to bite it off."

I could hardly believe this was the same Mike talking, after the way he was when we first met him. Eric responded bravely and dressed himself without further fuss. He looked at home in Johnny's clothes. Peggy advised him that no one wore short pants out here. She reached in the cupboard for a comb and

Douglas Hargreaves

brush and combed Eric's hair. He looked quite smart now and certainly very happy. He was smiling from head to toe.

"No wonder Mike is always talking about you Skipper and your Aunt Peggy. You are so nice and kind to us." he said.

"I would ask you boys to supper but your mother would be worried." Peggy said.

"Our mother is in Calgary again." said Mike. "She catches a ride whenever she can. She doesn't want to stay here."

"Have you got food at home?" Peggy asked.

"Oh, we can find something, Peggy. I think we have some cereal left over and Skipper gives us milk every day."

"Fine then." said Peggy. "You're staying for supper. Come on you guys, get the table set. One thing we have lots of is home-grown food and it's good for you."

I asked Mike if he thought his mother would be home tonight.

"I don't think so Skipper. She's looking for a job and it's too hard to get back and forth from here."

"Why didn't you tell us?" said Peggy. "You poor little guys, there all by yourself."

"It's really quite all right Peggy." said Mike. "We know Skipper and Ken live just across the road, so we aren't afraid. Well, most of the time we aren't."

Ken and Olie came in and Peggy talked happily about the two boys who had moved into our midst.

"Mike is getting to be a real help with the team." Ken said. I remembered when Ken would never say anything good about me for so long a time. The only

The Cowboy

real contact we had together was his hand whapping my rump. Now I was his boy.

Ken seemed worried as he looked over at the English kids. We told him where their mother was and that she was looking for work. "Well, she's going to need a lot of luck. It's damn hard to find a job in that city." he said. We always had a good time at supper. I usually got the job of blessing the food. This time I asked a special blessing for Mike and Eric and their mother. I was surprised when Mike thanked me and I could see he was holding back a tear. Things with this family were not all they should be, I thought.

We all helped with the dishes as usual and Peggy folded up Eric's clothes and handed them to him. Mike and Eric thanked Peggy for her kindness and her great meal and we got on our horses and rode home. Ken, Mike, Eric and I rode up to Old Jim's place to see if the boys' mother had returned.

"She isn't coming, I am sure." Mike said. "She just isn't taking things very well, you know."

"Ken, can they stay with us tonight?"

"They gotta sleep with you Skipper and you know how you snore." Ken laughed.

It was a tight fit but we all slept in my bed, with me on one side, Mike on the other and Eric in the middle.

WHERE'S MOTHER?

Michael and Eric stayed the next day and we kept them busy with our haying work. Mike was very helpful driving the team and the loaded hay wagon to the barn. Eric more or less came along for the ride.

There was still no word from Mrs. Stacey-Barnes. We had a hard time understanding how she could just take off like that, not showing up at meal times or at least by nightfall. The boys ate with us that evening and were very reluctant to go home afterwards. We decided to walk up to Old Jim's cabin and leave a note in case their mother came home and wondered where her sons were. She had been gone three days now. Eric worried that something might have happened to her. Ken too was concerned. Here he was, responsible for three boys now. He said they were well-behaved, really, and not a lot of bother. Coming from Ken, that was something. I wished he had said things like that about me when I first arrived at the ranch. On the other hand, I reckoned his experience with me taught him a few things.

We finished Olie's haying and moved the stacker to Grandpa's. We figured on getting his fields done by the end of the week if the weather held. The days stayed very warm and we sure got dirty. We worked up a sweat and washed off at the end of the day in Peggy's swimming hole. Peggy looked after washing the boys' clothes, as they only had the one change. They couldn't be wearing those short pants of theirs. She loaned Eric some of Paul's old clothes while his were in the wash.

Douglas Hargreaves

Peggy looked after the boys just like they were her own. Like she looked after me.

The boys adjusted well and hard work didn't seem to bother them. Ken had been afraid at first that they wouldn't want to get their hands dirty. Well, they sure proved him wrong. We used to laugh at how the boys were picking up Canadian slang expressions. With their English accents, it sounded funny. Horse manure was now just plain old horse shit and the horse's posterior became a horse's arse. How quickly they learned all the naughty words! I still got a dirty look from Ken every time he caught me using them. We even got used to sleeping three in a bed. None of us moved much during the night, which sure was a good thing or someone would have ended up on the floor. I had always been a quiet sleeper and Ken told me I never bothered him the times I slept beside him. That's more than I could say for him--he was the snorer, not me.

Eric attended school each day and fit in quite well, considering. Miss Snowdon thought he was very bright.

But where was Mrs. Stacey-Barnes? No one had the slightest idea. Ken got more worried every day. He decided that come Saturday, we would all go to Calgary to see what we could find. They would be setting up the Stampede rides and all that stuff and that would interest the boys.

Michael and Eric looked pretty good in the western outfits we had put together for them. But it seemed like a waste of time getting cleaned up and looking our best, just to get all filthy again from the drive into town. All the roads to Calgary were gravel and the dust

The Cowboy

just poured into Ken's old truck. We had to leave the windows open or we would suffocate from the heat.

We parked the truck at Williams Brothers store. "You boys look around the store for awhile while I try and get some information on Mrs. Stacey-Barnes." said Ken. "You fellas stay out of trouble, or you-know-who's backsides will burn."

"Does he mean a spanking?" Eric asked me.

"That's what he means, all right. Ken has the biggest hand you'll ever see."

"Do you get spankings, Skipper?" Michael asked.

"Yeah, sometimes, but not very often any more. I don't give him any cause. And I'm older too. You do as you're told and you won't get into any trouble. Just watch me."

Mr. Williams came over to us with his usual smile. I really liked him.

"Hello there, champ."

"Hi, Mr. Williams. These are my friends from Millarville, Mike and Eric Stacey-Barnes. They're just over from England."

"How do you do sir." said Mike. I told the boys that Mr. Williams owned the store.

"You have an awfully nice store Mr. Williams." Eric said with a big smile. "You must have everything here."

"Well thank you Eric. It would almost seem that way, wouldn't it? Skipper, you see the new trophies we have on display by the office? They're for all you junior participants this year." I told him that we were just heading that way. "Well, I must be off. Nice to have met you boys. See you later Skipper."

Douglas Hargreaves

We wandered over to the office and peered into the large showcase, filled with all sorts of trophies. "Hooollyy, will you look at the new junior trophy?" I said excitedly. It looked to be about twice the size of last year's. I remembered Ken joshing that if I won again this year, the trophies were going to have to go in the workshop.

"Skipper, are you going to win that one this year?" said Mike.

"I sure hope so Mike. Isn't that the neatest trophy you ever saw?"

Ken came out of the office where he had been using the phone. "Ken did you see all the new trophies for this year's events?" I exclaimed.

"Darned thing's too big. Can't think of where we'll put it. We ain't got any room for it. I think you'll have to get rid of some you already have." He sure sounded serious. He was confident I'd win. I wasn't.

"Well, I gotta go to the police station." said Ken. "I'll see you boys later. Remember what I said about staying out of trouble." Why did Ken keep on about us getting into trouble, I wondered. I guess he was saying that for the boys.

"I guess we had best behave." Eric ventured.

"That would be very wise Eric." I agreed. "Ken has a bad temper. Sometimes he can't control himself. He just explodes. You do as you're told and you'll get along just fine."

Ken returned an hour later and told us he had no further information. He told us we would drive down to the Stampede grounds and have lunch there. I could show the boys around the place while he could see what he could find out about Mrs. Stacey-Barnes. It

The Cowboy

was always fun to eat at the grounds. That was where all the ranchers gathered to talk and fun each other. Besides, we got the most food for half the price of anywhere else. Ken gave us each a quarter and told us not to spend it foolishly. He didn't want us buying stuff that wasn't good for us. I looked at the quarter and joked, "I don't think there's any fear of that Ken." He gave me one of those very special looks he reserved for me.

I took off with the boys in tow to look around. There were still lots of empty stalls, as the Stampede didn't open for a while yet. It was very exciting watching the rides and the game booths being set up and the tractors pulling tents into the grounds. Mike and Eric were all eyes as we wandered from building to building. They didn't miss a thing and asked lots of questions. With all the people rushing around, I wondered if Mrs. Stacey-Barnes would be one of them. I kept that thought to myself.

After we covered most of the grounds, I decided we should stay by the horse barns. Ken would know that's where he'd find me. The horse barns were where I would meet all my friends. I learned a long time ago to keep a low profile around here. Little kids couldn't get into much danger if they stayed clear of trouble areas and made themselves inconspicuous.

We continued walking through the main barn. I knew a lot of the kids who were busy helping their parents get their horses ready for infield events and chuckwagon races. I introduced the boys to the kids I knew as we walked along. Mike and Eric tried very hard to hide their accents, with little success. A few of the kids mimicked them.

George Sylvester saw us coming and overheard their accents. "Oh, I say, Skipper old top, who have you brought along for your outing today?" he said.

"George, this is Mike and Eric. They're just over from England and they've been helping us hay." I was trying to be as polite as I could, although I didn't like George. He always entered the steer riding events but never stayed on long enough to start the clock. Ken had told me George Sylvester's dad only had one oar in the water and lost the other one. I was too young to figure out what boating had to do with George's father, so Ken had to explain it. Come to think of it, George was kind of like that too.

"You mean that these kids are really working for you and Ken?" said George. "How are you guys sitting these days Skipper? You chappies had your ass smashed yet?" Ken's reputation for child discipline was well known. We moved on without answering, ducking in amongst the crowd.

We were walking along the stalls when Mike drew up beside me and told me he thought he heard his mother somewhere in the crowd. Well, there must have been a million people walking around laughing and talking. There was a place at the back of the building that was private. At least everyone told me it was. It was for grown-ups only--no kids allowed. I would often see guys trying to look inside through the stall rails. I never saw anything, but Billy Wilson told me once that that was the place cowboys came to get their oil changed. I couldn't figure that out, because there was a sign on the building doorway saying no cars or trucks were allowed. Come to think of it, I never once saw any cars there. I asked Peggy about it and she told

The Cowboy

me that one day Johnny and I would be old enough to take our cars there.

We kept looking around every stall to see if Mike really heard his mother back there.

"Wouldn't you recognize your own mother's voice if you heard it?" I asked Mike.

"I guess I would Skipper, but with all the noise ,it was simply not possible to tell very clearly." Mike said.

"Come on," I said, "let's get outside into some fresh air. Boy, this heat is killing me."

Phillip Wilson came running up to us as we were leaving the building. "Skipper!" he shouted. "You got your name on the roping roster already. That's 'cause you were the winner last year. You have to defend your title or give your trophy back. Eric, I guess this is your brother, Mike, huh?" He stuck out his hand to Mike. Phillip was a real gentleman, not like his low life brothers. "Are you enjoying all the sights?" he asked.

Mike answered in a low voice, trying to disguise his accent. "It's really some show, huh, Phillip? Skipper has told me all about you and Gordy."

"Well, I'll bet he never told you that he was the junior roping champion. I'll bet he never said anything about that, did he?" Phillip went on.

"Don't listen to him Mike. Phillip is always exaggerating things." I said.

"He's the junior champ Mike. You wait and see what he does next week. When are you going home Skipper? Want to come for a swim after?"

"We'll see what time we get home. I'd sure like to get cooled off."

Douglas Hargreaves

"So would I Phillip." said Mike. He was still trying to hide his accent.

"I gotta go Skipper but I'll see you guys later." said Phillip as he disappeared into the crowd.

We met up with Ken in the cafeteria and he got us all a huge tray of food. He sat down beside us and told us of his findings.

"Mike, it seems your mother has been around the town and lots of people have seen her. No one knows where she is at the moment." he said. I expected to get some sort of a reaction from the boys. They just kept their heads down as they ate their dinner.

After a while, Mike said, "Do you think she could have gone back to the ranch? Perhaps we passed her along the way."

"That's possible Mike but I doubt it. We only met a couple of trucks coming in." I said.

"Gosh all Friday, you guys are sure putting away a lot of food for little britches, ain't you?" Ken joked. "Anyway, I left our post office number with the police, just in case they hear something." he went on. "The police were concerned that no one was looking after you but I told them you were staying with me. They wanted to put you in the children's aid centre. No way you're going there." The boys smiled at Ken and I could see the respect they had in their eyes for him. He was so gentle when he talked about their mother, even though he was plenty annoyed with her and the way she had just left them.

We drove home afterwards and went straight to Old Jim's cabin. The note was still there where we had left it.

The Cowboy

"Okay, let's get home and get the chores done." said Ken. "Then we'll go to Peggy's for a swim." We all piled back into the truck and drove home. I changed into my old clothes and started milking. Ken wondered how it was that when I wanted to go some place, I could milk faster than him. Mike and Eric busied themselves with chores I had assigned them.

I laughed when Ken asked me how the boys were doing. Were they pulling their weight? As if it mattered. I knew he had an opinion already but I felt important when he asked me anyway. I could read his moods pretty well by now and could tell whether or not it would be wise to offer an opposing view on things. I was sure Ken was feeling pretty good about the boys. They were a little frightened of him but then so was I, even after all this time. I knew he loved and cared about me, as he was now caring for them.

Chores completed, we all headed to Peggy's to cool off at the dam. Peggy was all questions about the boys' mother and our trip. Ken told her there wasn't much to tell other than that some people had seen her. None knew where she was staying.

Johnny and Paul asked me who I would be roping against this year. Well, that was one question I couldn't answer, as the complete roster had not been posted yet. I wouldn't know until the day before the events. There was a boy from Nanton I roped against in the Little Britches. He did very well in the Lacombe rodeo. I knew I'd be roping against him in the Juniors. I always got excited when the list came out but it was scary too, especially if I thought they were better than me. Olie would kid me that there were lots better than I was-- they were just too busy to enter into amateur events like the Stampede. Hoooolly! There was no rodeo bigger than the Calgary Stampede. Everyone knew that. Olie would laugh at my reaction and cough as he lit up another cigarette. He was always kidding me about something, and he always had a cigarette in his mouth. I think he went to bed with a cigarette in his mouth. His lip was stained brown from his smokes.

We had our swim and came back up to the house for supper. This time Peggy didn't steal our clothes but she chased us all out to wash our hands and comb our hair.

"Peggy, we just got out of the pond." Eric squeaked. "Do we have to wash again?"

Ken overheard and said in his scariest voice, "What did you say young feller?"

By the look on his face, I thought Eric was going to pee his pants. We started to laugh. Eric didn't know whether to laugh along with us or not. He just shrunk up like a little toad and quietly replied, "Nothing, really, sir."

"Best not be anything." said Ken.

I was having a hard time figuring out how come the boys were taking their mother's disappearance so well. They didn't talk about her very much at all. If anything, they were feeling more sorry for themselves than they were for their mother. One thing was for certain, they were having a good time with us.

I chuckled to myself as the boys would look at Ken before they took any food, as if asking permission. I remembered I did that when I was a little kid or at least smaller than I was now.

We finished supper and washed and dried the dishes. "You fellas had better get a move on home

The Cowboy

before it gets too dark." said Peggy. She picked me up and pinched my behind as she usually did to let me know she loved me. And I laughed to let her know I loved her right back.

Though we were tired when we got home and crawled into bed, we talked quietly about roping and the days events. I couldn't sleep and asked Mike and Eric why they weren't worried about their mother--or at least didn't seem to be worried.

"Our mother can look after herself Skipper." said Mike. "She told us that she wouldn't take any advice or back-talk from any man." There was a bit of arrogance in his voice and I wondered where he thought they would be if it hadn't been for Ken taking them in. It sounded to me like Mrs. Stacey-Barnes could stand some advice right about now.

"So it's okay if she leaves you without any clothes or food?" I said.

Eric's jaw jutted out and he told me that their mother knew exactly what she was doing. It was her business how she handled things.

I was getting a little annoyed. "Well I don't think she thought this out very well." I said.

Eric started to cry and Mike just turned over and lay still. Immediately realizing I had gone too far, I said, "Look, I'm sorry I said that. I don't know anything about it and I'm sorry." Mike confessed that he was frightened. His mother had done some pretty dumb things in her life but had never left them like this.

Eric said, "She used to leave us with neighbours sometimes. Do you suppose something terrible has happened to her?"

We let it drop and soon drifted off to asleep.

ERIC TESTS KEN

In church the next morning, Ken and I sat with Michael and Eric in the middle of the pew, with Grandma and Grandpa on either end. The boys looked uncomfortable. They felt everyone was staring at them. Eric started to fidget until he glanced at Grandma--her look settled him down in a hurry.

Outside, after the service, Tom Wilson came over. "Got yourself another batch of kids, huh, Ken? I thought you would have learned your lesson after your first one. You're sure a sucker for punishment or maybe your boys are." he laughed.

"Tom, you're just jealous that I got boys who can work and are smart in school." Ken replied.

"I got Phillip and he's as good as Skipper. They're good friends, you know." said Tom Wilson. Grandpa always said Tom Wilson was a real dumballo. I think that was an old country expression.

When Grandpa and I were standing alone, I asked. "Grandpa, if he's so dumb, how come he has so much money?"

"His family paid him a ton of money to leave his home in Britain and to come out here to homestead." said Grandpa. "He is called a "remittance man". He's had a lot of luck and a whole load of money to keep him going. When you got money Skipper, you can easily make more of it, so it seems." I thought about it and realized that, with the money my parents had been sending, we had tripled the size of our herd in only three years. Now that was making money!

Douglas Hargreaves

As usual, we went to Grandma and Grandpa's for dinner after church. There wasn't a lot to do on Sunday, so I got to practice roping and showed off a little for Mike and Eric. Mike learned quickly how to keep an open loop and could even rope a fence post. We helped Grandma pick some vegetables for us to take to Peggy and then we left for home. When Grandma wasn't around, we could do some work on Sunday. But we weren't to let her know, that's for sure. We emptied the rest of the hay rack into the loft. We would be ready to bring in another load first thing in the morning.

Mike and Eric instinctively knew what had to be done and were always ready to help. They used common sense about most of the things they did. They were good workers. I really liked them and we all got along well together, like brothers.

We completed the balance of Grandpa's hay during the week. There was still no word on the whereabouts of Mrs. Stacey-Barnes. The boys had settled into a regular routine for the chores. I assigned them the horse feeding and the egg collecting. They were quite happy with that--they didn't mind those rotten birds. Of course, Ken had to make a big thing about how scared I was getting the eggs. Michael and Eric just laughed.

During the day, I ran the stacker while Mike drove the hay wagon. Eric kept busy doing odd jobs for Grandma. She was becoming quite attached to the little boy. I always used the word "little" with some reservations, as I was just an inch taller than Eric.

It was settled that we would all go in early next Saturday morning to watch the Calgary Stampede parade. This was a highlight in the life of all Valley

The Cowboy

kids. The next days went by quickly. We were so busy we didn't have time to think about Mrs. Stacey-Barnes. We would get home dead tired and still have the chores to do.

Because haying was such a dusty and dirty job, we had a bath in our creek every evening. Bath time was generally a time for fooling around--splashing and chasing each other. Ken was there with his bar of soap for our ears and neck. The creek refreshed and cooled us after a hot, hard day's work. At bedtime we were so tired we were practically asleep before our heads hit the pillow. We had been sleeping three in a bed for some time now and one night Ken asked me if I wanted to crawl in with him. He didn't have to ask twice because it was sure crowded in my bed. I had only slept in his room a couple of times. I would miss my nightly chats with the boys, whispering until it was late. I decided that I could slip into bed with them for a little while until we got tired of talking then I'd quietly crawl into Ken's bed. I think he would rather have had his bed to himself but I was a quiet sleeper. Ken would pretend he was asleep and make snoring sounds. When I was getting under the covers he would surprise the daylights out of me by grabbing and tickling me. "Gosh all Friday boy, but you make a lot of noise when I'm trying to sleep." he'd scold. "You keep laughing like that and I'm going to make you sleep in the barn." Then he'd tickle me some more. I would whisper in his ear. "I love you Ken." Then we would go to sleep. Friday evening we were all bathing and talking up a storm. Tomorrow was going to be a big day, the Stampede parade. We were making all sorts of plans about what we were going to do. I had been practising

Douglas Hargreaves

my roping every morning before chores and Mike was there beside me. I had dug up one of my old ropes for Mike to use and he was a happy learner.

All in all, Mike was getting to be a little more aggressive, not quite so timid. I guess he was getting used to us. He was starting to take a few liberties, assuming things. That was okay--after all, he was getting to be one of us. I spoke to him about a few things I thought he should watch, like getting up from the table before being excused and moving the horses around without asking. Ken let him know once or twice that he had to check with him first.

Eric was making himself completely at home, thinking he had an in with Grandma. He did too. He was expressing dislikes for things he had to eat and things he was asked to do. My advice to Eric was that he better be careful or watch his hind end. He hadn't experienced Ken's wrath yet. Eric's behaviour was out of character for him. I think it had to do with his mother's disappearance.

One evening we all walked down with our towels to take our baths. Ken told Eric to bring the soap. When we got down to the creek and in the water, Ken asked Eric for the soap.

"I forgot it." he replied.

Ken got testy. "Gosh all Friday boy, can't you follow a simple order? Now get the heck up there and get the soap. Now!"

"Why should I be the one who has to get the soap, anyway?"

Mike and I knew at once that this would be Eric's undoing. We knew exactly what was going to happen.

The Cowboy

Ken waded over to Eric, grabbed him by his arms and had him over his knee in a second. The fastest hand in the West gave Eric his first real spanking, right there in the water. Eric was shocked and surprised, to say the least. He hollered and screamed and wiggled around in horror and utter pain, like he was falling apart. Mike just stood beside me with his mouth open. He knew this was between Eric and Ken and he had best stay out of it.

Eric cried and howled and fell down in the water. Ken picked him up and carried him to the edge. "Now little man, you get your little arse up there right now and bring down the soap."

Eric was still holding his behind as he ran up to the house. He was back in a minute carrying the soap, still sobbing. He handed the bar to Ken and exclaimed. "How come you spanked me? You had no right do that."

Aw Eric, you've done it again, I thought.

Hooollly! Over Ken's knee again, and again the big hand landed, and again Eric howled. Eric continued to cry for a while, standing up to his knees in the water, sobbing quietly to himself, while Ken scrubbed his neck and his ears.

Mike and I stayed clear, waiting for our turn to get a scrubbing.

Eric looked first at Mike, then at me. Then he walked over to Ken and held out his arms. Ken picked him up and hugged him. Ken was very gentle with him.

"Ken, I am awfully sorry I behaved so badly." he sobbed. "I'll never do that again, I promise."

Mike said to Ken, "Thank you for all you have done for Eric and me. Eric was just testing. He wanted to make sure you really cared what happens to us. We know you do."

I almost cried when I heard Mike's sincere thanks. I felt we were really getting close to both Eric and Mike. We had tried to keep them busy so they wouldn't have time to worry about themselves. Yet I could feel their loneliness for their mother was getting to be too much for them.

CALF ROPIN' AT THE STAMPEDE

The night before the big parade, as we lay in bed, Ken said we'd have to watch the boys carefully and make sure they didn't get lost. It was easy to get separated, what with the large crowds everywhere. I knew Ken was feeling badly for the boys too.

The parade, of course, was just the beginning of the Calgary Stampede--there was lots more excitement to come. Still, the parade itself struck Michael and Eric with such awe that they could hardly speak. They were all eyes, not wanting to miss a thing--the horses, clowns, chuckwagons, Indians, cowboys and big marching bands. The oil industry rolled out their huge rig-moving equipment. We all waved at Phillip as he rode over to where we were standing.

Some time later, Phillip and Gordon came running up to ask Ken if we could come to the parade dispersal area. We could get a better look at the floats and all the participants. "As long as all of you watch out for Mike and Eric." he said. "I'll see you guys at the grounds for registration. Remember, keep an eye out for those boys and make sure they stay right beside you all the time. I'll meet you about 1 o'clock." he warned again.

And away we went, the five of us, ready to take on the world and the Calgary Stampede! Everything was in place and the famous gates had opened to proclaim the greatest outdoor rodeo show in the world. We could feel the electricity and excitement all around us. There seemed to be people by the thousands crowding to see everything that was going on. No matter where

Douglas Hargreaves

you went, you had to wait in line for tickets to the various rides and attractions. It was really more than anyone could take in all at one time.

"Skipper! Oh Skipper, over here!" It was Eilene, Johnny's sister, hollering and making her way through the crowd to us. "Skip! I just saw the roster and it looks like you're roping against some boys from Montana and two others from up in the Peace River country. It sure looks like you got some competition this time, huh?" She was as excited about the event as I was.

"Who are the entries from Montana?" I asked her.

"Wayne Schlosman. He's fourteen. And a Dereck Porterfield. They're listed in the roping and the bull riding too." Trust a woman to get all the gossip before anyone else.

Well, now I knew who I'd be up against in a few days. I thought about all the things that led up to the junior roping competition. The time would drag by so slowly it was almost unbearable. I would get so nervous I couldn't sleep. Ken would scold me and tell me there just wasn't all that much to get excited about. Well, he wasn't in any of the events, so he could talk. "Skipper," he'd say, "you settle down now, or else you're going to have a fit. Either you cool your heels a little or I'm going to have to pull your entry for this year." Well, I knew he would never do a thing like that but it showed me how worried he was that I might blow my chances. I had been working all year for this day and now it was here.

Peggy told me she had never seen me so riled up about my event. "Skipper, you been up against some

The Cowboy

tough ones before. Why all of a sudden you making such a deal of it this time?"

I remembered how upset Ken was with me when he found me out working a calf at four in the morning. "Gosh all Friday, ain't you got enough to do without getting up at this time of the day?" he scolded.

"Ken, I know about Wayne Schlosman and he's won the Butte Rodeo three years in a row. That's why he's coming up to try the big time." I explained.

"So what? You're better than him and a few extra hours of practice ain't going to make any difference at this stage of the game. Remember all we talked about and you'll be just fine."

"Ken, don't forget, Donny Porter is entering. You remember him from Nanton in the Little Britches Rodeo? He sure gave me a run that time."

I wished I had as much confidence in myself as Ken did in me. Right now, on top of everything else, all the excitement was giving me stomach cramps. All I needed now was to get sick. It seemed that every time I got excited or under some stress, my old stomach problem came back.

A few days before the Stampede, I found myself holding my stomach when Mike and Ken came over to the corral. "See?" said Ken. What did I tell you boy? Now you've gone and got yourself all plugged up again and all for nothin'. Better go up to the house and I'll fix you up." He looked after my bowel problem with the usual soapy water method and I felt fine again. I sure wished it would go away once and for all.

Another thing that worried me was having to use Gordon's horse, Blaze. Nixon had developed a slight limp and Ken said we shouldn't strain his foot. I had

Douglas Hargreaves

ridden Blaze in other shows and I knew he was real good for roping. It was just that this was a change I hadn't planned on and I really wanted to win this time. It would probably be my last competition. I didn't want to let my friends down. "Skipper, all you gotta do is remember what you've learned." Ken lectured. "The only thing you have to beat is the clock. Nothing else and no one else."

Everybody had something to do or say about my event. Grandma always saw that my clothes were as near to new-looking as she could get them and that my boots were polished. "You gotta look good for the picture-taking, Skipper."

Bath time before the Stampede competitions was always hilarious. Ken would scrub twice as hard as usual. We had to be spotless and looking our very best for the big show. I often wondered if the fish that swam in our creek ever got to blowing bubbles from all the soap we were putting into the water.

The night before the event I slept soundly for a change. Ken woke us up by pulling off all the covers.

"Up and at 'em, cowboys. Today's the day Skipper brings home number four, right Skip?" he laughed.

"I sure hope so. I sure been worrying about this one, I'll tell you."

"Remember to get him as close to you as you can. Then you got it made." We had been over this a thousand times before. "Rope him fast, keeping your rope short. Then when he falls down, you land right on top of him. Simple as that." Ken drilled this into me over and over again. It should've been him in the competition instead of me, I thought.

The Cowboy

Our trip into Calgary was a quiet one. Each of us were lost in our thoughts, me about the rodeo, Mike and Eric about their mom, and Ken about all of us. I knew it wouldn't be Ken's fault if I didn't win because he had sure spent many long hours working with me. He was just as tired from all our practising as I was.

At the main registration gate we paid the entry fee and Ken signed as my parent.

"Well Skipper, you got a little competition this time, I see." the registrar noted. "You know Wayne Schlosman from Montana?"

"No Mr. Carter, I haven't met him. Has he signed in yet?"

"Yup, he just signed in and he wants to meet you. He's over there by the Number Two gate. That's him standing with his dad." Hoooollyy! Wayne was about as small as I was. I wondered if he really was fourteen.

Mike and I walked over and I said, "Hi, Wayne, I'm Skipper Scott and this here's Mike. We're sort of brothers."

"Nice to meet you, Skipper. Hi, Mike. I sure heard all kinds of things about you. In fact, every time I turn around, it's Skipper did this or Skipper did that. Golly, you sure are a busy dude, ain't 'ya?" he laughed.

"Wayne, how come you're so short? I hear tell you're fourteen." I said.

"Ha! I was just going to ask you the same thing. You're even smaller than me!" We both laughed. I liked this guy and I think he liked me. "I don't expect to beat you, Skipper," he said, "but Pa thinks the experience will be worth the trip up here. And to rope against you is even better."

Douglas Hargreaves

"Wayne, to tell you the truth, I haven't had too much competition those other years." I was trying to be humble. "Maybe once or twice, I think."

"Skipper, I ride before you because I came from farther away and that worries me."

"Just do the best you can and I'll bet you can kick my behind." Naturally I hoped I was wrong.

Mike decided to say his piece. "Wayne, you're going to have one awful time beating Skipper this year. This may be his last year here before he goes home."

"I gotta go now." said Wayne. "My dad's waving me over to the stalls. I'm really glad I met you Skipper. I'd like us to be friends. Can we see each other after the rides?"

"Sure Wayne and it was my pleasure getting to meet you. And all the way from Montana too. Good luck." And I meant it.

"You too Skipper." Wayne said as he walked away.

"Skipper, how can you compete against a friend?" said Mike. "Doesn't it bother you a shade?"

"Yes it does Mike but I have a feeling Wayne wants me to win, just as I would like to see him do it. But we both can't, so we just do the best we can."

Ken would have been proud of me if he'd heard the line I was handing Mike. He would have called it bullshit.

Mike and I walked over to our stall and to the gate where I was assigned my calf. Hooolllyy! I couldn't believe the size of that sucker. Almost the size of Old Bossy. I'd never topple that monster, that's for sure. I got on Blaze and started making practice dashes here and there like we were taking after a stray. Blaze knew me almost as well as Nixon did. I looked around for

The Cowboy

Ken. He was sitting astride the top rail talking to Gordon.

The announcer called out the roster and the times already chalked up by other riders. I heard Wayne's name and saw him wave to me as he headed into his gate. He had drawn a medium-sized calf. I didn't think he could possibly lose with such a little one.

The horn sounded, the crowd roared and away went Wayne after his calf. The calf changed direction and started running toward Wayne's horse. Wayne had to swerve hard to get a decent roping angle. His rope sung out and captured the calf but Wayne was a long way from where his calf lay. He flew out of the saddle and ran for all he was worth, throwing himself on the calf. But the calf had regained his footing and that made it harder for Wayne to throw and tie him. Wayne finally managed to get the calf over and tied but his time wasn't going to be good.

"Time, 10 seconds." came the announcement from the loudspeakers. There was tremendous applause for the young Montana cowboy. His time was pretty good, considering the trouble he'd had with his calf.

Next came Roger Flett from the Yukon Territory. He was big for only fourteen, I thought. He must have been eating steaks for breakfast every day. Well, he was older than that. "Fifteen-year-old Roger Flett from Dawson City, Yukon Territory." the announcer called. Loud applause.

The gate opened and out came one fast calf, hell bent for the other side of the corral. Roger's rope snared his calf all right but his horse didn't stop. The horse kept moving into the calf, releasing tension on the rope. Roger fell down and got caught in his own rope. The calf shook free and walked calmly away.

Then the horse started pulling towards the corral, dragging Roger with him. Roger couldn't get on his feet. Wayne and several others came running to Roger's rescue. Wayne pulled out his pocket knife and cut the rope to free Roger. That was quick thinking, although someone probably would have stopped the horse before Roger suffered too much damage.

And as for damage, there was more done to Roger's ego than his rope. "You stupid Yankee bastard!" Roger yelled at Wayne, who just stood there with his mouth wide open, trying to figure out what was happening. "You cut my best rope, you idiot!" Having seen the whole thing, I thought that was a terrible way for Roger to talk to someone who had just saved his butt from getting dragged around in front of the whole grandstand.

Now it was my turn. What I had witnessed had unnerved me some. Ken gave me a pat on the behind as I slipped into the saddle. He told me to think of how the calf must be feeling right about now. That made me laugh. Wayne was standing nearby as they let the calf into the stall. I looked down at the calf. He didn't look up at me. Hooooolllyyy, he was sure big. How was I ever going to set this bugger on his behind? Ken had me take my tie rope and put it through a leather thong bracelet he had made for me. I would always have the rope handy at my finger tips no matter what happened.

As the horn blew, I heard Wayne holler. "Good luck, Skipper!" My gate opened and the calf charged out. Blaze had the calf all sized up. We were right on top of him in a second. I passed a low small loop that

The Cowboy

caught calf's neck just right and down he went. Blaze came to a dead stop. The forward momentum shot me over his front quarter, smack dab onto my calf. The calf was still down, thank goodness. All I had to do was just sit on him and tie him up. I had him tied in--

"Five seconds!" the announcer called out.

Hoooolly! I had beaten my best time by three seconds! It was a new junior record! The crowd roared its appreciation. So did Ken, who jumped up and down and carried me around on his shoulders. "That's my boy, huh!" he yelled. "Beat that if you can! Ain't he somethin' else?" Well, I was embarrassed as usual.

I saw Wayne, standing with his dad along side the gates, waving at me. I waved back and Ken put me down. I ran over to Wayne and could see his eyes were red.

"Wayne, did you ever see such fool luck in your whole life?" I said.

"Skipper, you were just great and you deserved to win. It wasn't just luck. It was darned fast thinking on your part. I thought you were going to fly right over his head." he said. We shook hands. I liked him because he was a gentleman and a cowboy. Wayne's dad and Ken were trying to talk above all the noise around us when Roger walked by and called me a Yankee Lover. Phillip and Gordon came running up just then and I introduced them to Wayne. No one talked to Roger. We all just ignored him.

Wayne's dad invited us all over to their trailer where it was quieter and we could talk. He gave us fresh, cool lemonade and cookies.

"Where's Mike and Eric?" Ken wanted to know. I looked at Gordon and Phillip but they just shrugged their shoulders. Now where had those boys got to? They had been with us--at least I think they had--right until I got on Blaze to start my run.

"Well we had best spread out and see if we can find them." said Ken. "They couldn't have gone too far." He had a worried look on his face.

"I met Mike but who's Eric?" Wayne asked.

"Well, they're sort of like my brothers." I replied. "We're kind of looking after them for awhile."

As we were getting set to go looking, along came a policeman with Mike and Eric. Naturally all of us were glad to see them.

But the policeman looked grim. It was pretty clear there was more to this than a pair of boys getting lost at the Stampede.

THE FOUND AND THE LOST

Mike and Eric had wandered off while we were getting ready for my event. We just got carried away with all the commotion and didn't notice the boys as they disappeared into the crowd. Well, a grounds guard saw them looking lost and he took them to the police station.

When Mike and Eric gave the police their names, the police brought them to an inside office. They questioned the boys about where they were staying and where Ken was. Michael asked the police if they had heard where their mother was. This got the officers' attention. They told the boys they would have to find Ken first. Then they could sit down and talk about any news they might have regarding Mrs. Stacey-Barnes.

Michael told the police that we were in the roping events, so it was easy for them to find us. The officer who brought the boys to us asked Ken to come with him for a private talk. He took Ken aside and told him that the boys' mother had been involved in some unsavoury practices with some other women. The police officer knew all about it because it had happened at the Stampede grounds.

Late one night, after closing time, Mrs. Stacey-Barnes was wandering around the grounds. The Elbow River runs alongside the Stampede site and Mrs. Stacey-Barnes, who was very drunk, apparently fell or possibly jumped into the river. The next morning, some vagrants who had been sleeping by the river found her body.

Douglas Hargreaves

Ken returned to us with a shocked and sad look on his face. At first I wondered if the boys had got into some kind of trouble. Ken told us he wanted to talk to us privately, just Mike and Eric and I. So we said goodbye to Wayne and his parents and thanked them for their hospitality. Phillip and Gordon said they would wait for us until we had our talk. I was sure something terrible was about to happen because I had seen that look on Ken's face before. He only wore that face when he had something to do that he didn't want to have to do.

We found a table that had been set up for the participants. We sat down and Ken told the boys that he had news about their mother.

"Did they find her, Ken?" Eric asked.

"Why didn't they tell us back at the police station?" Mike wanted to know.

"Well, it ain't quite as easy as that Mike." Ken began slowly. "You see, your mother fell in with some bad company. She was drinking pretty heavy. Well, she got lost, wandering around the grounds after everything closed down. And she accidentally slipped into the river over there." Ken pointed towards the river. "I guess she didn't know where she was or what was happening and she wasn't able to get herself out again. The police found her the next morning. They've taken her to a special place. They want you boys to come and see if the lady they found is your mother."

Ken was trying hard to keep that quiver out of his voice. "Michael, there isn't much I can say about how sorry and sad we are for you and Eric." he continued. "We want you to know that you have nothing to worry about. You're with me and Skipper and that's where

The Cowboy

you'll stay until we can find any of your relatives back in England."

Michael's eyes were full of tears. "Thank you Ken." he said. "I gather that our mother has passed away and that we will not have her to look after us any longer."

Eric wept quietly. Then he said, "Ken, do we have to go and see her?"

"Mike can go, Eric." said Ken. "It will only take one of you then we'll head for home. You know you are at home with us, don't you?"

Looking at the faces of Mike and Eric, I felt sadder than I ever had in my whole life. It was the uncertainty of their future that was the most upsetting for them, I thought. They really needed assurance that they were, in fact, coming home with us and that we would look after them.

We got up from the table and went over to where Gordon and Phillip had been waiting. Michael and Eric walked along with Ken, holding his hands tightly. I followed with Gordy and Phillip and told them what had happened. They felt terrible and wanted to know what they could do to help. I told them to just be friends to the boys. That was the best any of us could do.

"Eric, I want you to stay with Skipper and the boys while I take Mike to the police station." Ken said. "We'll meet you at the horse barn as soon as we can. It shouldn't take too long."

Ken and Mike returned a short while later. Mike looked terrible. He had been sobbing. Gordy and Phillip said they would see us at Peggy's swimming hole after chores. We departed sadly for home.

Douglas Hargreaves

Ken insisted that we do everything the same as we usually did. So we completed our chores as usual and then we all headed for Peggy's. She was there at the door to meet us. Gordon and Phillip had already told her the news about Mrs. Stacey-Barnes. She put her arms around the boys and hugged them. She told them how sad she was for them but their mother was in good hands and would be watching them from where she was in heaven. We were all crying.

Peggy wanted to do something to ease their sadness. "All right, you monkeys," she said, "all of you get down for your swim. By the time you're done, I'll have supper on. And Eric, you better watch where you put your clothes!" A little smile came over Eric's face and we all took off down to the pond. Ken stayed to talk with Peggy.

Gordy and Phillip were waiting and ready to splash us as we undressed. The water felt good. I hoped it might somehow wash away our sadness. I think it did a little. For a few minutes the boys seemed to forget their troubles.

That night, as we were getting ready to go to bed, we knelt down to say our prayers. Michael prayed, "Dear God, please look after our mother and look after us. Thank you for Ken who has been taking care of us. Mother, if you're watching us now, you can see that we are all right and we know you're all right now too. Don't worry about us. We'll be just fine, now that we know where you are. Mother, I know you will find it a lot easier where you are. Goodbye Mother and thank you Lord. Amen."

Michael was crying as we crawled into bed. We hugged and wept until we finally went to sleep.

The Cowboy

Winning my trophy had no importance compared to the tragedy that had befallen Michael and Eric.

Ken came into the bedroom and motioned me to get up. I crawled out of bed without waking the boys. Ken picked me up and carried me into his room. "Skipper," he said, "I am so proud of you, I can hardly tell you. This was a big day in your life and it was spoiled by this terrible accident. You're my special kid you know." He had tears in his eyes.

THE BIG ROUND-UP

At the beginning of September, Ken and I went with Michael and Eric to enrol them in school. We wanted to make sure everyone there knew those boys were to get the same respect as the other kids. Well, we didn't have to, as it turned out. Michael and Eric had been in the community for the past two months and most everyone knew all about them. There was sympathy for their loss.

Ken and Peggy did their best to help Mike and Eric through their horrible ordeal. Ken's experiences raising me proved very helpful to him in dealing with the boys. They took to our love and caring well. All of us still got our backsides heated every now and again but we all knew that was Ken's way of showing us he wanted us to learn and that he cared.

Sometimes I questioned in my own mind Ken's "big handed" method of discipline. One thing I learned was never to brood over my punishments. I was able to convince Mike and Eric that it was best to learn what Ken had to teach and to learn from their mistakes. After all, Ken forgot about it right afterwards, so we should too. He never carried a grudge.

The boys did learn, quickly and willingly. So when it came time for school they were excited to get started. Miss Snowdon had married over the holidays. She was now Mrs. Barr.

She wanted to know Mike and Eric's actual grade level so she gave both of them a departmental exam. Michael was twelve so he wrote the Grade Seven exam. He passed with a mark of one hundred percent.

So Mrs. Barr gave him the Grade Eight test. Again, he scored one hundred percent! On the Grade Nine exam, Mike scored seventy percent. Mrs. Barr told him he would start in Grade Nine.

I knew all along that Mike was smart--not your average Grade Sevener. He asked me very intelligent questions about ranching, cattle, branding and marketing. He could figure out exactly how much we stood to make on our herd.

Eric also scored very well. He did well enough on the Grade Seven exam to start in that grade. Not bad for a ten-year-old, going on eleven. Mrs. Barr was excited over the prospect of having two new intellectuals, as she called them. The boys were very modest and humble about their good scores. Mrs. Barr explained to the school why the boys were being advanced. The rest of them should try and do as well, she advised.

Phillip was going into Grade Eight and Gordon into Grade Nine. I would miss them as I was starting Grade Ten at the high school in Turner Valley.

Eric rode to school on the back of Michael's horse. Gordon met them each morning at our gate to make sure they got to school on time. Michael complained that he was quite capable of riding to school without someone watching over him. He was, too. The real reason was that Ken wanted Mike and Eric to meet all the kids through Gordon and Phillip.

With the beginning of school came the beginning of fall. The leaves turned their gorgeous colours and the ranchers made plans to move their herds back home. We always looked forward to this annual event.

The Cowboy

Some of my memories of the round-up were bad ones, such as the time Johnny and I had our run-in with Wilf Krause from Tom Wilson's ranch. I wished I had told Ken what had happened but he might have sent me back to my parents if he figured it was more than he could handle. Well I didn't tell Ken and just put it out of my thoughts. Johnny had wiped it from his mind as well. Phillip and I talked about it once in a while when we were alone. The events of the past were long gone but not the memories.

Ken, Tom Wilson and Olie started the round-up by riding to the lease lands around Square Butte to see if they could spot our herds. The cattle were farther back than we figured so it was going to take more than a week to get them rounded up and home. Eric and Mike were so excited about the coming ride that they forgot about everything else. Gordon, Phillip and Willie would be joining the drive. Even Johnny, young as he was, had managed to convince Peggy and Olie that he should join us as well. Mrs. Barr was used to the boys leaving each fall for the round-up. The poor school looked deserted.

Billy Wilson and I were released from high school. So, with Tom Wilson and his two hired hands, his four sons, plus Gordy, Olie and Johnny, Ken, Mike, Eric and me, that made up the drivers, as Ken called us. Fourteen in all. Ken had some reservations about Eric but he thought the boy would feel really left out if he couldn't join in. Eric wouldn't be doing any real driving, only watching and moving along with us.

Lynn Spence, my friend from Turner Valley, offered Eric his new bay mare to ride, along with a saddle and all the trappings. Lynn wanted to join in on the round-up too. His dad, an oil man, said Lynn could join us on Friday after school. Lynn and I had been room mates in the local hospital two years before when I got knocked out chasing a stray. Nixon had taken me under a low branch--I didn't duck soon enough.

Fourteen was a large crew. We had to take along a cook wagon with our food supplies. Ken and Olie had taken the wagon out before we arrived and had it set up just below the butte.

We spent the first three days finding the herds and moving them to our camp. We were split up into groups and were assigned areas to search and times to report back. Olie, Ken, Johnny, Eric and Mike made up one group while Phillip, Gordon and I were assigned to one of Wilson's hired hands. Phillip and I looked at each other, remembering the last hired hand we had been assigned to.

Well, our man turned out to be a real worker and he made sure we did our share. We found our herds quickly and moved them to the butte. We could hear Ken and Olie, with Michael shouting at the top of his lungs in his soprano voice. We laughed, even though we were doing exactly the same. Tom Wilson and his crew found some of our herd and Olie's mixed in with his.

It was a sight right out of those cowboy books I read as a little kid in Winnipeg. Fourteen hooting and hollering cow pokes moving all those cattle along. We worked hard and were ahead of schedule. Two more days would see us to the road and then home. Lynn joined us Friday afternoon and told me that this was the greatest experience of his life. Well, he hadn't been sitting in the saddle for a week. If Peggy were to pinch

The Cowboy

my butt, I would have hollered bloody murder. Both Eric and Michael were real helpers, as though they had been ranching for years. Mike worked cattle well, considering it was his first time. Johnny and Eric teamed up together, chasing the odd stray that got away. Lynn, having the time of his life, talked non-stop about the drive.

By Saturday afternoon Ken decided we could just leave the herd where it was. We would pick them up again on Monday and have them home by Wednesday. Lynn hadn't expected to be home so soon and was some disappointed. He wouldn't be picked up until Sunday night so he would stay the night with us and would see his parents at church.

As we all went our separate ways, we said we would see each other in church on Sunday. We arrived at Peggy's and immediately headed for the beaver dam for a swim. Cold or not, we were going in. I noticed that Eric and Mike hid their clothes this time. Poor Lynn seemed a little surprised to see us all strip down to our nothing and dive in. He waited about five seconds, then undressed and dove in.

Back at the ranch, Mark and Eilene were sure glad to see us. They had been doing our chores.

We were all pretty tired as we got ready for bed. Both Mike and I offered Lynn our place in bed but he said he would rather sleep on the floor. That way, he would appreciate his own soft bed when he got home. We all laughed. Lynn and I rolled out two bed rolls on the floor by the bed.

Before we went to sleep, Lynn asked Mike to tell him about his home in England. Mike had a lot to say about where he lived and his friends back in his home

Douglas Hargreaves

town. We could hear the sadness in his voice as he related his stories. Both Lynn and I hoped Mike and Eric would see their home again. There had been quite a few letters written to relatives and whoever else might be concerned. There was a grandfather somewhere back in England. The boys had never seen him but they knew he was still alive.

"Would you want to go to live with your grandfather, Mike?" said Lynn.

"I've been wondering that too." Mike replied.

"Well, I wouldn't." said Eric. "I want to stay right here and be a cowboy with Ken and Skipper."

The next morning we all dressed for church. The boys wore their borrowed outfits, all washed and ironed.

The visiting pastor told us he had written to England regarding the plight of the boys. He was waiting for an answer. I was glad someone was doing something. Eric and Mike didn't mind much.

Back at the herd on Monday morning, something was wrong. We were missing some cattle. They must have strayed during the weekend. Or did they? We counted and recounted and still came up twenty head short.

"Twenty head just gone!" Ken spat. "Gul darn it! They didn't wander off. Look at them tracks. There were trucks here!" We decided that the stolen cattle were mostly from our herd. Ken was positively furious.

As we moved our herds toward home, Ken hollered at Mike and me almost continuously. "Gosh all Friday Skipper, you're slower than the second coming!" I decided to just watch my step really close.

The Cowboy

"Mike! Get your arse in gear and keep those strays off the fence!" Mike looked over at me, then did as he was told. He knew well enough what to do and not make noises about it. "You want your backside tanned?" Ken hollered at Mike as two strays tried to break through the fence. Mike looked downright scared as he hustled to move up between the strays and the fence.

Ken was sure owly. I guess he had reason to be but Mike wasn't used to Ken taking it out on us like that. Losing those twenty head had nothing to do with us. I was used to Ken's temper and wasn't afraid. Mike was having trouble with the strays. For a minute I thought he was going to get squashed between the strays and the barbed wire fence. I came down the fence line from in front, which was the way to handle that situation and the strays headed back to the herd. "Thank's Skipper." Mike said with real relief.

Johnny, Paul and Olie were way ahead and were not aware of what had been going on.

We took the short cut through Olie's and Peggy's place on the way home. There was dust was everywhere and we were sure dirty. I wanted to swim real bad, and we were just about to pass the dam. "Keep those bastards moving!" Ken hollered. So much for having a swim.

Johnny and Paul rode up and asked us to come for a swim but I told them we had to get the herd home.

"Okay Skipper, we'll ride along and give you a hand." said Paul.

"Boy, Ken can sure get mad, can't he?" said Eric.

"Well, he's real upset with what's happened." I said.

"I heard about rustlers in western movies." said Mike. "I hope he isn't upset with me."

"Naw," I assured him, "he's just mad about losing the cattle."

ERIC VANISHES

We tallied up our losses. It wasn't as bad as we first thought but it was still a big blow. We were missing eleven head, Wilson lost eight, and Olie lost one. Losing the cattle was bad enough but to have them rustled right from under our noses was outright insulting.

Ken reported the loss to the Royal Canadian Mounted Police in Turner Valley. A few days later, several Mounties from Calgary arrived to investigate. They took reports from Ken and Tom Wilson. Ken was not pleasant to be around. It wasn't that he was mad at us. He was mad at himself for letting it happen. Grandpa told us there hadn't been any rustling in this area since he first came here. He had heard that rustlers operated from time to time west of us, in the more isolated areas, more towards the Kananaskis country.

The Mounties were very interested in the truck tracks the rustlers had left in the dirt. They made plaster casts of the tracks in case the rain or other cattle wiped them out. The Mounties asked us if we had seen any strangers in the area, any trucks, wagons or anything unusual. We hadn't. "One thing's for sure," said Ken, "those bastards are going to have one hell of a time getting rid of our cattle." Everyone would know there were cattle missing and would be on the lookout for them.

We tried to cheer Ken up but all of us were feeling down. It was terrible to think that there were rustlers around, right in our midst. Mike, Eric and I were on our best behaviour around Ken, making sure we didn't

Douglas Hargreaves

give him any cause to get upset with us. Ken gave us a talking to about watching out for strangers and staying together until the rustlers were caught. Lynn had left his horse at our place for Eric and we told him to stick around and not go riding off on his own.

I was unhappy that Ken was so mad at himself because I didn't know how to make things better. It was as though Ken took the rustling personally. Mike and Eric were afraid Ken might send them away. I knew how they felt because I had felt the same way for quite a while. It was a terrible feeling to think you wouldn't have someone to care for you.

Mike and Eric rode to school each day and were usually home before I was and would start the chores. The Wilsons and Ken took turns driving Billy and me into the Valley to school. They'd let me off at our gate and I'd walked home, change, and head down to the barn to start heaving hay for the horses. Mike was usually busy shovelling manure onto the stone boat. When it was full, we'd hitch up the team and haul it away. Eric would be feeding and watering the chickens.

"How was school Mike?" I asked one day.

"Great, Skipper. I really like the way Mrs. Barr conducts her classes. I wonder how she is able to handle us all, with so many things going on at once in that small room."

"Well, she's had lots of practice and never seems to mind it."

I climbed down from the loft and started to fork hay out into the barn corral where we kept the horses. Nixon was always nearby, especially when I came home and was working in the barn. He knew I was

The Cowboy

there and he would get fed. A few cups of oats, some hay and he was happy. Boots, Lynn's horse, was not in the corral.

"Mike, where is Boots?" I said.

"Eric hasn't come home yet. He was going to ride part way home with Gordon and come back by Peggy's."

Hoooollyyy! I almost had a heart attack. Ken would be furious. "Mike, why did you let Eric go with Gordon? You know what Ken told us about riding alone. Ken's going to have your hide, I can tell you that."

I was really getting scared. What would we do if something happened to Eric? "I'm going to ride toward Peggy's." I said. You stay and get your chores done. I'll milk when I get back." I put Nixon's bridle on and hopped on bareback. Nixon knew I was in a hurry and started to gallop. I just let him.

I got to Peggy's and ran inside.

"Peggy, has Eric been here?"

"Slow down Skipper." said Peggy. "What are you talking about? Why would Eric be here?"

"Well, he rode part way home with Gordon and was to cut across through your place and then home." I was shaking. "Peggy, Ken's going to skin me alive."

Johnny came in from doing his chores and I told him what was going on. "We better ride back along his trail." he said. "Maybe he went all the way with Gordy."

"Yeah, well, he better not have done that. Boy, will he ever get it." I was feeling terrible between being scared of Ken and frightened for Eric.

Douglas Hargreaves

Johnny and I had gone back almost all the way when Gordon rode up. He had been moving his cows. "What you guys doing here?" he asked.

"We can't find Eric. We were coming to see if he had gone all the way with you." I said.

"Well," said Gordy, "he left me just past the lease gate and I told him he had to go straight to Peggy's. He knows the way. He's been over it often enough."

"He didn't come home and he hasn't been to our place." Johnny said. He was scared too.

"Help me move these cows home, then I'll help you look." said Gordon.

Well, we really moved those poor cows. I think we might have churned some butter. If Ken had seen that, we would have been in even more trouble than we were already.

We rode along the trail that led to the lease lands. There were horse tracks around but anybody could have made them.

"Eric!" Johnny called.

"Eric, Eric!" we all started calling.

I was responsible for this, as I was in charge when Ken was not home. "I think we had better get hold of Ken." I said. He's been branding at Wilson's. He should be home by now."

"I'll do my milking and then start looking again." Gordon said. I thanked him and told him not to go too far, as I didn't think Eric would be so stupid as to ride away into the leases. That would be dumb because there was nothing there. He could sure get lost.

We rode back to Peggy's and she was some upset. "Skipper, how could you let that little boy ride off there by himself like that? I'm surprised at you." Peggy

The Cowboy

was not in her usual joking mood, to say the least. There was no use telling her that I had nothing to do with it, that Mike was the one who let him go. "You better get your little behind home pronto and get Ken in the picture." she warned. Your name is MUD, little man." I knew that. Johnny filled in his mother on where we had been and what we saw. I took off for home.

When I told Mike we couldn't find Eric, he was terrified. " Oh shit, Skipper! What am I going to do?" He was crying.

"You better not let Ken hear your filthy mouth, either." I said. "No time to cry. We got to think about what's happened to Eric."

Ken drove up. "Gosh all Friday, boy! Don't you have those damned cows milked yet?" he yelled at me. I knew I was in for it good.

"Ken, Eric hasn't come home and we can't find him. He rode part way home with Gordon, as far as the lease gate." My voice broke but I went on. "He was going to ride through Peggy's and then home. He hasn't shown up there either."

"What the hell you telling me, Skipper?" Ken shouted. "Eric is lost?"

"It's all my fault." Mike interrupted. "It was me who told him he could ride with Gordon." Mike was really sobbing now.

"Stop that blubbering," Ken barked, "or I'll give you something to blubber about.

Ken peppered me with questions. We went over everything we had done to find Eric. Ken was worried and bloody furious. "You finish your milking and then get something for us to eat. I'm going to drive over to the lease gate and see what I can find." he said. "Gosh all Friday anyways." he muttered to himself. I knew someone was going to get tanned when this was sorted out.

"Skipper, I'm really frightened that something terrible has happened to Eric." Mike said. "What would I do without my brother?"

We finished milking and took the milk up to separate. We had food on the table when Ken drove into the yard. He never said a word, just washed up and sat down to eat. He never looked at me or Mike. I didn't really want him to look at me--I could usually tell what was coming by the look on his face. I asked to be excused and got up and cleared the dishes. Mike followed suit and we started to wash up.

Even though I didn't want Ken to look at me, I hated it when he wouldn't talk to me. Finally, I said, "Ken, did you find anything at all?"

"Get your gal-danged homework done before I decide to tan you both." he fumed. No more questions for now. I got my books out and lit the lamp. Mike and I got to work.

"Mike you can count on one lickin' you'll never forget." Ken growled. "I trusted you and you fouled up. You let me down and now we've lost Eric. Let me tell you something else. Someone has taken him. Gordon found boot prints just inside the lease. Eric wasn't anywhere around but there are car tracks. How come you missed seeing those, Skipper? You blind or something? Why in tarnation would anyone take Eric? Gosh all Friday, someone's gonna pay for this. As if I ain't got enough to do without chasing down a kid that ain't even mine."

The Cowboy

Mike had been silently weeping to himself and tried to cover up his tears behind his homework books. But with that last remark of Ken's he got up enough nerve to say, "He may not be your kid, but he's my brother."

"You shut your mouth!" Ken lashed out. I thought he was going to lay one on Mike right then. "You want you and me to settle up right now?" Mike backed down and sank deeper in his seat behind his book.

It was dark when Tom Wilson drove into our yard. Right behind him was a Mountie from Turner Valley. The officer had been to the lease gate and examined the tracks. "We don't know what to think about this Ken, but you're right about one thing. Whoever was in that car took the boy." said the Mountie. "We found the boy's footprints and a couple of men's tracks on both sides of where the car had been parked. We'll get bulletins out and try and find out everything we can. We don't have much to go on."

Tom Wilson and the officer left and Ken told us to go to bed and not one word from either of us. We whispered quietly so there was no way Ken could hear us. Mike wanted to take off and look for Eric on his own. I talked him out of that as being a stupid idea.

"I wish he would punish me and get it done with, rather than making me wait." Mike said.

"Yeah, I know what you mean. He's just upset. He'll probably forget about it when we find Eric." I tried to assure him. We were talking about the spanking to try to keep our minds off the real trouble.

I don't think anyone slept that night. Mike cried on and off and I couldn't have slept anyway. We were all worried about Eric. I could hear Ken walking back and

Douglas Hargreaves

forth in the kitchen. I prayed for Eric, that he was going to be all right and that we would wake up and find it was all a bad dream.

The next morning, while we were doing the milking, Gordon and his brother, Morris, rode into the yard. Gordon was carrying a piece of paper. He had found it stuck on a tree limb just inside the lease gate. How did we miss that, I wondered. The note was printed in big letters and said:

KEN, IF YOU WANT TO SEE YOUR BOY AGAIN, YOU JUST QUIT LOOKING FOR YOUR LOST CATTLE.

Ken was livid. "Bastards! Goll-damned bastards. How the hell are we going to find that kid?" He pounded his fist on the corral fence. "They better not touch a hair on his head or they're dead, that's for sure." He turned to me. "Get on with your bloody milking or you'll be late for school."

"Can't I stay and help?" I asked.

"You and Mike stay the hell out of my way until we find him, you hear? I might be away for a day or so. You go and eat at Peggy's and tell her what's happened. I'm going to Calgary."

Three days later we found Boots, Lynn's horse that Eric had been riding. Still no Eric. We hadn't heard from Ken but Peggy figured he would be searching the Calgary Stockyards. Maybe even the Stampede barns.

Mike and I did our chores letter-perfect and right on time. We ate our suppers at Peggy's. Finally, on Friday, right after we had got home from school, Ken drove up. Eric was not in the truck. Hooolly! What a terrible thing this was turning out to be.

The Cowboy

Ken and Morris had gone directly to RCMP headquarters in Calgary. The Mounties told them here had been a lot of rustling reported in our area and the police had a few leads. Our brand had not been spotted anywhere so far. Ken told us he had a hunch that the Stampede auction stables might be involved.

One night around midnight, Ken said he and Morris had gone down to the Stampede barns to look around. It was pitch dark. Ken saw a few people but no truck. Ken was walking along behind the big barn that ran alongside the Elbow River where Eric's mother had died. He heard a whimpering sound coming from the bushes. There was Eric, all rolled up in a ball, trying to stay warm. He was dirty, bleeding and badly bruised all over. Eric saw Ken and jumped up and ran to him. Ken picked him up and the little guy just cried and cried and hung on to Ken like nothing would ever pull him off.

Ken tried to find out what had happened, but it was too hard to make sense out of what Eric was trying to tell him. Ken carried Eric up through the barns and the boy just kept crying. He told Ken not to let the men see him. Ken had figured that out already and took a back street to the truck where Morris was waiting.

They drove Eric to the hospital just across the river. The doctors examined him thoroughly, patched him up and put him to bed. He begged Ken not to leave him. He was exhausted and didn't need anything to make him sleep. Ken stayed with him all that night. Eric was well enough when he woke up the next morning to fill in Ken and Morris about what had happened.

Douglas Hargreaves

Eric was riding home when he came across a car with some men in it parked by the lease gate. One man got out of the car as Eric approached. Eric thought he could outrun them but before he could turn around to get started, the driver used the car to corner Eric against the fence. One big guy pulled Eric off Boots. Eric couldn't get away and tried screaming until one of the men slapped him in the face. Eric assured Ken that he fought as hard as he could but they just kept hitting him all over.

Eric thought they must have knocked him out because he didn't remember much about where he was or how many days had gone by. Then he found himself in a smelly horse stall. He told Ken he recognized the smell as being the same smell from when we had been in the Stampede horse barns.

The men tied him up with rope and stuffed a rag in his mouth. They told him if he wanted to ever see his family again, he had best shut up and be quiet. Eric said he bit one of the men on his finger and made it bleed. That really got the guy mad, so he hit Eric in the stomach and knocked the wind out of him.

Eric said he couldn't breathe and he even threw up.

During the night Eric managed to get his hands free from behind his back and untied himself. There was a man at the front of the barn and the back door was locked. Eric climbed up the wall onto the overhead trusses. Then he crawled along to a window opening onto the roof. It was a ventilation skylight. He crawled out and onto the roof. He tried his best not to make a noise.

Eric crawled along the edge of the roof towards the back end of the barn. He lost his balance and he fell to

The Cowboy

the ground. That knocked the wind out of him again. Eric admitted he had a hard time keeping from crying.

He heard the men rushing around inside the barn and out in front. He crawled over the manure pile at the back of the barn near the river. He figured the men who were looking for him wouldn't want to crawl through a manure pile. He found some bushes to hide in nearby and it was there by the river that Ken found him.

He told Ken that these were the guys who had taken the cattle and that the cattle were somewhere near the barns.

The way Ken was telling the story, I could tell that someone or something was going to get a pounding pretty quick or he would burst. That's how upset he was.

The doctors decided to keep Eric in the hospital for a few days to let him heal. They wanted to keep an eye on him. Eric had a front tooth pushed through his lower lip and needed some stitches.

The newspapers carried the story and reported in no uncertain terms that the boy knew what the rustlers looked like. When we read that, we were all scared.

The Mounties knew exactly what they were doing. They wanted to scare the rustlers into doing something foolish to get rid of the cattle. Sure enough, they did. They tried loading a truck full of the stolen cattle in with some auction cattle. They tried to cover up the brands with paint to make them look like another brand, at least from a distance. The police caught them red-handed.

We figured the rustlers never would have returned Eric. They just wanted to get Ken off their backs until

Douglas Hargreaves

they got rid of the cattle. Eric said they had tried to get him to promise he wouldn't tell anything about them or else they would kill Mike and maybe me. Eric told them he was going to tell everyone exactly what they did to him and how they had stolen the cattle. They hurt him again for that.

Mike and I felt terrible for poor Eric. "The only guy with any guts around here." Ken said. But at least Eric had been found and was now safe. We could get him home in a few days.

Ken took Mike and me with him to get Eric. We were shocked to see how terrible Eric looked. He smiled at us, just the same as he always did. "Mike," he said, "I tried to get away from them but they hemmed me in with their car. I didn't want to hurt Boots."

When we got home and got Eric settled, Ken called us outside. Hooooolly! Here it comes, I thought. I wondered if Mike would be up to it because he was sure shaking. He was terrified. He was already starting to cry.

Ken walked us down to the barn and I had it figured that this would be the lickin' of all time. Ken told us to sit up on the oat bin.

"You know what you got comin', don't you?" said Ken.

Mike just hung his head and his whole body shook from his sobbing. "Yes sir." he said.

"Do you know how much you mean to me?" he said. His voice was breaking a bit. "Do you see how breaking the rules and disobeying me nearly caused us to lose Eric? We almost got him killed. Think about that hard now. You see why I gotta punish you every

The Cowboy

now and again, 'cause you won't listen otherwise? Do you know how I feel having to do this to ya? You're really too old to get a spankin', but you behave like little children and they learn best with a smack on the bum. You're too old to have to be treated that way. Don't get the idea you're too big, 'cause you ain't. I think you shouldn't have to be treated like babies any more. You should be more responsible and know what it means to obey. I'm very disappointed in you, Michael. You should have had more sense than to let Eric go off on his own after I told you against it. I can't trust you any more. Well, what do you have to say about all this?"

Mike was weeping silently to himself. The tears were rolling down his cheeks. "Ken, there seems like there isn't anything I can say. I am sorry and I promise never to disappoint you again. I deserve to be thrashed and I would feel better if you did. Eric and I would never have been able to get along if it hadn't been for you and Skipper." Mike sobbed. "Ken, I love you and thank you for saving Eric." He jumped off the bin and put his arms around Ken and hugged him.

I was crying a bit too but Ken had said it all just the right way. We were not responsible enough for our age. I thought I would never get in this situation again.

"You boys are part of my life." Ken said. "How would I get along without you?" Ken had a tear in his eye. I always knew when he was feeling like crying because his voice would start breaking. "You ain't going to get a whippin' this time Mike. You've learned your lesson the hard way. But you're going to have to earn my trust back again." he said.

Douglas Hargreaves

We walked up to the house hand in hand. I felt about ten years older than my thirteen years just then.

"Where you guys been?" Eric hollered as we came in the door.

"Oh, just talking things over. You okay?" Ken said as he strode over to where Eric was looking out the window. Ken put his arm on Eric's shoulder and hugged him. Eric knew all along where we had been. He had seen us.

"Ken, can I tell you something?" Eric said.

"Sure. What's up?" Eric motioned Ken over so that he could whisper in Ken's ear and mumbled something to him.

Ken answered out loud, "Well, he really deserves it but I think he's learned his lesson, don't you? And remember, little man, you knew that you weren't to go by yourself, right? Maybe I better tan your behind 'cause you danged-well disobeyed my orders, right?" Ken half smiled as he said it.

Eric jumped up out of his chair and flung himself into Ken's arms. Ken held him tightly and kissed the boy on the cheek.

"You're all right now." Ken told him.

I was feeling just about as good as I had ever felt.

"Eric, are you okay enough to ride to Peggy's?" Ken asked.

"Yes please, Ken. I can't stand Skipper's cooking." he replied and we left.

CHANGING TIMES

Ken bought a radio and we would all gather around to listen to it after the boys and I had done our homework. Charlie McCarthy, Jack Benny, Fred Allan and others made us laugh. We sure needed cheering up. Everyone was going around with long faces as the news about what was going on in Europe got worse. Sometimes we would hear news broadcasts from the BBC in England. The announcer would tell us what Germany was doing in Europe and how Neville Chamberlain, the Prime Minister of Great Britain, was going to bring peace in our time.

Grandpa, Ken and Olie would sit around talking about what they thought was going to happen. The teachers at our high school in Turner Valley had us writing reports and opinions about the current news items, especially what direction Great Britain might go. It got so that every time we turned on the radio we heard that the Germans had bombed some town and were about to storm another.

When you're thirteen, your mind is on things other than some war going on way over there, several thousand miles away. The only problem was, the war was coming to the Valley. Many of the young ranchers and oil men were preparing to enlist. They wanted to help England and Grandpa said that Canada would be the first to offer support.

Grade Ten was going pretty well as far as the school work was concerned. But my classmates discriminated against me because of my size and my age. I found I was a little kid amongst what seemed to me to be young adults in my class. I only called them young adults because they were so much bigger than me. Who wasn't? Their view was that I had no business being there with them, period. So they just tolerated me and that's about all. Some of them didn't even consider me a person. The only exceptions were the classes my friends attended. There was Lynn Spence and a few other ropers I competed against in the summer rodeos.

Most everyone knew me or at least knew who I was but that didn't make any difference. They would talk to me when we were alone but it became embarrassing for them when their friends joined us. They still wouldn't go out of their way to be friends for fear of what the others might think. No one wanted to chum around with a little kid. I was known as a "Smart Ass" to almost everyone. That was the part I really hated about being in high school.

In order for me to participate in sports programs and in phys-ed, the school transferred me to the Grade Eight program. I played baseball and hockey but not football. I had to make up my credits with music. That seemed to suit everyone--more the little kid's style. I really wanted to be in the sports programs because music was considered a girl's activity and I had had a belly full of girls already.

Ken was even more upset about what was going on at school than I was. I decided I wouldn't say anything about it unless he asked me. He usually did ask, wanting to know how my day went. I begged him not to visit the principal because it would only make matters worse for me. We knew why I couldn't play sports in my own grade. It irked him that they would

The Cowboy

discriminate because of my size. I was sure slow in growing and all because of my stupid stomach problems. It was all in my genes the doctor told us. I wondered who in my family had given me that gift. Grandpa kept all of his grandchildren's heights marked on the kitchen doorway. I was now a whopping four foot ten.

I enjoyed the Eighth Grade sports and made the lineup on several teams. Playing with the younger (since you had skipped a few grades would they not be the same age as you?) kids didn't bother me. My pride could take a little bashing. The kids in Grade Eight treated me a lot better than the ones in my class. That was the reality of being pushed ahead mentally as opposed to physically. Academically, I was in the top three in my Grade Ten class and that didn't sit well with the others. I had been recommended for the Governor General's Scholarship.

My roping skills continued to improve, although with winter coming on, I had less chance to do much practising. Ken taught me all he knew and even looked for someone who could help me advance further. He was bound and determined I was going to retain the trophy for as long as I was living at his ranch.

I was having mixed feelings about the future. Ken was thinking about giving up the ranch he had been renting. He felt he should be helping his father because Grandpa was getting too old to do some of the heavy work.

We built a new log addition to Grandpa's ranch house and got some new furniture. There would be lots of room and Michael and Eric would have a room of their own until they returned to England. We also

Douglas Hargreaves

made a lot of improvements on our place. We built a spare bedroom for visitors and even got a power plant. It was a used one but it gave us electricity for the first time. We had trouble getting used to it and would forget to use the electric lights. I still lit the coal oil lamp in my bedroom.

Ken even wired a light out in the crapper so we could see in the dark. What would anyone want to see in there, I wondered. We never had a light out there before and got along okay. Now that it had light, there was no reason for me to pee out my window. Ken put a stop to that disgusting practice.

My old problem with my stomach persisted. We had been told it would. Nevertheless, the doctors tried to find a cure and would prescribe medicines that I couldn't keep down. I wished their cures would have worked as fast on my bottom end as they did on my top end. Throwing up was such a bother. Peggy and sometimes Ken looked after my problem and kept me healthy and that was all that mattered. Sometimes I could go a whole month without a stomach ache and I thought things might be improving.

Ken and I often discussed my returning to Winnipeg, now that my family was back from Europe. They had written to tell me they wanted me back to finish my remaining two years of high school in Winnipeg. I didn't like having this particular conversation with Ken because it always went the same way.

"I don't want to talk about it. Why do you talk about it all the time? Do you want me to go?"

"Skipper, we have to talk about it. They are your parents and they want you home."

The Cowboy

"Ken, they don't even know me. Why do they want me home after all this time?"

"You're their kid and they want you to finish school in Winnipeg."

"I am not their kid. I'm your's. I really belong to you. You're the one who really cares about me. Grandpa thinks so too."

"Skipper, you're just going to make it harder for all of us when it comes time for you to go. Wouldn't you rather it be your idea to leave than for them to actually come and drag you away? I can't keep you against their will. You know that. Your mother hates me as it is. She feels I've turned you against them."

What a big stupid joke it all was, to my way of thinking. My parents no more wanted me home than they wanted me to fly to the moon. If they wanted to have me around, it was only so they could ease their conscience a little. Show me off to their high and mighty friends. I hated all that phoney stuff. Mother hadn't changed. She was still climbing the social ladder. She even sent me a newspaper clipping announcing their arrival back from England. There was a big party thrown for them.

I wasn't their kid any more. I belonged here. Peggy knew more about looking after me than they would ever know.

And as for Peggy, she was taking this as badly as Ken and I. I conspired with her about how I could escape my family's plans for me. Just stay around here and maybe change my name. No one would be any the wiser. Everyone thought I was Ken's son anyway. After all, I had lived with him since I was ten and now I was almost fourteen.

Douglas Hargreaves

Christmas was coming. I knew it was going to be a hard time for me. I usually got so excited about big events coming around--my birthday, the Stampede, Christmas. I'd count the days. But not this Christmas. I wasn't looking forward to it because I thought it might be my last with my ranch family.

The snow fell heavier than it had for some years. There were days when we couldn't get out to the road and had to miss school. The snow got so deep on the road to Millarville that they had to get a Caterpillar snowplough to open it. For quite a while, they didn't get around to lowing the road up to our place.

If we couldn't get to Millarville, then we didn't go anywhere, only to Grandpa's or Peggy's. All the people out our way took turns taking the kids to school in an old caboose on sleigh runners. It wasn't all that cold but it was hard to get through the snow. One time, the caboose nearly tipped over. Everyone said it was the worst year for snow they had seen in ages.

As far as I was concerned it sure was the worst. I never shovelled so much snow in my life. It was a good thing we had lots of hay in the loft and a stack beside the barn. We would have enough for the winter without having to haul any.

Nixon sure got his exercise that winter. I rode him wherever I could. Often the snow was just too deep and it was too hard on him. Ken said we shouldn't strain the horses. A horse could break a leg in the deep snow. So we shovelled pathways through the deeper drifts. Eventually we were able to ride our horses most places.

Ken found some old snowshoes and we fixed them up so we both had a pair. We made a neat trail to

The Cowboy

Peggy's and sometimes we would hike as far as Grandpa's. We were always in touch with Grandpa and Grandma and were always there on Sundays. Grandpa would meet us at the door and say, "Well, good grief, who are you and where did you come from? Can't remember seeing you before."

"Come on Grandpa, you know who I am." I'd play along.

"Well, just take off some of those clothes so I can see what's hidden under all that stuff." Ken and I would be smothered in scarves, sweaters and overcoats. We wore moccasins with felt lining and two pair of soft, warm, woollen socks. "Wellllll! I'll be go-to-heck." Grandpa would laugh in mock surprise. "Look everyone, it's Skipper!"

The trails we had made hardened in the cold weather. After a while they were so hard we could walk on them without snowshoes although I was getting pretty good with those snowshoes.

A chinook wind blew in one day and melted a lot of the snow. Even our pathway disappeared. I got soaking wet. Everything melted and water was running everywhere. Then, overnight, everything froze solid again.

Close to Christmas the ploughs finally got through and we were able to travel by vehicle. The snow was piled so high along the roads it seemed like cars were driving through tunnels.

We heard on the radio that Canada and England were going to go to war against Germany. Morris, Gordon's brother, was talking about joining up. Ken too talked about it. Morris came home one day and told us about the interview he'd had with the army in

Douglas Hargreaves

Calgary. He was real excited. The more he talked about it, the more interested Ken looked.

"Ken, with your knowledge of heavy equipment, you could probably get in as a sergeant." Morris said. "They wanted to know what my skills were. I told them I was just a poor rancher. Just cow skills. They said that if I had been a driver or a mechanic, I could have qualified for stripes. Ken, you could sure get them." "Well, I might see them sometime I'm in town." Ken said. Things aren't going to get any better for a long time, I'm thinking." Ken said.

"Ken, how can you talk about joining up?" I asked.

"Well, Skipper, you're going to be going to your folks soon. Mike, Eric, and I will be moving over to Grandpa's. There ain't nothin' to hold me here."

"Grandpa needs you to help him Ken." I said. "How can you if you join up?"

"What's to stop me from going?"

"We've mixed both the herds. We bought those extra steers. That's more than Grandpa can handle, don't you think?"

"Mike and Eric can help Grandpa." said Ken. "So we'll see. Lots of things can happen before then, huh? We ain't officially at war yet." he laughed. "Don't you worry your little head about such things now, you hear?"

"Ken, please--if you join up, then I'm not going to Winnipeg and that's final."

"Hey, listen here, little one. You do exactly as I tell you, right?"

I knew that tone of voice, so I let it be.

A letter came from England advising us that an uncle wanted to take in Mike and Eric. He was their

The Cowboy

mother's brother and had just heard about his sister's death. It was the first anyone had heard from their relatives in England. Mike and Eric were not the least bit interested in leaving us. They felt this was their home. Ken told them there wasn't any choice. Their uncle could look after them better than he could. And besides, with Ken probably going into the services, Grandma and Grandpa were too old to look after a couple of young ones. I would sure miss them. They were like my brothers.

This Christmas was breaking my heart. Somehow I knew it would be my last one on the ranch. Things were a bit testy. Everyone knew what was going on in the minds of both Morris and Ken. They were the same age and both would be highly sought after for military service. And now the government was talking about the possibility of conscription. You'd have no choice-- they'd just send you a letter and tell you where to report. At least if you joined up on your own accord, you would have some say about what you would like to do.

As usual, we all gathered at Grandma and Grandpa's place for Christmas. Grandpa was looking older to me and Grandma fussed over him more than ever. I though about Johnny as he and I sat by the fire. I sure would miss him. He was younger than me but we were still the best of friends, sharing each other's secrets and concerns. He told me his mother would cry quite a bit when they talked about my leaving. "She thinks of you like the rest of us kids." Johnny said. "She loves you Skipper." He started to sob.

"Well, she is a mother to me." I said. "I know that and that's what makes it so hard to leave. She got real close to me over the years when I needed a mom. She was the one who always looked after me."

"Yeah Skipper, you and your problem. She won't be able to steal your clothes when you're swimming any more. Or pinch your butt."

It was more than I could handle. Who said Cowboys don't cry?

Peggy came over to ask us to set the table for Christmas dinner. "What's bothering my boy?" she asked.

"Skipper just feels bad about leaving, Mom." said Johnny.

"Come on son, let's not think about such things at this time." Peggy said. "We're supposed to be happy not sad at Christmas time, remember?" She gave me a big hug and knelt down beside me.

"Peggy? Why does it have to be this way?" I said to her through my tears. "Ken talking about leaving, Morris talking about it, and even Gordy's thinking about it too."

"It looks like war for certain, Skipper. And everything is changing. Even you're changing. Nothing ever stays the same forever, as much as we'd like it to. You're entering another part of your life and you're too big a boy now not to be able to roll with the changes. You're too smart to let something like this throw you." I hugged her even more.

Ken came over to us. "What's eatin' you, Skip?"

Peggy told him I was upset about all the changes that were taking place and about all the talk about him joining up. There were quite few of these sad little conversations. We did a lot of sitting and gazing into the fireplace over Christmas. All of us kids were

The Cowboy

growing up and we were not as excited nor as rambunctious as we used to be. I knew the other kids were feeling the same way about everything as I was. We all dealt with Christmas as best we could under the circumstances. Some of it we even enjoyed. But it sure was different from other Christmas times.

Grandpa, as usual, read the Christmas story. We drank to a happy Christmas and a safe journey for Santa Claus. We had the orange punch Grandma made. This Christmas was a little special on that matter too. Grandpa gave me a drink that was different from what the other kids were drinking. I don't think anyone noticed. Grandpa gave me a wink and offered a toast for everyone. "Well, here is to a Happy Christmas and a Happy New Year ahead for Skipper, Michael and Eric."

I choked a bit, either from my spiked orange juice or the lump in my throat. I wasn't going to blubber, as I had been doing so often lately. Ken wouldn't think too much about my weeping like a little kid. Mike and Eric were unusually quiet,as they too were leaving. Their Uncle was coming to Canada to return the boys to England,in spite of the threats of war. They didn't want to leave either.

Grandpa commented that it was sure going to be quiet around the place with his boys gone.

As for Christmas gifts we all received much more than we deserved. There was no doubt about what I wanted for Christmas and that was to continue to live on the ranch. All I wanted was to stay here forever.

About the Author

Douglas Hargreaves was Born in Winnipeg, Manitoba Canada in 1925. He spent the first 10 years of his life there, later moving to Alberta. He lived in the area for several years then joined the Royal Canadian Airforce in 1943. He served a tour of operation with an RAF Bomber group, completing his tour of 35 operational missions over enemy territory. He returned to Canada and later obtained a job flying locally out of Pine Falls Manitoba. He then moved into to Northern Canada and became a part time Hudson's Bay Post employee and Bush pilot serving North Saskatchewan. He is married with two sons and their families. He has written many articles and short stories. His first published novel was *The Cowboy* now in its third printing followed by its sequel *From Cowboys to Cockpits* in its second printing.

The books, although fiction, are based on the many interesting experiences and adventures of the author as a young boy growing up in the foothills of Alberta, and his experiences while in the services and in Northern Canada.

The author resides in Abbotsford, British Columbia, but spends much of his time in Blaine, WA with his wife on their sailboat into the Georgia Straits.

Printed in the United States
22432LVS00001B/124-132